MR LONELY

'Sid Lewis came into this world exactly the same way as any other child. He weighed eight and a half pounds and had a shock of black hair ... His childhood was normal – lumps, bumps and mumps. His schooling was average – sums, bums and chums. He left school when he was fourteen and went to work behind the counter of a tobacconist's shop earning fifteen shillings a week and all he could inhale...'

So begins the Sid Lewis story, a tribute to that great and incomparable comedian who achieved stardom as Mr Lonely...

MR LONELY

Eric Morecambe

METHUEN LONDON LTD

A Methuen Paperback

MR LONELY
ISBN 0 417 07340 2

First published in Great Britain 1981
by Eyre Methuen Ltd
Reprinted 1981

Copyright © 1981 by Eric Morecambe

Lyrics from *Do-Wacka-Do* by Roger Miller
are quoted by permission of Tree Publishing Company/
Burlington Music Company Limited.

This edition published 1982
by Methuen London Ltd
11 New Fetter Lane, London EC4P 4EE

Printed and bound in Great Britain by
Cox & Wyman Ltd, Reading

This book is dedicated to my first grandchild,
Amelia Faye Jarvis.

Foreword

Dear Reader,
This is not a biography of Sid Lewis written by someone who never really knew him. These are some wonderful stories and memories of a much loved man, who, when he appeared on our screens, most of the country would watch. I remember one Christmas show he did when thirty-five million people watched, and the repeat was seen three weeks later (by public demand) by no less than twenty-eight million. Put these two figures together and that show alone was seen by sixty-three million people. To me it proves how much we all loved him and always will. I well remember Sid once saying to me, 'Eric, old palamino. What do they (the public) see in me?' He gave me his Glenn Ford type grin and his eyes filled up as I told him, 'Sid, I don't know but be thankful they do.' I was with him on many of the occasions mentioned in this book. Obviously there are a few, when, in all honesty, I could not and should not have been there, but these were retold to me by Sid himself or, in some cases, by the male or female involved. I have not put myself in Sid's story. The story is about Sid, not me. My pleasure and happiness come from writing about him. I am offering you a few snatches from his life, nothing more; some funny, some sad. After reading this book I hope you will remain a fan of Sid's and a friend of mine. All the photographs are from my own private collection and have never been shown publicly before. Here, I would like to say a special thank you to Miss Victoria Fournier for long nights we had to spend together in her flat trying to get it right. Also to my darling wife, Joan, for her understanding. As Bela Lugosi said in the film *Dracula* (1931), 'Listen to them, children of the night. What music they make.'

Harpenden
England 1981

Mr. Lonely

By SID LEWIS

1. The spot-light wa-vers un-til it picks up the sin-gle_____ clown
2. A bro-ken fi-gure, head in hands, the spotlight stresses the_____ pain

His stage is empty and the audience gone; it's hours since the curtain came down.
An hour ago he had them crying for more, now only the memories remain.

Hey Mr. Lone-ly, Why can't you see,

Why can't you see, Success is no guar-an - tee.

3. Success and se - cu-ri-ty have never e - lu-ded his grasp.
4. But it's his life, it runs in his blood as the theatrical philosophy states,

But it's love and it's hap-pi-ness that he could see but not quite clasp.
You'll kid yourself you'll throw in the towel but in reality you'll wait for the breaks.

Hey Mr. Lone - ly, Why can't you see,

Why can't you see, Suc-cess is no guar-an - tee.

(repeat Vocal Chorus)

Sid's song. Perhaps the most famous signature tune in show business.

Prologue

Sid Lewis came into this world exactly the same way as any other child. He weighed eight and a half pounds and had a shock of black hair. The trouble was, as he used to say, 'It wasn't on my head, it was all under my left arm.' His childhood was normal – lumps, bumps and mumps. His schooling was average – sums, bums and chums. He left school when he was fourteen and went to work behind the counter of a tobacconist's shop earning fifteen shillings a week and all he could inhale. Twice a week he went to dancing class in the evenings. He was, apart from another fourteen year old boy called Ashley (that was his first name), who became quite well known as a ballet dancer, the only other boy, with twenty-two girls between thirteen and eighteen years of age. He learned more about girls in four weeks, or eight lessons, than was good for a young lad of fourteen. The thirteen to sixteen year old girls wanted to practise with him, while the sixteen to eighteen year olds wanted to practise on him. His mother did say to his father, 'He must be working hard at that dancing class, he comes home exhausted.' At eighteen he went into the army and worked his way through the ranks from private to captain of the ATS. Private Betty Grassford and Captain Maureen Collins. He always wanted to make major but she wouldn't let him. He remained a corporal. He came out of the army at twenty-two, took a month off, then got a job for a while as a postman, and slowly, through singing, doing a few jokes and reading the 'Wanted Ads' in *The Stage*, came into show business via pubs, clubs and church halls, working to OAPs, talent competitions and one summer as a Red Coat at Butlin's Holiday Camp in Clacton.

He was now hooked. Performing was the only thing he wanted to do and a comedian he wanted to be. For a few years, including the early part of his marriage, Sid found it difficult to make ends meet. It's sad to say that his wife Carrie was no real help to him.

9

She never thought him really funny and on the rare occasions she saw him work he always seemed to 'die the death'. She loved him, though, and when things were tough she worked as a waitress or in some kind of job that would bring some money in. The first year of their marriage she earned more than he did, but she didn't understand his wanting to be in show business. She never complained, yet she never understood. Carrie just wanted him to be the type of husband that brought in enough money to live on, to pay the rent, and to go to Yarmouth for a few days every year, the same as her father had done. Sid used to say, 'We only had one child because she found out what caused it.'

I don't think there was very much passion between Carrie and Sid. Just a gentle love that never gave out any real heat. What Sid wanted to do all through his married life was 'To become a Star'. He wanted to be a star for Carrie but she couldn't understand that. What she wanted was for him to be average. He couldn't understand that. They both became reconciled to each other and over the years their early, youthful love slowly developed into fondness. It was a great sadness because both of them deserved better from each other.

1

It was Tuesday morning. Sid came into the kitchen for his breakfast. He looked at the electric clock on the wall – nine-fifteen. Carrie, his wife, had already taken their daughter, Elspeth, to school and was now back in her kitchen making her baggy-eyed, unshaven husband his breakfast. Sid sat down with the ease of a still tired man in that part of the kitchen that was known as the breakfast area. He picked up half a dozen lumps of sugar, picked out two special ones, put the others down and, like a Mississippi gambler, threw the two lumps of sugar towards the packet of Shredded Wheat. As they hit the box and stopped rolling he shouted in a loud voice: '*Craps!*'

Out of the corner of his eye he could see Carrie adroitly avoiding hot bacon fat and, at the same time, breaking two eggs to fry. In competition with the bacon and eggs was a male radio DJ of the older school, who was allowing an actor to tell all of this particular DJ's audience how good the play he was appearing in, was, and how good all the other actors and actresses in it were, and that the producer, although still quite young (a breathless twenty-two) was nevertheless, 'my dear', only quite brilliant, and the director, 'my lambs', a genius, and younger than Noel was. The music? Well – all of the best the West End has heard since Cole and, of course, Ivor. The show, 'my loves', was the best thing to hit town in Zeons and why people weren't coming to see it in droves baffled him.

The older-type DJ was doing all his 'of courses' and 'Good Lords' in all the right places, finishing up with, 'Well, I just find that too hard to believe, Randy.'

'Don't we all, darling,' purred the actor.

11

'But after what you've just told me, I shall go and see *Cosmo, The Faceless Goon* myself.'

'Moon,' whispered Randy.

'Moon,' shouted the older-type DJ, who then announced the wrong theatre followed by the wrong performance time.

Sid thought, Older-type DJ, in this last ten years you have become an institution, and now that's where you belong.

Carrie thought, Randy. I wonder if that's short for Randal? She said, 'How many eggs?'

'One,' said Sid.

'One?'

'Yes.'

'But I've done you two.'

'So I'll have two.'

'You've no need to have two, if you don't want to have two. You can have one if you only want one.'

'I'll have two.'

'Are you sure?'

'Look, if I only have one, what will happen to the other one?'

'I'll have it.'

'Do you want it?'

'Well, I'm not bothered, but I'll have it if you don't want it.'

'Give them both to me before I go off the idea of either bacon or eggs. Have you grilled any tomatoes?'

'No.'

'Well, that's a relief. That means to say that if you had and I didn't want them, you won't have to have them now.'

'Are you ready for them?'

'Yes, if they're ready for me and incidentally ...'

'Yes?'

'I don't want the tomatoes.'

Carrie give him his bacon and eggs. 'What time did you come in last night?' she asked.

'About three. If you're going to do any tomatoes, I'll have them.'

'I didn't hear you. I didn't hear the car.'

'I turned the engine off before coming down the drive. These eggs are great. I'll take bets they were brown eggs.'

'One of each.'

'Oh, I would say the one on the left was the brown one.'

'I didn't feel you get in the bed.'

'You should have done. I made love to you twice.'

12

'I don't think that's at all funny. You're getting crude in your old age. Pass me the plate when you've finished.'

'It was like a joke,' he said, passing the now empty plate.

'Coffee?'

'Yes please, but without tomatoes.'

'You probably see all the tomatoes you want at the club,' Carrie said, putting the plates in the sink. 'Do you mind instant coffee this morning as I'm in a bit of a hurry?'

'Instant coffee's fine,' Sid said, undoing his dressing-gown cord. 'But what's that about the tomatoes at the club business?'

'Do you want cold milk or half and half?'

'I'm easy.'

'We'll have the cold milk then.' Carrie got the cups ready and started to pour the coffees. 'Three o'clock's late. You're usually home by two.'

'Lard asked me back to his room for a drink after he'd finished.'

'Who?'

'Lard. Lard Jackson. He's the star this week.'

'That black man, who was on *Nationwide* the other night?'

'Most likely.' Sid picked up his two special sugars and dropped them into his coffee. 'He's a nice fella.'

'What does he do?'

'He's got a number in the Top Ten. He finished his act with it.'

'What's it called?'

'Let me do it to you again, baby.'

'Good Lord.'

'It's a song.'

'Hmmm.'

'No, it is.'

'Is he married?'

'I don't know. I never asked him. How can I say, "Hello, Mr Jackson, are you married? I'm asking for my wife"?'

'Is his first name really Lard?'

'As far as I know – yes.'

'How does anybody call themself Lard?'

'Well, he says, "What's cooking?" a lot.' Sid looked at her over the rim of his coffee cup. After fifteen years of marriage he knew when she was on edge. She wasn't happy about him coming home late.

'I suppose his dressing-room was full of women.'

'Packed,' Sid smiled to himself. 'We counted them. Seven black

13

and seven white. All the black women were dressed in white and all the white women were dressed in black, otherwise we couldn't have told them apart.'

'Very funny.'

'I thought so.'

'Do you want another cup?'

'Nope.'

'Elspeth saw something this morning,' said Carrie.

'Pardon.'

'Elspeth. She saw something.'

'Oh.'

'Yes.'

'Good.'

'What do you mean – good?'

'Well, I'm glad for her sake.' Sid was at a loss. 'I will have some more coffee if there's any left.'

'She's twelve.'

'I know.'

'Well – she saw something.' Carrie whispered, 'You know, she *saw* something.'

Sid looked blankly at his wife.

'Her periods have started,' Carrie said.

'Good God. She's only twelve.' Sid was embarrassed. 'I mean – she's twelve years old.'

Carrie smiled to herself for the first time that morning. Now she felt in charge. 'I was thirteen.'

'Yes – but you are older than her.' Sid wanted to get off the subject as soon as possible. 'Er. Is she all right?'

'Fine.'

'Good.' That was final as far as Sid was concerned. 'What was that you meant about the tomatoes? You said, "You see all the tomatoes you want at the club." Do you mean tomatoes as in women or as in thrown?'

'Nothing.'

'If it's women, I'm flattered. If it's thrown, I'm hurt. But if it's women, which women? The waitresses, or the bar ladies, or the disco dancers? And what about all those young women who work in Boots or Marks and Spencers? If I'd had as many women as you seem to think I've had, I should have died a long time ago from a rare disease called ecstasy.' Sid stood up from the small breakfast table and put the chair back under it, picked up his cup and walked

14

towards the sink. 'And if the term is thrown, I'd like you to know I'm good enough not to get anything thrown at me, and if you would come to the club and see me work sometimes you would find that out. I've been working there for the last two years and you haven't been once. Half the staff think I'm a widower.' He was rinsing his cup under the tap.

'I don't like nightclubs.' She picked up the drying cloth and took the cup from him.

'Sweetheart, there are times when I hate the sodding place.'

'Don't swear!'

'But I work theatres, clubs, TV and kiddie shows. I sometimes work seven days a week.' Carrie gave him back the cup. 'And I do it for two reasons. One is that I enjoy working and the other is that I do it to earn money so I can give you and Elspeth a nice home. There's not many other comics who work as regularly as I do.' Sid washed the cup again. 'But I still get the impression that you want me to have a nine-to-five job.'

Carrie said, 'That's twice you've washed that cup.' Sid put it down. 'I'm going to Sainsbury's.' Carrie didn't want to get caught up in a quarrel because she never did win a verbal argument with Sid anyway. He was much too devious. It was all the practice at the club. She put her coat on. Sid wiped the cup dry. There was a little bit of silence now, except for Glenn Miller belting out 'Little Brown Jug' for a senior citizen of ninety-seven. 'Mrs Gerry will be here about ten. She's having her hair done. I said it would be all right. Don't stop her from working by telling her how hard you work. Could you pass me the plastic carrier off the doorknob?' Sid did. 'I'll be back about one o'clock to get you a bit of lunch.'

Carrie left by the back door to get to the garage. Sid watched her go. She's still an attractive woman, he thought. He had to smile to himself. She was going to Sainsbury's with a plastic bag that told the whole world how good Macfisheries were. Maybe she had a sense of humour after all.

The elder DJ obviously had a sense of humour. He was now talking to some idiot who had written a new book on diet and health called *Fry Your Way To Fitness*. The DJ got in a good ad lib. He said, 'I'm a stone overweight. Fry me.'

2

Sid opened the left door on the third floor and walked out of the Tardis towards the door with MGM Agency on it. He took the advice of the sign that said, 'Enter'. A young, attractive woman was busy typing directly opposite the door. To his right on the carpeted floor was a comfortable bench seat fully occupied by the three it would take. Nearest to Sid sat a sixty-eight-year-old, once famous film star screen lover, Gavin Wright, now hoping for any small part, but it must be a part – 'I will not do extra work'. He was seated next to Lennie Price, the very latest black comedian from the new wave of black comedians. His style was to knock his own kind, his own people, make out he was white. Next to Lennie was an actor with a small 'a' whom millions of people had seen on television at least once a fortnight for the previous five years and yet not one of them would recognize him if he offered to pay their income tax. He had the kind of face that made people say, 'Just a moment. Aren't you ... er? You know ... the, er. My wife thinks you're ... You do the ... er. You're on every ... night. Yes. You're what's his name.'

Sid had an appointment with Leslie Garland, the 'G' part of MGM, Mitchell, Garland and Maybank. He had been with Leslie now for about six years. Leslie did the light entertainment side, clubs, one-nighters, theatres, summer season and pantomime. Stan Mitchell was the straight side – West End plays, straight plays on TV – while Richard Maybanks was the overseas rep; Singapore, Hong Kong, the States and Australia. Sid had never seen Maybanks.

The girl looked up from her typing and smiled. 'Good morning, Mr Lewis. I'll tell Mr Garland you're here.' The others in the waiting-room looked at Sid as he gave a nod. She phoned through to

Leslie's office and told him: 'Mr Lewis is here.' Sid waited for the reply. 'Mr Garland says five minutes, Mr Lewis.' Another phone rang. She put it to her ear. 'Yes?' She put the receiver back. 'Mr Mitchell will see you now, Mr Wright.'

The sixty-eight-year-old, once famous lover of the silver screen creaked through the waiting-room towards the big red leather door and disappeared behind it. Sid sat next to Lennie Price on the still warm seat left vacant by the old screen lover. Lennie looked at Sid and, with a smile, said, 'I'm Lennie Price.'

'Sid Lewis.'

They shook hands.

'I saw you at the Starlight Rooms, when the Three Degrees were there. Great,' Lennie said.

Sid didn't know whether he was saying that Sid was great or the Three Degrees. He took no chances. 'Yes, they were.'

'Fantastic.'

'Great.'

The actor with a small 'a' was reading the television part of *The Stage* and never once looked up.

'Does Leslie do your work then?' asked Lennie.

'Yes. I've been with this office over six years now.'

'I'm hoping to see him. I'd like him to do my work. Do you think he's any good?'

'Kept me in pretty regular work.'

The red leather door opened and out came the ex-silver screen lover. You could tell by the look on his face that work was not coming his way that day. He left the waiting-room without a word.

'Who's at the Starlight Rooms this week?' asked Lennie.

'Cliff.'

'Cliff?'

'Richard.'

'Great.'

The actor asked, 'What time is Mr Maybanks due?'

'I'll ask his secretary,' said the pretty typist. She dialled a number and asked, 'What time is Mr Maybanks due? I see. Thank you.' She put the receiver down and looked at the actor. 'Not till Thursday. He's been delayed in Canada.'

'Oh. I thought he was due back yesterday.'

'He was, but it's snowing in Canada.'

'Yes. Well, I'll call again on Thursday.'

'Fine. Who shall I say will be calling?'

'Colin Webster.'

Of course, thought Sid, Colin Webster.

'Goodbye, Mr Webb,' said the pretty secretary.

Exit stage left, thought Sid.

Behind the big red leather door Sid and Lennie heard male and female laughter. Leslie held the door open for a woman called Marcia Vaughan, the best stripper in the country. Well, if not the best, certainly the fastest. The star of all the sexy revues.

'Hello, Sid,' she said. 'How's Carrie and Elspeth?'

'Fine, thanks. Reggie okay?'

'As good as he'll ever be. That's not saying much. I think he thinks it's fallen off. He's put on so much weight. I see it more than he does. Goodbye, darling.' A kiss was exchanged that wouldn't have shocked a vicar's maiden aunt. 'Bye everyone,' she said and left.

'Bye, darlink.' Leslie smiled at everyone in the little room and they all dutifully smiled back. He seemed to be enjoying a certain power. Slowly he lit a small seven-inch Havana cigar. 'Sid,' his voice cracked. Sid jumped up to follow him through the red door. He noticed it wasn't held open for him as it had been for Marcia.

'How's Coral?' Leslie asked.

'Carrie's fine, thank you.'

'Good.' They were now half way up the small corridor. 'And the kids?'

'She's fine.'

'Good.'

They entered his office. It was very large. A beautiful desk was placed so that Leslie sat with his back to the window and a couple of easy chairs were on the other side facing him. On a bright day you had the sun in your eyes so that you could not see him clearly. You were always in an inferior position. You were being looked down upon. A psychological advantage. A beautiful, small carriage clock was facing you. It had a loud tick. Leslie always kept turning it towards you and he always gave you the impression that you were wasting his time.

'Sit down, Sid,' he said.

'Thanks. I ... er ... won't keep you. I know how busy you ...'

'Good.' Leslie turned the clock full-face towards Sid and rested his hand on it.

'It's ... er ... just to ... you know, er ... to ... er. How's Rhoda?'

'Who?'

'Rhoda. Your wife.'

18

'Haven't you heard?'

'What?' Sid asked, with fear in his voice.

Leslie Garland's eyes raked Sid's now almost quivering face. 'No matter.' He looked at the clock again.

Sid wondered whether to ask about Rhoda or to carry on about himself. What he said was, 'Oh, I'm really sorry about that.'

'About what?' Leslie asked.

'Rhoda,' answered Sid, giving a sickly grin.

'What about Rhoda?'

'What you said,' Sid said, with a nervously drying mouth. 'Carrie will be upset.'

'Who's Carrie?'

'My wife,' Sid replied through an almost closed mouth.

'What is it you want to see me about, Sid?' Leslie asked with a small sign of temper.

'Well,' Sid began, 'I've been working at the club now for two years or so and I thought ...' The phone rang.

Leslie raised his hand from the clock and picked up the phone. 'Yes?' he shouted.

Sid stopped talking and tried to give a non-listening look.

'Shirley who?' Leslie bellowed. 'Okay. Put her on. Hello, Shirl. Yeh. Fine. How's Warren? Good. Give him my very best. And he should live to be 120. Rhoda? Haven't you heard? We've split. Yeh. She took off with the chauffeur. Yeh. Last week.' He nodded to the phone. 'Don't worry. Everything you've asked for has been done. I promise.'

Sid was looking at some pictures around the walls.

'Yeh, the orchestra. Everything. The advance? Great. It's great.' Leslie smiled for the first time. 'You'll be a sell out. I'm telling you. Yeh. The dressing-room's been altered to your specifications. A bathroom with a shower. Yes. A TV, and a bar – all in blue and gold. Yeh. Yeh. Yeh. Ah ha. Yeh. Sure. Of course. Yep. Okay. Sure. Natch. Anything, why not? Of course you're not being difficult. If you don't deserve it, who does? A what?' Leslie's eyes almost glazed over. 'Yeh, surely, but that could be a little difficult. Yes. A coloured maid. I'll try. You don't mind if she's a Jamaican, do you? A Jamaican. You know, West Indian. Sure they speak English. An ice maker? Yes. Air-conditioning? Yeh. Okay. A what? A Teasmade. Yes, they are cute. And a limo. A Rolls. Fine. Of course, with a driver. A black one. Is that the Rolls or the driver? A white Rolls with a black driver. What?!! Sixteen seats on the front row on opening night? For your relatives? That's a lot of money. Oh, sure. Of course, I'll see that the theatre pays for it,' he said, turning heart-attack grey.

Sid had, by this time, seen all the pictures on the walls and read all the 'Thank you, Leslie's' on them. One day, he thought, my picture will be in here and I'll just put, 'What's the time, Sid?'

'What's the weather like in Hollywood?' Leslie asked Shirl. 'What do you mean, you don't know?' he looked at the clock and then at Sid. 'Oh, you're in New York.'

Sid moved over to the window and looked out on a busy London street.

Leslie continued his transatlantic conversation. 'Yeh, at the Savoy. A suite. What? But what's wrong with the Savoy? All right, darling,' he smoothed. 'Sure. I'll see to it. The Oliver Mussel. Yeh, Messel.' 'Messel, Shmessels,' he whispered to himself. 'At the Dorchester. Okay, kid. Yeh. And to you. Goodbye. Sure. I'll give Rhoda your love.'

Leslie put the phone down in a small state of shock. He then picked up the other phone and dialled one number. After two seconds he said, 'Stella, get the Oliver Messel suite for Shirl. I know you've booked her in at the Savoy. So get her out and in to the Oliver Messel suite at the Dorchester. Look, I don't give a Donald Duck how you do it. Do it.' He slammed the phone down.

Sid was now standing at the edge of the desk with the clock facing away from him. Leslie turned it back so Sid could see it very clearly. Sid took the hint and carried on with, 'So I thought it was time I had a rise.'

'I'll have a word,' Leslie almost growled.

He then put his hand out to be shaken and left Sid to find his own way out. Sid looked at his watch. Seven minutes in all he had been with his agent to talk over his future and that included a five minute phone call from New York. Christ, Sid thought, that's what I call looking after your artist. He saw Lennie still waiting. 'A word in your ear, son,' he said. 'If and when you get in, speak quickly.'

Lennie did not know what he meant, but he would.

Sid walked out of the office entrance into a windy Piccadilly. It was still early. There was no rush to get home and he need not be at the club until about eightish. He looked at his Snoopy watch and thought he saw Leslie Garland's face ticking from side to side. It was only three-thirty. He put his head down to face the wind, pulled his overcoat more closely around himself, and, at a fair pace, walked down Piccadilly into the Circus, along Shaftesbury Avenue, and then across into Soho itself. He slowly lifted his head out of the top of his overcoat and looked at some of the pictures outside small clubs, cinemas, sex shops, and bookshops with magazines that made *Health and Efficiency* look like something the verger handed out with *Hymns Ancient and Modern.*

Unbeknown to Carrie, Sid had won a hundred and odd quid at the club on a Yankee bet. At this moment it was burning a hole in his pocket. He stopped to look at a small ad frame. Sid looked at one particular card in the small frame. He read it twice. He had to. He could not believe it. It read:

> Miss Aye Sho Yu – Oriental Massage – Number 69.
> Three flights. Two masseuses. No waiting.
> Your joy is our pleasure. Please knock.

Sid looked around just to make sure nobody was actually looking at him, eyeball to eyeball, before he entered. He had one more look at the frame. Should it be, he thought, Aye Sho Yu, or the other next to it: Turkish Delight – 'not like that – like that. You get the *massage*' – written on a fez? No, thought Sid, Aye Sho Yu.

As he started his walk up three flights of stairs he thought, Of course – the reason I'm doing this is in case I get a good idea for some gags or a sketch for the club, or maybe even TV. He knew that what he had just said to himself was a complete excuse and really about the weakest he could have thought of. No way would he be able to use one line, one thought, or one iota of an idea in his professional work. I'll turn back. I'll leave. Why? Because I am right. It's wrong. But suppose somebody actually saw you coming into the building. So? So. I'll tell you so. If you leave now and he's still there outside, he's going to look at you and say to himself, 'Good God. He didn't last long,' isn't he? That's true. Yes, it is, isn't it? Yes. Then keep going. Okay.

He had one flight to go, past a man coming down the stairs. Sid stopped and looked towards the wall as the man passed him and then turned his head to watch the man as he staggered down the stairs. Sid thought, he's either drunk or exhausted.

On the landing of the third flight were four doors, numbered 68, 70 and 71. Where was 69? Oh – there. 69 was printed on its side. Clever. Sid took a deep breath and knocked on the door, softly, so softly in fact that had there been woodworm in the door they would not have heard him. Door 70 opened and a man's face furtively looked out. Sid turned, but only just in time to see the door close quickly. From the fourth floor a fat man appeared. He continued his way downstairs. He was about eighteen stone. If he had forgotten anything on the fourth floor it would have to remain there as it would have killed him to go back up those stairs. Sid knocked harder. Number 69 opened and he came face to face with a pretty Chinese girl.

'Yes?' she asked.

'I ... er ... saw your ... er ... advert in the frame downstairs.'

'Massage?'

'Er ... please ... yes.'

'Would you please enter. I will ask Miss Yu if she can help you.' She put both hands together and bowed her head. 'Please to wait.' She pointed to a small couch. 'Please to sit.'

Sid sat. The wall at the back of the couch was decorated with a red dragon that looked as if it had been painted by the PG Tips monkeys. The girl was dressed in a long black nightgown as far as Sid could tell. She left the tiny hall and, after one knock on a door, went through into another room. On the back of her nightgown was embroidered a golden dragon. Instead of fire there was a number 69.

Sid looked round the tiny hall. On the door that Miss Takeaway had gone through was a full-sized poster of Bruce Lee kicking the Eartha Kitt out of about thirty Chinamen, all armed with guns, knives and hatchets. Bruce had only his bare hands and his bare feet. He suddenly disappeared as the door opened and in his place stood Miss Takeaway.

'Miss Yu will see you please.'

Sid stood up and hit his head on the swinging paper lantern. He walked past Bruce Lee and Miss Takeaway into a room with a bed in the middle of it that was very reminiscent of an operating table. It was covered with a white towel. Everything looked clean and the air was pleasantly perfumed. The square room was completely painted in willow pattern style and looked like some of the plates his grandma used to have.

Sid thought, If I stripped off and lay on that table, I'd look like a chip.

A door opened and in came Miss Yu. She also had the look of an Oriental and was wearing a long dress that was split down one side from the floor to just under her left arm. She looked an old twenty-six, about thirty-two, but she looked good. Well – good enough, when money's burning a hole in your pocket.

'You would likee massage?' she asked in the phoniest accent he had ever heard.

'Well, yes. You know – just to get rid of a few aches and pains.'

'You wantee normal or special massage?'

'What's the difference?'

'A tenner,' she replied in perfect English.

'How much is a normal massage?'

'A tenner.'

'And what would I get for a normal massage?'

'The same as a special massage only quicker.'

'American Express?'

'Balls!'

'Okay then.'

'I take it honourable gentleman would likee special?'

Sid expected Edward G. Robinson to walk in at any moment and the whole thing to develop into a Tong war.

'I will leave you to get undressed,' she went on. 'If you would let me have the twenty qui ... pounds, I will not embarrass you by remaining. Of course, if honourable gentleman pays twenty-five pounds, my beautiful younger, virgin sister helps to makee you relax more in longer time.'

'Twenty-five?'

'Only if you wishee complete relaxation, but if master only desire ... er ... quickee ... er ... I alone am willing to accommodate.'

Sid said to himself, That fella going downstairs wasn't drunk or exhausted. At twenty-five quid he was probably broke. However, after the win he had the cash to spare and the urge to spend it. 'What's your sister's name?' he asked.

'Why.'

'Well, I think for twenty-five quid I'd just like to ...'

'Her name is Why.'

'Why?'

'Yes, Why.'

'Not Why Aye Sho Yu?'

'All is arranged.' She crossed herself. Sid looked slightly surprised at a Chinese Roman Catholic, but in Soho ...?

'Were you recommended?' she asked demurely.

'No, no, no. I would put myself down as a one off.'

Miss Yu waddled over to a small gong on a pair of wedgies. If she had any wish to commit suicide she could have jumped off them. She hit the gong with an object that a book like *Family Planning* or *Getting Married* would have called a phallic symbol. What Miss Yu called it she kept to herself.

'Please undress and lie on table,' she said. She started to walk away from him, then turned round to add, 'Face upwards.' She smiled.

'I thought Chinese people didn't laugh.'

'It all depends on who they are with, oh great one!'

She threw Sid what Carrie would have called a face flannel, with which to save himself any embarrassment. She then left the room, walking through a river in the willow pattern. Sid began to undress. Through a loud speaker, which was painted so as to blend in with the willow pattern, and rested on a Chinaman's head, came a noise that made Sid almost jump out of his pants. It was very loud and sounded like what a Cockney would call in rhyming slang 'a jam tart'. Then, as it settled down and the sound was lowered, it became some sort of Oriental music; although quite modern, it was to Sid's mind Japanese. A Jap group was singing songs like 'The girl from Okayama' and 'Oh Yokahama, where the wind comes sweeping down the plain'.

Sid was now in his Y-fronts. The small towel Miss Yu had given him was laughable. He hoped there was a shower for later and also a bigger towel with which to dry himself. He kept on his Y-fronts and also his socks as, although the white carpet looked clean, he was more than a tiny bit afraid of verrucas. He sat on the edge of the white, towelled mattress and swung his legs. It might make a good sketch, he mused. Lies, all lies, Sidney, and you know it. That's true, he murmured back to himself. How about Carrie, you rotten sod? Have you no conscience? He smiled. Ah, he answered, conscience doesn't stop you from doing it. It just stops you from enjoying it. He started to swing his legs from side to side. Does that mean to say if you don't do it you'll enjoy it? he asked himself. He was now on his back, cycling his legs in the air. That doesn't make sense, he replied. He leaned forward to touch his toes. You see, he continued. He pulled his feet towards him like a footballer with cramp. What? He grimaced for the trainer to be sent on. Exactly.

A gong sounded and through the river of the willow pattern entered Why. She carried a tray on which were oils and perfumes. The thing that puzzled Sid was that earlier on she had left him via Bruce Lee and had now come back via the river. Did that mean that rooms 68, 70 and 71 had connecting doors? Had she gone

24

through room 70 to get to 69? His mind went back to reading the advert outside. Next to him, he remembered, had stood the biggest Negro he had ever seen in his life, big enough to make Mandingo look like a black Ronnie Corbett. He remembered also seeing another ad: 'Madame La Rochelle, MBE. French taught the easy way. Guaranteed satisfaction. Room 70 – third floor.'

Sid looked at Why. She did not look overworked. He noticed as she put down the tray that she had changed her dress. She was now wearing very little everywhere. She did not speak and, as she walked away from him, he looked at her lovely little firm, round bum and thought, I'll never eat another hot cross bun again.

The gong sounded. Sid looked towards the river but nothing happened because Aye came through another door which was painted as a rice planter. As the door opened Sid thought he saw a pained expression on the face of the painted rice planter as the whole of his arse was moved from the rest of his body.

Aye was carrying a folder. Her outfit – well, with Why you could see through what she was wearing, and with Aye you could not see what she was wearing. To Sid twenty-five pounds was a lot of bunce, but at least they were working for it. Judith Chalmers would have difficulty in describing Aye's costume – two pieces of elastoplast and a cork.

'Why you no undressed?' Aye asked Why.

'Well, you see …' Sid started to answer.

'I was asking my sister, Why. Why you no undressed?'

'Oh.'

Any moment Sid expected Aye to say, 'Did white man arrive in big iron bird?'

'Why? Please.'

Why went to the leg end of the high mattress, while Aye went to the other end, placed her hands on Sid's shoulders and easily and professionally forced him down. Why grabbed his underpants and, with one deft movement, whipped them off and his socks too, with such speed and dexterity that would have made a hospital nightnurse applaud and many a magician go home and practise. Sid's first reaction was to reach for the towel, but that was by now in the same place as his underpants and socks, wherever they were. So, as he first thought, he felt like a chip.

Aye handed him the contents of the folder. 'Please to take plenty good look at Chinese art,' she said.

God, she was a bloody awful actress. Sid was given six ten-by-twelve blow-ups of what were once known as French postcards – the kind of thing all men looked at but would not have on their person in case they ever got knocked down or run over.

'Are you showing me these for a reason?' he asked.

'To help patient relax,' Aye answered.

'Well, that's the last thing they're going to do.'

Why started to massage Sid's big toes very gently, while Aye held his head up so he could see the Chinese French postcards without having to lift his arms in the air. The pictures were of hands and things. Sid recognized Why by the ring on her finger. After looking at the pictures twice through, Aye took them from him and let his head fall back hard on the table, which made his Adam's apple bounce up and down fast enough to make cider. Why was now massaging the back of his knees. Aye put the pictures back in the folder and put them on the tray. She then picked up a tin of Johnson's Baby Powder and powdered him with it, as if it was a salt-cellar and he *was* a chip. Aye and Why were now standing either side of his shoulders. The lights started to dim on their own. Sid wondered, Am I being watched? Am I part of room 70's French lesson? He tried to look round for an eye hole but, from his position, could not see one. Powder and hands were everywhere. At one stage he thought he felt five hands, but he dismissed that thought.

'Please – you have name?' Aye smiled.

'Er … Dick.'

'Dick. Very nice name.' Why said shyly, 'You have number two name?'

'Barton.'

'Dick Barton. Velly nicee name,' Aye said, with a resounding slap.

This woman must be the worst actress in the world, Sid thought. The nearest she'd ever been to the East was Ley Ons, the Chinese Restaurant in Wardour Street, and, as far as 69 was concerned, that was the special fried rice on the menu.

Powder was now settling. Another hard slap.

'Please vill you turn ofer.'

That was the third accent she'd used. Sid did as she commanded just in case she said, 'Ve have vays of making you turn ofer.' Forget Edward G. Robinson, Sid thought, as Why tried to walk up and down his spine. But keep an eye out for Curt Jürgens rushing in to tell us all that the allies have invaded France and the Führer is insane.

'Over again, please.'

Sid turned, but a little too quickly, before Why could get off the table. She landed on the floor flat on her hot cross bun. Why came out with some language that Sid had only heard once before, when a red hot rivet had landed on the inside of a ship builder's leather apron.

'Sorry,' Sid said and got up to try to help Why off the floor. As he did this the lights started to get dimmer. The room was now almost dark, obviously from some timing device. Why put out her hand to grab what was, she thought, Sid's helping hand, but Sid's helping hands were under both of her arms. Sid let out a scream that would have sent both Edward G. Robinson and Curt Jürgens running out of the room.

By this time Aye was making her way round to both of them, when, on cue, the room went into complete darkness. Aye tripped over Why's legs and fell with arms outstretched. Nature being what it is, self preservation took over, and she held on to the first thing she grabbed. Sid let out yet another scream.

The music got louder and faster. There was a knock on the rice planter and a female voice shouted: 'Are you all right, Doreen? Doreen, Stella, are you all right?'

'Switch the bleeding light on,' Doreen or Stella shouted.

The lights slowly came up. The rice planter was once more in his painful broken position and Sid saw what he took to be Madame La Rochelle standing in the doorway with the eleven foot negro, both naked.

'Shut that door,' one of the girls shouted.

What a great catch phrase, Sid thought. I must remember that.

Madame La Rochelle shut that door. The rice planter must have been in agony. Sid, Doreen and Stella were still on the floor.

Sid laughed painfully. 'Well, at least it's been different. Original even. Stella?'

'Yes?'

'How do you feel?'

'All right.'

'Probably more shock than anything,' Sid grinned. He stood up. 'Well, Doreen,' he asked. 'Do I get a refund, or do we do a deal?'

'Refund?' She said the word as if she had just heard it for the first time, as in 'Me Tarzan – You Refund'.

'Well, it was you who had the thrills. Both of you grabbed me by the orchestras.'

27

'Orchestras?' they chorused.

'Yes. Orchestra stalls. Now do I get a refund? Let's say half, or do I tell the police you both tried to rape me?'

All three were standing up. Stella, Doreen and Sid.

'No refund,' said Doreen.

'Okay then,' Sid mused, 'we carry on where we left off.'

All three smiled. Doreen nodded, Stella rubbed her bruises and Sid said, 'Lights, music, action. Doreen?'

'Yes.'

'Don't keep doing that. It doesn't help,' Sid said in the darkness.

3

Sid's way of earning a living was, to say the least, hard. The idea
of his job was to entertain the people, who had paid sometimes
£3.50, sometimes £15 per person, for what was loosely called dinner. Dancing was thrown in, rowdies were thrown out, and, now
and again, dinner was thrown up. Gambling, if permitted, was
always kept well away from the entertainment because the management did not like the audience to hear the cheers of a man who
had just won seventy quid, or the screams of a man who had just
lost seven hundred quid, although they were less against the
cheers than the screams. If the star name was big, so was the business; if the star name was not big, neither was the business. Service
was normally slow but what's the rush anyway. The waiters were
mainly foreign, the waitresses were usually British, and the customer
was often hungry. Invariably the room was dark; only the staff could
see their way around because God has given all nightclub waiters
special eyes. The toilets were sometimes as far away, or so it felt,
as the next town. The sound system was the nearest thing to all
the bombs falling on London during the last war condensed into
two and a half hours approximately.

Sid's job was to come out on to a small platform or stage and
try to tell you how much, thanks to him, you were going to enjoy
yourselves. The nightclub audience is not prudish but it will not
laugh at a dirty joke unless it is filthy. So the comic feels that he
has to gear his material to that audience for safety, the safety of
his job. No one is going to pay a comic good money if the laughs
are not there, so laughs have got to be found and the safest way
is the oldest way – give them what they want. That maxim still
applies, from the shows at Las Vegas to opera at Covent Garden.

If they do not like it, they don't come. In this side of show business it's called 'arses on seats'. If the seats are empty, so is the till. So Sid had to walk out and face a basically uninterested audience and get laughs with the first of his four or five 12–15 minute spots, and, of course, have something prepared in case the lights failed, the star got drunk or the resident singer had not turned up because she had had a row with the fella she was living with and her husband had ever so slightly changed her face around a little when she went back to him. Not a lot, she'll be fine when the swelling goes down!

Sid was on the side waiting to go out there for the first of his spots. The group were on their last number, which received its usual desultory applause. Sid's music started – 'Put on a happy face'. He checked his flies and walked out as if he was the biggest star in the world. Wearing a well cut, modern evening dress suit, mohair of course, and a pale blue frilly dress shirt that d'Artagnan would have been proud to wear, he timed his walk to the mike so that he could take it out of its socket, put it up to his mouth, and sing the last line of the song 'S . . o . . o . . o . . o put on a happy f . . a . . a . . a . . c . . c . . e. Thankyouladiesandgennelmengoodevening.' The end of the song and the welcoming words corresponded volume-wise with the air raid on Coventry. Three quick blows into the mike to check that the sound was working. 'Now first of all ladiesandgennelmen can you hear okay?'

'No,' shouted a voice from the blackness.

'Then how did you know what I've just said?' He tapped four more times on the mike top with his fingers. 'My name is Sid Lewis ladiesandgennelmen. The most important thing is – are you enjoying yourselves?'

'No,' was the shout from the same voice from the same blackness.

Sid put his hand up to his forehead and looked into the distance, reminiscent of Errol Flynn as Robin Hood saying to Alan Hale as Little John, 'Run, it's the Sheriff of Nottingham.' What he did say was, 'Don't worry about him, folks. He's only talking to prove he's alive.' He put his hand down. 'I'll tell you something about him. He's a great impressionist – drinks like a fish. His barber charges him 80p – 20p a corner!'

He had no worries about the voice coming back at him again from the darkness because the voice was a plant, a stooge. By the time Sid had done his barber joke, the stooge was backstage drinking a pint, paid for by Sid.

Sid was now into his act, walking about with the mike. 'Let me tell you something else. No, listen. A father and son. Got that? A father and son walking in the country. Now, listen. A father and a son. It's all good stuff this. When suddenly a bee lands on a flower. The little boy kills it with a rock. No, listen, you're laughing in the wrong place. His father says, "For being so cruel you won't have any honey for a year." Walking a bit further, the boy sees a butterfly land on a flower. He cups his hand around it and squashes it. No. Not yet. Don't laugh too early. Soon. I promise you. S .. o .. o .. o .. o .. n. The boy's father says, "For doing that you won't get any butter for a year." Then they went home. His mother was in the kitchen making dinner, when she saw a cockroach. She stamped on it and killed it. The little boy said, "Are you going to tell her, Dad, or am I?" ... Cockroach ... Do you get it? *Cock*roach. C-o-c-k ... Oh, well, it's up to you.'

Sid kept moving around the small stage, looking at nearby tables. 'Here's one. The same little boy. That's right. The same little boy ran towards his mum wearing a pirate outfit. His mum says, "What a handsome-looking pirate. Where's your buccaneers?" The little boy says, "Under my buccanhat." Now, listen. Here's another one you might not like. You've got to listen to me, lady. I work fast. The same boy, same boy. He's on a picnic with his mummy and daddy and he wanders off. No, not for that, lady! Just for a walk and he gets lost ... Aw ... Aw ... Come on, everybody. Aw ... Sod you then. Anyway this little boy's lost, same little boy, so he drops to his knees to pray. "Dear God, help me to get out of here." A nice prayer. Straight to the point. Now then, as he's praying, a big black crow flies overhead and drops his calling card right in the middle of the little boy's outstretched hand. The little boy looks at it and says, "Please God, don't hand me that stuff. I really am lost ..." Now, listen ... Here's one. You'll like this one, lady. I can see you have a sense of humour. I can tell by the fella you're with. Now, listen. This one's for you.'

Sid sat down on the stage close to the table where the woman was and helped himself to a glass of her wine. 'A girl hippy said to another girl hippy, "Have you ever been picked up by the fuzz?" The other girl hippy says, "No, but I bet it must be painful!" Now, listen. A poem. I know you like poems ...

A lovely young girl called Lavern
Was so great she had lovers to burn.

31

She got into bed with Arthur and Fred,
But didn't know which way to turn.

Now, listen. Don't get carried away ... You'll like this one, sir. May I ask? Is this your wife? Is she your wife, sir?'

The man nods.

'I took my wife to the doctor's this morning and he said to her, "Open your mouth and say moo." You'll like this one, sir. This could be you. A handsome husband ... Why is your wife laughing, sir? A handsome husband, whose wife was a raver. I said you'd like this one, sir. "I've found a new position," he tells her. "Great," his wife says, "which way?" He says, "Back to back." She says, "Back to back? How can that be done?" The husband says, "I bring home another couple." I knew you'd like it. I have to go now. One more poem before I go and lie down. Poem ...

A ballerina with very big feet
Would give all the stagehands a treat.
But if they asked for a ride,
She'd blush and she cried,
"It would ruin my nutcracker suite."

See you later, folks.'

The music would start and Sid would run off to a fairly good response. They would not go mad for him because they realized he was coming back throughout the evening.

Twenty minutes later, Sid was back on stage, and happy. 'Always happy when I'm out there working.' He had been on for maybe ten or twelve minutes, handing out bouquets of flowers to the silver weddings, the twenty-firsts, the eighteenths, newly-weds and the engagements. As a matter of fact, Sid could present a bouquet to anyone. He was good at that. He'd been at it now for almost two years, night after night. He knew his audience, but more important, his audience knew him. They accepted him. It had been said that Sid could present a bouquet to a dead body and have the body go off smiling. The hard part was getting the body to come on, there being very few places on that small stage for it to lean against.

Perspiration was beginning to dampen his shirt collar. He undid his tie and opened his top shirt-button. It gave the impression he was working hard. He walked about the stage in the spotlight that followed him like the light of the top tower in a jail break at Sing

32

Sing. The mike was almost glued to his lips. He never stopped talking. He was never at a loss for a word or an ad lib. His style was fast and full of energy. Nothing subtle and no fear. If he saw a woman in the audience with a large bust, he would go straight to her, look directly into her eyes and say, 'We have our own bouncers here, lady. But I see you've brought your own, or are you just breaking them in for a friend?' The table she was on would erupt into gales of laughter, the tables close-by would look and laugh, while the rest of the audience would carry on eating and talking, but Sid would walk around and within a second would come out with, 'Here . . . no . . . listen. Have you heard the one about the Irishman?' Then he would go into *his* latest Irish joke, this being the one he had heard from the petrol attendant on his way to the club that night.

'I do POWER comedy,' he used to say. 'Never give the punters time to think.' He would walk, talk, ask, beg and shout at the punters to help him get a laugh.

On stage with him were a young couple.

'So, Sharon, your name is Sharon, isn't it, Sharon?' Sid put his mike to her mouth and Sharon nodded. He put the mike back to his own lips, 'And your name, sir?'

'Mar'in.'

'Martin. Well, it's nice to have you both with us. Sharon and Martin.'

The young couple shuffled about, Sharon on her six inch wedgies and Martin on his size twelve Kickers.

Sid looked into the blackness of the moving, eating, talking noise. 'Because tonight, ladiesandgennelmen, Sharon and Martin are here to celebrate their engagement. So how about a round of applause for Sharon and Martin?'

A table thirty or forty feet away from the stage whistled and applauded.

'How old are you, Martin?'

'Nine'een.'

'Nineteen,' Sid bellowed. 'And Sharon, how old are you?' he asked in a much softer voice.

'Seveneenanaalf,' she giggled.

'Seventeen and a half.'

Sharon tried to hold Martin's hand. Martin, embarrassed, slimed out of her grasp.

'So what are you going to do with these lovely flowers, Sharon?'

33

'Givem to me mum.'

'Give them to her mother,' Sid told everyone. 'What do you say to that, Martin?'

'Sawrye.'

'Well, we hope you'll both be very happy. How about a big hand ladiesandgennelman for The Two Ronnies?' Sid handed Sharon the bouquet. 'Sharon and Martin, ladiesandgennelmen.'

The young couple headed towards the dark safety of the audience. Martin, in front of his future wife, suddenly stopped, while still on the edge of the bright circle of spotlight, and put both arms above his head and thumped the empty air in the same way he had seen football players do after scoring the only goal of the game with no more than thirty seconds left for play, including time added on for stoppages. He seemed to realize that this was probably the last time so many people would be watching him at one given moment. Then Sharon and Martin were enveloped by the blackness and the nothingness of the future.

'Here, now listen,' Sid said. 'Have you heard about the Arab and the Jew shopping in Golders Green?' He told his latest Arab and Jew joke. It got its quota of laughs. 'And now ladiesandgennelman ...' Without turning round, Sid pointed to the drummer, who gave a cymbal crash followed by three rim shots like a machine gun that only had three bullets left. Sid then changed his voice to a much lower and more serious tone, as if he was going to introduce Dean Martin at the Sands in Las Vegas. 'The management of the Starlight Rooms, East Finchley, would now like to present ...' A slight pause; an attention getter, an old pro's trick to make the audience think maybe the star is coming on. A few heads turned towards him, still chewing their chicken-in-a-basket. 'A special bouquet,' Sid smarmed. 'The last bouquet.'

The few heads turned back and tried to find their food.

'I know it's the last bouquet because it's eleven-thirty and the cemetery across the road closes at eleven.'

The noise was getting louder because the punters were getting bored with bouquets. The bar at the back was packed with people trying to get all their drinks to take back to their tables to swim in while the star was on, because in the star's contract there was a clause forbidding the bar to remain open while the said star was performing. The punters knew this. They even knew how much the star was getting and, in some cases, how much in 'readies'.

Sid carried on, 'To someone you all know and love. The ex-resident singer of the Starlight Rooms – Miss Shelley Grange. HowaboutabigroundofapplauseforShelleyladiesandgennelmen?'

Sid's delivery was now getting louder and faster. It was almost like Kermit the frog. He knew nobody out there was interested in Shelley Grange. Hell fire – she even talked off key! He was now having to battle, but the management, Manny and Al Keppleman, had insisted he did this because Manny, unknown to Al, and Al, unknown to Manny, had both been having naughties with Shelley, known to everyone. So tonight she was being thanked publicly. Even the group was smiling, all except the drummer as he'd joined after Shelley had left.

'Come on up, Shelley,' Sid said, putting his hands together as if in prayer.

Shelley made her way up from one of the front tables looking completely surprised, which made Sid think, She's a good little actress as well, seeing that it was all planned yesterday.

The group were playing one of her songs, 'I did it my way'. Shelley – her real name was Minnie Schoenberg – glided on to the small stage, her candy-floss hair so lacquered it almost cracked as she walked. She had a good figure, leaning slightly towards plumpness. Her dress was a mass of silver flashing sequins, and as she made her way towards the stage she reminded Sid of a very pretty Brillo pad.

She was now on stage with Sid and the dutiful applause faded very quickly. A few voices from the area of the bar shouted incoherent ruderies, followed by loud guffaws of beer-brave laughter.

Sid boomed, 'Welcome back, Shelley. It's great to see you again.'

Shelley smiled at Sid and the audience. Her blonde hair crackled in the spotlight. She turned to the group, the Viv Dane Stompers, affectionately known as the V-Ds. The boys grinned back. In the wings, another blonde in a tight blue flashing dress watched Shelley. She was Serina, the new resident singer. They looked at each other with exposed teeth and four dead eyes.

Sid shouted, 'Ladiesandgennelmen, we've invited Shelley back to the Starlight Rooms tonight because a little bird has told us that Shelley is getting married next month to a –'

'Next week,' Shelley said.

'Why? Can't you wait?' Sid spurted out. He went on, '– next week to a friend of all of us, our own bar manager, Giorgio Richetti. How about a round of applause for GiorgioRichettiladiesandgennelmen?' Apart from Shelley's own table, the loudest applause for Giorgio came from just outside the office door – Al and Manny.

'Come on up, Giorgio,' Sid shouted.

Giorgio was guided by his eight friends at his table, all men, all Italian, all in tuxedo suits, all applauding, all looking as if they were waiting for Jimmy Cagney to walk in and say, 'Okay you dirty rats.' Giorgio was up there with Shelley and Sid. Six foot two inches, black shiny hair, black dress-suit, a full black moustache and a large black bowtie. He stood there looking like a rolled umbrella.

For all the audience cared, Shelley and Giorgio could be in Manchester. Waiters were trying to clear the plates off the tables, waitresses, in their bunny type costumes, were leaning forward showing cleavage at the front and white, tailed bums up in the air at the back.

'What was that, sir?' one of them asked.

'Four pints of lager, two large whiskies, one with American Dry, one without, both with ice. A dry martini and lemonade and ... What's yours having, Bert?'

'A snowball.'

'And a snowball for the lady.'

'We haven't got any snowballs, sir.'

'No snowballs, Bert.'

'What? Right – a Babycham.'

'I'll be as quick as I can, sir.'

'Good girl.'

Sid was now sweating. He welcomed Giorgio aboard.

'Thatsa very nice.'

'Where are you going for your honeymoon, Shelley?'

'Give her one for me, Giorgio,' echoed around the club, followed by laughter from an understanding friend.

'Well, actually, we were thinking of going ...'

'We go to Italy to asee ma Mamma,' Giorgio told the microphone. 'Then we're staying ina Rome to open the restaurant.'

Yes, with oneze twoze money you've stolen from the club. Sixty for the till and forty fora the pocket, Sid thought to himself. He said, 'How wonderful. Will you be singing for the customers in your restaurant, Shelley?'

'Shella have no time for the singing. Shella be helping Mamma with the cooking.'

'So ... er ... yes, how about tonight, Shelley? How about doing a song for us tonight?'

The front table jumped up as if they had been given a command and started to applaud. The group went into the intro of 'Blue

36

Moon'. Serina almost stood on the stage to see Shelley work. Sid gave two bouquets of flowers to Giorgio, one from Al and one from Manny. Giorgio returned to gangland and Sid walked off backwards to the protection of the curtains, where he downed an already-waiting cold lager. In twenty minutes he would have to be out there again to introduce a star, the new recording sensation from America – Loose Benton. One hit record in the States and now struggling. That's why he was in England. He couldn't get himself arrested in the States. His gimmick was a gravel voice and every few bars he would drop to his knees and move around the floor singing like a doped-up limbo dancer.

Shelley finished her last note of 'Blue Moon' and the punters moved around talking to each other. Shelley did very well for applause, mostly from the eight Italians. Serina walked away thinking, She won't be hard to follow!

Shelley returned to the Mafia. A waitress said, 'I got a snowball for you.' The group were already on their second beer before the echo of the last note of 'Blue Moon' had died away. The stage was empty.

Sid had gone to say hello to Loose Benton in his dressing-room and ask him if there was anything special he would like him to say when he was being introduced. He walked past his own room towards the star's dressing-room. In the Starlight Rooms, like most of the other clubs up and down the country, there were four or five dressing-rooms for the artists and the band, group, etc, but there was always one star dressing-room. The other rooms had the look of broom cupboards. In the Starlight Rooms there were four. One for Sid, one for the singer, and a third for the group, but usually they came to the club already dressed for the show so theirs had become more of a pub than a dressing-room. It was the room in which everyone stubbed out their cigarettes and left their half empty and empty tins of beer. If you happened to get cornered by anyone in that room for any length of time you came out smelling like a very old Guinness.

Sid had reached the star's room. This room was large, beautifully decorated, private toilet, changing room, lounge, drinks cabinet with drinks, including champagne, fridge, mirrors with lights all the way round them, colour television, wall-to-wall carpeting, very comfortable settee and easy chairs. Sid knocked on the highly-polished door just below an enormous star with 'Loose Benton' written in the centre of it.

'Yeh?'

'Sid Lewis.'

'What?'

'Sid Lewis.'

The door opened about two inches and a big, male, brown eye looked into Sid's pale blue one.

'Huh?'

'I'm Sid Lewis, the compère, you know – the MC. May I ask someone what Mr Benton wants me to say about him to the audience before he goes on, or will he leave it to ...?'

The eye left Sid's eye and the door closed. Sid heard a muffled version of what he had just said. The door opened wider this time. 'Come in,' said old brown eye.

The door was closed behind him. Everyone in the room was black, with the exception of a white waiter dispensing drinks. They all turned their faces towards Sid.

Sid smiled. 'Good evening, gentlemen. I'm Sid. Sid Lewis. I'm the MC.'

A man walked towards him. 'Hi, Sid. I'm Loose Benton.' They shook hands.

Loose, as his name implied, was loose. He moved like a sack of coke, tall, elegant, an easy smile, and teeth as white as half the keys of a new Steinway. He was wearing a white three-piece suit, black open-necked shirt, black crocodile shoes, and a large brim-down-at-the-back-style white hat, with a black headband. Bloody hell, Sid said to himself. He looks like a negative.

Aloud he said, 'Er, is there anything you would like me to tell the audience while I'm introducing you?'

'Anything you wanna say, man.'

'Just get the name right, kid,' a black manager said.

'He'll get the name right, Irving.' Loose grinned Beethoven's Moonlight Sonata. 'How about a drink, Sid?'

'That's very kind. I'll have ... er ... a Scotch on the ... er ... rocks, please.'

'Waiter, get our guest a drink.'

Loose left him and went to join the others. Sid was given his drink by the most miserable looking man he had ever seen. He said his 'Cheers' and began to sip his whiskey and ice. He tried to figure out who the other people in the room were, whilst, at the same time, trying to hold polite conversation with anyone who would look at him and answer. The big fella with the pink, frilly dress-shirt – He

38

must be about sixteen stone. He's walking about tidying things –
he'll be his minder, Sid said to himself. To no one in particular
he said, 'Terrible weather.'

'Pouring down when I came in,' the waiter replied.

'Yeh,' muttered Sid into his drink.

'Waiter, fill up the glasses!' This command came from a middle-
size man wearing thin checked pants of bright red tartan, brown
and white two-tone shoes, a thin blue tartan jacket, and a pink tee-
shirt with 'I'm a fairy' written on it. Obviously his dresser, thought
Sid.

The waiter unhappily refilled the drinks. Sid said, 'No thanks.'

The waiter whispered, 'I hope it's stopped raining.' He looked
even more miserable. 'I hate that bloody moped when it's raining.'

Sid nodded.

There were two more left to figure out. The first one; dress-suit,
smart, middle-aged, hardly smiles, hardly speaks. Sid had a bet with
himself – musical director. Got to be. The other one; day-suit, talks
in a whisper – manager/agent.

The waiter slid over to Sid. 'If you go to the toilet, look out of
the window and see if it's still raining,' he whispered.

'You worked here long, Sid?' Loose asked. The waiter scuttled
away.

'Two years now.'

'Good audience tonight?'

'It's packed,' said the day-suit.

I was right, Sid smiled to himself. He's the manager. Aloud he
said, 'Yes, they're great and just waiting for you. Anyway, I'll go
and stand by so I'll see you in about five minutes. Oh . . . and thanks
for the drink.'

'Any time, man. Come back after the show.'

Loose put his hands out to be slapped. Sid was slightly confused.
He had only ever seen that done on television so he played safe.
He put his own hands out to be slapped. Loose looked at them,
then back to Sid, smiled the Emperor Concerto, slapped his hands
and went in to the toilet.

Sid walked towards the door. As he opened it he came face to
face with the most beautiful girl he had ever seen – black is beautiful
– and very tall. He was at a loss for words.

Someone said, 'Hi, baby.'

The waiter walked over to her and said, 'Is it still raining, miss?'

'It's pissing down, turkey,' she smiled.

4

Sid walked past Serina's open dressing-room door. Serina had been with the club for a few weeks or thereabouts. As Sid glanced in, he saw twenty-five years of body, forty-five years of experience, and thirty-eight inches of bust. He said his usual evening 'Hello'.

Her answer was usually, and without looking up, 'Hi.' But tonight it was, 'Hello, Sid. Good audience. You did well. Got some enormous laughs.'

The sentence was long enough to make him stop and answer back, 'Yes, they are good. A lot of coach parties. Have you settled in?'

'I think so.'

'It's a great place to work. Al and Manny are a couple of nice guys and, if you're on time, easy to work for.'

Sid was blocking the narrow corridor. Two or three people were trying to squeeze by. 'I'm sorry,' he said to a ventriloquist.

'That's okay,' said the ventriloquist. 'Just greathe in and we'll all ge agle to get kassed,' said the ventriloquist's dummy.

'You'd better come in,' Serina smiled. He did. 'And close the door. I'm sorry. The room isn't really big enough for two people. If you sit here, Sid, I'll be able to take my make-up off.'

'Thanks.' He sat down.

'You put a few different ones in tonight,' she said. 'What was that one about "together at last"?'

'Oh, that's the prostitute one. You know, about the scrubber who dies, and on her gravestone she had written "Together at last", and someone asks if she has been buried with her husband, and the scrubber's friend says, "No, dearie, she means her legs!"'

Serina laughed out loud. It was one of the dirtiest laughs Sid could remember. It sounded like the last quarter of an inch of a squirting

40

soda-siphon bottle. 'That's funny. Oh, yes, I like that one,' she coughed. 'I thought you worked well tonight.'

'That's very kind, Serina,' he said, slightly embarrassed.

'Could you pass those tissues?' He did as asked. 'Thank you. Do you like my work?'

'Oh, yes,' he said, a shade too quickly.

'I've never seen you watching me.'

'You wouldn't. I always go out front to watch you,' he lied.

'Drink?'

'What have you got?'

'I've got half a bottle of whiskey, or a full bottle of Scotch.'

'And you?' Sid asked.

'Maybe.' A slight pause. 'Later.'

Nudge, nudge, hint, hint, went through Sid's mind.

'I have to change. Please help yourself.'

'To what?' Sid smiled.

'You'll find all you want under my slip, the one on the table,' she said slowly. 'You have to hide the drinks in this place.'

'Don't I know. Mine's under the sink in a locked suitcase and the suitcase is chained to the wall.'

Serina made her way to the corner of the room. 'Turn round while I change. No, darling, not towards me, the other way, and don't look in the mirror. It could steam up.'

Sid poured his drink, turned his back and relaxed. No way was he going to look in the mirror, when, if he played his cards right, he'd be able to see the real thing. After a few audible tugs and pulls, sounds of opening and closing zips, followed by clicking of wire hangers, Serina said, 'Pour me a small one, Sid angel. I'm almost dressed.' Sid did as he was asked, never once looking in the mirror.

'Okay to turn round?'

'Didn't you even peek?'

'You told me not to.'

'Do you always do as you're told?'

'It depends how big the bed is.' He gave her the drink.

'There isn't room for one here. That's for sure.' She sipped the drink. 'Well, I'm through for the night. How about you?'

'Yes, if I want to, or I could go on and thank them after Frank's finished but I don't have to. Al and Manny like me to do it. They say it's good policy.'

'They're not here tonight,' Serina said. 'They're in Stoke. They've gone to Jollees and they're staying overnight.'

'Oh.' A slight pause. 'How do you know?'

'You'll have to take my word for it,' she smiled.

'You going home now?'

'Yes. You?'

'Er ... yes,' answered Sid.

'Where do you live?'

'Not far – Friern Barnet. You?' He stood up.

'Ballards Lane,' she said.

'Ballards Lane. I go past there every night – near the Gaumont, North Finchley.'

'That's right.'

'Good God.'

'Pass me that umbrella, sweetheart.'

Come on, Sid, think quicker, she's almost leaving, he thought. Aloud he said, 'You live there with your folks?'

'No.'

'Husband?'

'No. I'm not married.'

'I am.' Might as well get that part straight.

'I know,' she said.

'Oh.'

'So?'

'Fella? You live with your fella then?' He tried to be casual, as if he asked all women that question every day, even his mother.

'I like too much freedom for anything like that.'

'Right!'

'I have a flat in Ballards Lane and it's mine.'

'Maybe I could drop you off?'

'I have a car, Sid.'

'Oh.' He was losing ground rapidly and she knew it. 'Oh, well. Maybe I'll see you tomorrow and I'll supply the booze.'

'What time do you normally get home?' She was fastening her coat. 'If you stay and do your bit at the end?'

'Any time. Two, three, three-thirty. Any time,' he said.

'What's the time now?'

Sid looked at his watch. It said eleven-forty-five. 'Eleven-thirty.'

'Do you fancy a drink?'

'At your place?'

'Where else? Unless you think your wife wouldn't mind you bringing me home to have a drink at your place and, of course, we could keep very quiet and only have a soft drink.' She laughed again.

42

This time the laugh was like a set of poker dice being shaken in a pewter tankard.

'Your place it is then,' Sid grinned. 'I'll get my coat and follow your car.'

'Don't make it too obvious, *chérie*. I'll leave now and see you back at my place. Number 447. It's on the ground floor. Bottom button.'

'Fine.'

'At about twelvish. Now off you go back to your room and incidentally, your watch has stopped.' They both looked at each other and grinned.

Sid left her room with an extra loud, 'Goodnight, Serina,' that Lord Olivier would have had trouble following. He went to his own dressing-room, had a quick electric shave, splashed some 'Henry Cooper' all over his body, 'Mummed' under both arms and talcumed everywhere-else. He knelt down below the sink, opened the suitcase with his key, and poured himself a good glass of Scotch.

Sid stopped his car in Ballards Lane, got out and looked at the house numbers. 459. I'll leave the car here and walk back, he decided. He looked down Ballards Lane and about six houses back saw a house with the front curtains drawn but not tightly closed. It was the only house with the front room lit. That's got to be it, he thought. If that light goes out before I get there, I'll break the window. He quickened his pace, looked at his watch – one minute to the bewitching hour. He found the bottom button of three, checked the number again and, with a thundering heart, pressed the button. The bell made no sound at all, not that he could hear. After maybe twenty seconds the curtains to his right in the bay window slowly opened, ever so slightly, and bright red, well manicured fingernails tapped on the glass. The curtain closed before he caught a glimpse of the face. He stood there, knowing how the Boston Strangler must have felt. At the back of the door bolts and locks were heard to be working. The door opened and Serina pulled Sid in.

She closed and rebolted the door, looked up at him and smiled. 'You must have had your watch repaired. Give me your coat and go in there,' pointing to the door leading to the front room. She left him with an, 'I've only just come in myself.'

Sid heard voices coming from the front room. Oh, hell, he thought. That's ruined the evening. He gently pushed the door open and in the far corner Ginger Rogers was telling Fred Astaire that she didn't love him in the least. Except for Sid, Fred and Ginger, no one else was there. The room itself was very nice, tasteful and comfortable. He sat down on the settee in front of a coffee-table with a coffee percolator in competition with Fred and Ginger singing 'Change Partners'. There were a few photos in frames on a sideboard. One in particular took Sid's eye: Al and Manny Keppleman with Serina, taken at a party.

Serina came into the room carrying a tray with two coffee cups, two glasses and a bottle of champagne on it. Style, thought Sid. She had also changed into the inevitable 'something comfortable'. Hell fire, he thought, she either really fancies me or she thinks I know where the bodies are buried.

'Do you like those old films?' Serina asked. 'I do. What I like about them is – you can watch the last fifteen minutes and still pick up the story.' She put the tray down. 'Next week, it's *The Fleet's In*. Coffee?'

'I'll do it. You watch the film.'

'Turn it off,' she said. 'Fred gets Ginger; Sid gets ...'

'What?'

'Coffee?'

He walked towards the television set. 'Which is off?'

'The white one.'

He pressed the button and Fred and Ginger left the room.

'Come and sit next to me.' She held her hand out and guided Sid next to her. As he sat down, Serina got up. That shook Sid a little. She turned out all the lights except the glow of the electric log fire. She switched on a tape of romantic music as if it had all been arranged, then stood in front of the glow from the electric fire. Sid could, or thought he could, see through her négligé. The tape was playing a very slow 'Girl from Ipanema'. Serina put both her arms out towards him. He got up and they danced very close together. They did not actually dance; they stood very close together and swayed to the music. Fred and Ginger danced; Sid and Serina swayed. She put her arms underneath his open jacket, kicked off her slippers and immediately dropped about three inches. She was tiny, top weight five foot, while Sid was a good six foot odd. His only worry was, as her head rested against his lower ribs, that she didn't think the noise of the coffee still percolating was coming from the region of his lower ribs. She very deftly took off his jacket and let it drop to the ground. Sid thought, I hope she doesn't dance on that jacket – my reading glasses are in my top pocket. She gently pulled down his head and with soft lips she munched

44

his ear-lobe. Her mouth slid from his ear towards his mouth. He hadn't been kissed like that since the party where a drunken Swedish masseuse had tried to swallow him whole. I've still got her card in my pocket, he thought.

Serina now, with her small, strong body, started to push Sid back towards the settee. I'll have to lift her over the jacket, he thought. He tried but the négligé she was wearing was satin and she just kept slipping out of his grasp. His foot was now in one of his jacket sleeves. As he slowly went back, so did his jacket. Gradually he made his way back towards the settee, until the backs of his legs touched the upholstery. He tried to sit down slowly but she was still kissing him and she gave him one final body push. Sid went backwards, their lips parted, but not their bodies. Serina was now on top of him on the settee. Her last push took him by surprise. He lost his balance, his legs went up in the air and the jacket left his foot, flying upwards over her shoulders. He saw the jacket land on the small chandelier above them. The top pocket of his jacket was now facing downwards. Slowly, through the swaying of the chandelier, Sid's thick, library-type, reading glasses were slipping out. Serina's lips were searching hungrily for his. The percolator was going berserk. His glasses dropped. He tried to catch them before they hit the back of her head but he failed as he could not see them without his glasses. They landed, both arms downwards, on the back of her blonde hair. She felt nothing, her hair having so much lacquer. The glasses were trapped and were now looking upwards towards the jacket on the small, almost stationary, chandelier. Her emotions were still high. Sid tried to reach the glasses with one hand but as he touched them she left his lips to moan, 'Don't touch my hair, Sid.'

'Heh?'

'Not my hair, darling.'

'Heh?'

'Anywhere else but not my hair.'

His hand drew away while her lips tried to find his mouth again, like a month-old piglet looking for the teat of its mother. The percolator was almost dancing on the table.

Sid freed his mouth and said, 'Do you fancy a coffee?'

'Turn the bloody thing off.'

'How?'

'It's electric. There's a switch. I'll do it.'

She got off Sid and flicked the switch at the bottom of the percolator to the 'down' position. Sid was still lying on the settee. She looked down at him and through a pouted mouth said, 'Would you like to see the rest of the flat?'

'Pardon?' Sid said.

'The rest of the flat. Follow me and bring the champers.'

She turned to leave the room, still wearing Sid's reading glasses on the back of her head. He picked up the bottle and said to his now receding glasses, 'The percolator is still percolating.'

'Leave it,' she whispered breathlessly. He followed her out of the room. 'Don't forget the glasses,' she added.

'You've got them. Oh, yes, the champagne glasses.'

'I love champagne. It really gets me going.' Sid dashed back for the champagne glasses on the coffee table. The percolator was still going strong. He unplugged the attached lead at the wall. At the door he looked back into the room. I wonder what the melting point of glass is? he said to himself.

'In here, Sidney.'

Sidney, he thought. I hate being called Sidney. My mother used to call me Sidney.

He went into the room the voice came from. It was just as nice as the other room and the bed was covered with one of those enormous pillows. 'Put the champers there, darling.' She pointed to a dressing-table. 'It's bigger than that stinking dressing-room, eh?'

'I'll say. Should I open it now?'

'Why not?'

'The best way to open champagne so it won't blow is to hold the cork and turn the bottle.'

'Oh.'

'I read that in my diary.' He undid the foil and the wire, then screwed the bottle round, while holding the cork. Serina sat on the edge of the bed. Sid wondered if she was still wearing his glasses. The cork left the bottle followed by a shower of two full glasses of wasted champagne. Serina laughed. It sounded like the scream of cattle on barbed wire.

Sid shouted, 'Oh, sod it.'

'I hope that gave you some ideas, Sidney.'

He held the bottle to her glass and filled it. The bubbles subsided. He handed her one glass. She was about to lie back. 'Don't lie down, darling,' Sid almost shouted.

'Oh, something different in mind, Sidney?'

He poured one for himself. 'Yes.'

'How do you do it with your clothes on?' Serina giggled. Her

46

giggle was softer than her laugh, very similar to a dentist's high-powered water drill.

'Slowly,' he grinned.

'Not too slowly, I hope.' From the other room the tape was going strong. 'Turn off the tape in the other room, cherub,' she instructed.

'Yes, okay.'

Sid left the bedroom and went back to the other room. He turned the tape off, and looked at the still-percolating coffee. He touched the glass. It was still very hot. If I hadn't turned that off, we might be in orbit by now, he thought.

He went back to the bedroom. Serina was now naked and pouring another glass of champagne. Her back was turned towards Sid and his reading glasses were still safe. She drank her champers down and passed him a full glass. He took it and drank it quickly. She was starting to get heady.

'Sid, you're lovely.'

'Yes, I know,' he said.

'Come to bed.' He undid his tie. 'Allow me.' She took off his shirt and slowly undressed him, drinking and laughing. Sid thought, This is going to be one hell of a night. A night to remember. I'll ask her for my glasses tomorrow.

Sid drove home with drunken care – the kind of driving a police patrol would notice instantly. Twenty-three miles an hour in a thirty mile an hour zone; twenty-nine miles an hour in the forty mile an hour zone; and ninety miles an hour in the seventy mile an hour zone. He had had a few so the best thing to do was to drive with all due care. It was two-fifteen am. The Rover cruised in a straight line, albeit in the centre of the road. The roads were empty and, anyway, he was only a few minutes away from his house. Past the Tally-Ho Corner and turn right at the Torrington Arms, into Friern Barnet and home. Twenty-two Peacock Lane. Every time he drove down Peacock Lane, he felt satisfaction, a feeling of achievement. It gave him pride. Tonight, as he drove back towards Peacock Lane, having missed the turning, he felt all three – pride, and the satisfaction of his achievement. He thought, if he had a family motto, it would be: Pri, Satis, Achi.

Soon now, he told himself. Slow down. Twenty-two, twenty-two, where are you – twenty-two? Oh, there you are. The white Rover slowly turned into the gravel path, through the ever-open gates, and went towards the closed garage doors. Carrie's car'll be in the garage, he thought, so I'll have to back up and open the garage doors. Cobblers. I'll leave it out. It's a nice night and she'll be able to take Elspeth to school in it tomorrow. I'll leave the keys in the usual place, under the tin of Cadbury's Lucky Numbers Assortment in the kitchen.

Sid said all this to himself in the car while fighting to get out of the seatbelt without unlocking it. A thought came to him. Stop. Unlock the seatbelt, son. That's a good idea. I know. Do it now. He did and the belt slid back and once again he was a free man.

He quietly closed the car door and locked it from the outside. He quietly opened the car door again and turned off the lights. He then banged the car door shut. He did not actually roll towards the front door and he did not exactly stagger, it was both, more of a rollagger. He looked up and above his front door saw the space for the immortal words – Pri, Satis, Achi. For a full two minutes he tried to open the front door with his car keys. After several deep breaths and a search of pockets, he found the door key and let himself in. The porch light was on, as always. He tiptoed into the dark kitchen, made his way across to the pantry and put the light on there, left the front door keys under the Cadbury's Lucky Numbers tin, turned out the pantry light, crossed the dark kitchen towards the porch light and switched the kitchen light on, thinking he was turning the porch light off as he closed the kitchen door.

Carrie, his wife, was at the top of the landing, slowly making her way downstairs. She was wearing a dressing-gown over her nightie. Sid looked up and at one glance knew there was something wrong. She looked so ill. She had obviously been crying. Her eyes were puffed and red. Sid became sober within a few seconds. He walked up the stairs towards her. Tears were welling up in her eyes. He gently put his arms around her shoulders and slowly guided her down the stairs. A hundred things went through his mind: His mother had died. Her father. They'd been robbed. She'd been raped. She's found out about Serina. How? Serina had phoned her. Why? What for? Spite. Balls. Use your head.

He took her into the best room and switched the lights on, sat her down on the sofa and held her hand. He knew he must not rush her, let her cry. 'It's all right, love,' he soothed. 'You cry.' He squeezed her hand. 'Would you like a drink? A cup of tea, darling?' She shook her head. 'Would you like to tell me what has happened?' He smiled to give her confidence, he hoped. Carrie seemed to have a little more control of herself now.

48

'Didn't you get my message, Sid?' she asked. 'It's Elspeth.'

Jesus, Sid thought. She's been raped.

'She fell off Pegagus,' Carrie said.

'Pardon?'

'She fell off the horse. She was out riding with a friend, the Wilsdens' girl, Eunice. Pegagus shied. Elspeth was thrown. She kept hold of the reins and, as he got up, the horse veered and kicked out with its back legs and hit Elspeth.'

'Where?' he whispered.

'In her face,' Carrie sobbed.

'Jesus Christ,' Sid almost shouted.

'Please don't swear, Sid.'

'Where is she now?'

'At the hospital.'

'Which one?'

'The Cottage.'

They were quiet now for a few seconds. They just sat there, Carrie thinking about Elspeth, and Sid thinking about retribution.

It's God's doing, he thought. He's made this happen because I had some naughty. Well, that's the last naughty I'll ever have. God works in mysterious ways, his wonders for all to see. Wait a minute! Elspeth had the accident this afternoon. Right? Yes. Well, this afternoon I didn't know I was going to have some naughty and Serina didn't know she was, and I'll lay even money God wasn't that sure.

'Sid?' He squeezed Carrie's hand again. 'Would you mind ringing the hospital now? Just to see if there's any news. Would you, Sid? Please.'

'Of course. Where's the number?'

'It's by the phone. On the pad.'

Sid left Carrie and walked over to the phone, picked up the pad and put his hand to his top pocket to take out his reading glasses. 'What's the number, darling?' he asked, handing her the pad. 'I seem to have mislaid my reading glasses.'

She read out the number.

Sid picked up the phone and dialled.

And the sins of the father shall fall upon the sons, he thought. Be sensible, Sid. God didn't know. He knows everything. How did he know I was going to have some naughty this afternoon? How could he have known?

'Hello,' Sid said. 'Oh. My name is Mr Lewis and my daughter,

49

Elspeth Lewis, was admitted this afternoon. Lewis. L-e-w-i-s. Lewis. Elspeth. E-l-s-p-e-t-h. No, not Elizabeth. Elsbeth. It's Elizabeth without the "z", It's an "s" where the "z" is in Elizabeth, and a "p" for the "b".' Sid put his hand over the phone. 'I've got some Paki – can't understand English.'

He looked at Carrie. He thought, Maybe it's the sins of the mothers shall fall upon the daughters. Maybe she's been having some naughty. Naw. She wouldn't do that to me. If I found out I'd kill her.

Back to the phone. 'Look, I know there is no Elizabeth Lewis. It's Elspeth. She fell off a horse this afternoon. Is there anyone else I could speak to? An English person. Oh, you are English! Yes, well, I'm sorry you sound a little Paki ... stan ... Oh. Indian.'

Sid put his hand over the phone again. 'And Chicken Biriani to you. Hello, oh hello, are you a nurse? Good.'

He said to Carrie, 'Sabu found a nurse.'

'I'm trying to find out how a Miss Elspeth Lewis is. She was brought in this afternoon after falling off a horse. I'm her father and I've only just come in from work so I thought I'd give you a ring. The doctor said I could ring you any time. Yes. Miss Lewis. L-e-w-i-s. E-l-s-p-. No ... p, as in parsnip. E-t-h. Thank you.'

He turned to Carrie, 'She said she'll see if there's been any change.'

'Hello. Oh, God. It's Ram Sing again. I'm holding on, son. I'm holding on because the nurse you found has gone to check on my daughter for me.

'Don't you cry now, Carrie. We'll soon know if ...

'I'm talking to my wife.

'I've got to keep him on the phone till the nurse gets back.

'Hello. I must say you people do a good service and er ... it was very kind of you to find that nurse for me. How long have you been English? Three weeks. Oh, knockout. Do you feel any dif –? Hello, nurse. No change. She's comfortable as can be expected and she's asleep. Yes, thank you. Thank you very much.'

Sid put the phone back on its cradle. 'Well, she seems to be resting.'

'Oh, Sid, her face was a mess. She's lost her front teeth and her nose is broken, Sid.'

'Yes, er ... well, you know, they can do wonders – dentists and doctors – nowadays and, not only that, I mean, a broken nose is nothing nowadays. Good Lord, how many doctors have broken noses. Anyway they have to break your nose before you can have a new one. Look darling, I'll pour you a drink and maybe ...'

'No, Sid, I won't have a drink. I'll go to bed.'

'Did you get anything from the doctor? At the hospital, I mean. Did he give you any downers?'

'Any what?'

'Downers. You know, something to make you sleep.'

'No. Anyway he was a black doctor.'

'Well, even black people sleep. Anyway you go to bed. I'll have a drink and a little thought down here. Okay? I'll take you to the hospital in the morning, see Elspeth, and then drive on to see my agent, pick you up on the way back, bring you home, have a kip, then go on to the club. But if you have anything else in mind, I'm quite willing to do it.'

'No, that's fine.'

'Okay. Off you go to bed.'

'Now don't you be late, Sid. You'll have had a hard night tonight.'

'Yes. Well, goodnight, dear, and I know it's silly but try to sleep and not to worry. I'm sure it will be all right.'

Carrie picked up a handful of tissues and then left the room. Sid sat completely alone for a few minutes thinking, What a night! What a bleeding, bloody, bastard of a night! He got up and from the drinks cabinet poured himself a large Scotch. He stood by the window, looked out, raised his glass and said, 'Here's to you, God. Look after my little girl, and while you're at it, my glasses.'

5

The car was parked in the space for parking cars, but cars for 'Doctors Only'. Carrie asked Sid if it was all right parking there and going through the door marked 'No Entry'. Sid said, 'Yes,' and that was that conversation shot to hell.

They walked through the 'No Entry' door into the hospital itself, asking the way to the reception area.

'First left, second right, past the smell of rice pudding, along the corridor, past the sluices, through the swing doors, ask again.'

'Certainly. Straight on and past the smell of rice pudding.'

'No, wait a minute. If you go through these doors and into the geriatric ward, go straight through there and you can't miss it.'

Fifteen minutes later they had found the reception desk by starting again outside and going through a door marked 'Entrance', much to Sid's annoyance and Carrie's looks of 'I told you so'. The desk was manned by a turban-wrapped Asian gentleman. Sid and Carrie walked up to the desk and waited and waited and waited, until Sid's patience started to run at a very low ebb.

'Excuse me,' Sid said to the Asian gentleman, who was sorting out some cards with deep concentration. No response.

This time a little louder. 'Ahem, excuse me.' Still no response from the counting, concentrating, turbanned, Asian gentleman.

Sid was now smiling, but with dead eyes. It was the type of look that even frightened Carrie's mother. 'I'd like to see my daughter.' The voice came from what was now a wrinkle under Sid's nose.

'Maternity is through that door, there,' the Asian gentleman said without looking up. In retrospect, that was the undoing of the Asian gentleman, the fact that he never looked up.

52

'She's not in maternity, son,' Sid said coldly. 'She's too old for maternity, cowboy.

'How old is she?' he asked Carrie.

'Twelve.' Carrie shivered. She didn't like Sid when he was like this.

'She's twelve, little brown man, and I'd like to see her.'

Carrie said, as quickly as possible, 'She came in last night.'

'Lady,' said the Asian gent, 'I'm very busy for the next few moments, and then I'm here to help you. I'm being very helpful soon.'

'Thank you,' Carrie said softly.

The card–counting gentleman then said, 'I am now finishing. Hello, hello, can I help you?'

A surprised Sid said, 'I'd like to see my daughter, Miss Elspeth Daphne Lewis.'

'This is not the hour for visiting.'

'I know, but at the moment it's the only time I can get here.'

'I see. Now – a Miss Elizabeth Delphi Lewis.'

'Miss Elspeth Daphne Lewis.'

The turbanned tiger started to look through another set of cards. 'There is no one here by the name you have stated.' He looked directly at Carrie, not once at Sid. 'You are probably at the wrong hospital.'

'I am not at the wrong hospital, young different coloured sir.' Sid spoke quietly at first, slowly building up to a small crescendo. 'And I don't care what anybody says. I don't care if she's asleep, or if the rest of the ward are on the verge of dying, I and my wife, here – this is my wife,' he said, pointing to Carrie, 'want, no *demand*, to see my daughter, Miss Elspeth Daphne Lewis.'

Sid's voice was getting louder and Carrie was trying to get smaller.

'Vhat you don't seem to understand, zir,' said the Indian or Pakistani gentleman, 'is ve have novon who answers to the name you are saying, zir.'

'Look, I know it's early, and we, my wife and I, realize you have a very hard and very difficult job to do, but if I don't see my daughter within the next, let's say fifteen minutes, you, sir, will be very sorry you left your tin hut in Poona or wherever you came from.'

Carrie put her hand out on Sid's arm. 'Sid, please.'

'Shut up,' Sid whipped back at Carrie. 'Look, Sabu, I want to

53

see my daughter. Now do you understand that, you bloody Asian berk?'

'Sid, sh.'

'Right now. Pronto. Quick. Understandee?' Sid stormed. 'Because if you don't find somebody who I can talk to in real English, you'll be needing that bandage around your head, son. Phone someone, now.'

This rather gentle Asian gentleman was now out of his depth. He picked up the phone and asked for a nurse called Miss Miandad.

'She'd better understand English, son,' Sid remarked, when he heard the name Miandad.

The Asian put his hand over the mouthpiece and very proudly said, 'She vos born here, zir. Thank you.'

A voice on the phone spoke and the Asian gentleman said, 'Hello, hello, could I speak to a Miss ... Pardon? I would like to speak to ... What do you mean – who's speaking? I am.' He looked at Sid and Carrie, took the mouthpiece from his mouth and said, 'There's some Irish people on the switchboard. Hello, hello. I would ... Yes, oh yes, I am understanding. My name is Haroon ... No, Haroon. Yes, Haroon, from the reception. I want to speak and talk to Nurse Miandad.'

After a few seconds, in which someone at the other end had gone to find Nurse Miandad, Haroon Amarnath tried to get into polite conversation with Sid. 'I see Chelsea lost again.' He half smiled.

Sid looked at him as if he was mad.

'I'm taking my vife to Vindsor at the veekend,' Haroon continued.

Carrie said, 'She'll like it there. The Queen goes there sometimes. Is it her first visit?' she asked rather slowly.

'No, ve go every veekend because ve live in Slough. Very close, you see. Hello, hello. Ah ... Nurse Miandad. Haroon. Yes, from the reception.'

Sid snatched the phone away from him, which Carrie thought hurt his feelings. After all, she thought, he goes to Windsor every weekend, which is more than we do, and we are real English.

'Hello, look my name is Lewis. Mr Sidney Lewis, and last night my daughter, Elspeth, was – What? No, Elspeth,' he said resignedly, 'Elspeth Daphne Lewis.'

Sid looked at Carrie and almost smiled, 'She's gone to check.' He looked at Haroon as he said, 'I think we've found an intelligent one.'

Carrie put her hand out to Haroon's and patted it. He smiled a smile of a surrendering man.

'Good. How is she?' Sid said into the phone. 'Ask her if she's ...' Sid waved his wife quiet. 'I see. I'm her father and her mother is here with me.' He spoke precisely and slowly, 'Now, if you can tell me where she is we'd like to see her. I know it's not visiting hours.' He enunciated crisply, almost losing control, 'But it's the only time I can get here.' His voice was getting louder and faster. Haroon looked nervously up, and then even more nervously down, at the cards he was trying to sort. 'All right. All right,' Sid seethed. 'Whom do I get permission from? I see. From Sister Lawton. Is that Lawton as in Charles?' he sneered. 'Hello, hello?'

The phone was dead. Sid put it down. He was beginning to feel his age – a hundred and eight. He put his arm around Carrie, took a long, deep breath, and went back into action. To a now rather bewildered Asian, who was only three inches away from this strange white man's face, because this white man was leaning over the reception desk, he once again spoke.

'Okay, sunbeam, how do I find Sister Lawton?'

The Asian dropped all the cards on the floor. 'Zister Luton?' he gulped.

'That's right, and if I don't see her within the next few minutes, you, my little friend, will have eaten your last chappatti.'

'I'm getting her on the phone for you now, right away, zir,' he breathed. 'Zister Luton,' he cried into the phone. 'It's an emergency.' He looked at Sid and pointed to the phone as if Sister Lawton was about to come out of it.

Sid looked unblinkingly at him.

''Allo, Zister Luton?' Haroon's face beamed and his black eyebrows shot up and almost disappeared under his turban. 'For you.' He almost shook with excitement as he handed Sid the phone. He looked at Mrs Lewis as if to say, I am being very privileged to watch the meeting of the Big Two – Zister Luton and The Wild White Man.

'Sister Lawton?' Sid asked, very pleasantly. 'Good. I would like to see my daughter, Miss Elspeth Lewis. She came in yesterday evening. I'm her father, and my job, I'm afraid, won't let me visit in the normal visiting hours. This is the only time I can make it today. I would so much like to see her. I know she's being looked after by the best,' he crawled, 'but if I, as her father, could just sit with her for a few minutes before what could be my last mission,

Sister Lawton. I'm sorry, I shouldn't have told you that. I mustn't say any more on those lines.'

Carrie looked at Sid.

Haroon looked at Sid.

'Government work,' Sid whispered, turning his back on both Carrie and Haroon. 'You are more than kind,' Sid smarmed. 'Yes, I understand. What ward? Gandhi ward, and there will be a nurse waiting for me. Sister, thank you very much indeed. Goodbye.'

Sid put the phone down and Haroon clapped his hands together and beamed his biggest smile since leaving India or Pakistan.

'Very good. Oh, yes, very, very good, zir.'

'Harold . . .' Sidney started.

'Haroon.'

'Haroon, could you tell me the way to the Gandhi ward?'

By the swing doors to Gandhi ward stood a big, very black, West Indian nurse. She wore a badge that told you her name was Coral Shivnarine.

'Hello dere,' she said. She gave a smile as big as Barbados itself. 'Sister Larton toll me to wait for you.'

Sid nodded.

'You come to see a payshant?'

Sid renodded.

'Well, right now, arm in ma coffee break,' she giggled. 'But I mean, if you know what she look like you'll find her by the far door.' She gave them both a great big grin and waddled off.

Sid looked at Carrie and asked, 'You okay? Do you feel up to seeing her?'

Carrie took a deep breath and very quietly said, 'Yes.'

Just before Sid held the door open for Carrie, Nurse Shivnarine waddled back and said, 'Sir, no longa an fiminutes.' Sid okayed her request. She laughed again and left.

Sid and Carrie went into the ward. He took stock and very quickly came to the conclusion that at the near end of the ward were the 'nearly betters', in the middle part of the ward were the 'doing all rights' and at the far end were the 'not so goods'. They looked down to the far end. In the last two beds, one on each side of the ward, were two patients completely wrapped in bandages – arms, legs, chest and face. Sid gripped Carrie's arm as they walked slowly towards them, looking sideways at every other bed to make sure Elspeth was not in one of the 'nearly betters', or even the 'doing all rights' beds.

As they reached the far end one of the heavily bandaged patients seemed to move an arm in slight recognition. They both went over and looked hard at this professionally wrapped-up person. As they looked into the dark, brown eyes, Carrie thought how much like a baby seal about to be bopped over the head she looked. Carrie sat on the edge of the bed and let tears stream down her face. Sid held Carrie's hand and slowly kept patting the top of the bandaged head.

Carrie composed herself and told the bandaged head not to worry. Grandma Lewis had sent her love, and Grannie and Boppo – Elspeth's baby name for Poppa – sent their love and would soon send her a tin of nuts.

They had been there about five minutes when Sister Lawton came down the ward and stopped by them. She was in her blue uniform and white hat. She was also very tiny. She was four foot eleven and a half inches tall, four foot eleven and a half inches wide and four foot eleven and a half inches deep. She looked like a small blue cube, but when she walked down the ward, frightened bones rattled.

'What are you doing here? And who are you?' she said in a whisper so fierce that the Ayatollah would have changed his religion.

'Oh. Hello, Sister. I'm Mr Lewis. I spoke to you on the phone about ten –'

'Ah, yes. Mr Lewis,' she hissed. 'But what are you doing here? And please, don't pat the patient's head.'

'I'm talking to my daughter.'

Sister gave a look that had about as much warmth as a mid-European's smile. 'This isn't your daughter. Your daughter is through those doors.' She pointed to the doors near them.

'Oh,' Sid said in a deflated tone.

Carrie looked at the bandaged girl and said, 'Don't worry. *I'll* send you some nuts.'

'Follow me please, Mr Lewis,' said Sister. 'I suppose this is Mrs Lewis.'

'Oh, yes,' Sid said.

'You never mentioned a Mrs Lewis when we spoke on the phone.' They moved towards the door. 'Goodbye, your highness,' Sister said to the patient. 'This way and you have five minutes.'

Sid gently waved to the bandaged person and Carrie smiled and gave a small curtsey. Sister opened the door for them. They saw

Elspeth and learned she would be out in the next three or four days. She was not injured as badly as Carrie had thought but she would have to be looked after at home and she would continue to be an out-patient for at least another three months.

As Sid and Carrie left the hospital, Sid said to Carrie, 'Some of these blacks do a good job.'

6

The theatre is at the end of the pier looking towards the sea. The stagedoor is on the right side of the theatre. If you come down a few steps from the stagedoor you are on the planks of the pier itself. If you turn left and walk a few yards you are in the literal sense on the end of the pier.

Every morning at about eleven o'clock Sid would walk slowly down towards the end of the pier to the theatre, to see if there was any mail at the stagedoor. Who knows me who could write? he would think as day after day he would look into his empty pigeon-hole at the stagedoor office. I even have an agent who's not on the phone.

Sid at that time was earning seventeen pounds ten shillings per week, of which ten per cent went to his agent, and six pounds fifteen shillings went to his landlady – a ninety-four-year-old woman who used to send her young, seventy-year-old daughter to do the shopping. Sid was playing straight man to an old, hard comic who, Sid thought, was about as funny as Frankenstein's monster with a cleaver.

This comic, Ed Low – known to the rest of the profession as Big Ed Low – always finished every sketch he did by dropping his pants, or Sid's pants, or one of the chorus girl's pants, just before the black-out at the end of the sketch. If a chorus girl played that part in the sketch and her pants came down, she did not get any extra money from Ed Low. He would tell her she would get a present at the end of the season in September, and Ed usually kept his promise, but the poor kid never saw the present until about the middle of the following June.

Ed would be earning around two hundred pounds a week. He

would be staying in digs or a very cheap boarding house. His outlay would cost around ten pounds ten shillings per week and on top of that there would be the odd extras, such as two or three sisters and at least two different wives and a few nieces. Strangely enough, no brothers ever came to see him and no nephews either. He would drink about half a bottle of Scotch a day, plus a few beers, then in the evening he would start buying his own. His most expensive item was Sid, seventeen pounds ten shillings per week, and he used to pay him out as if he was a partner – a pound at a time – one, two, three, four and so on. Never once did he give Sid his money in bulk; always one, two, three, four, as if they both earned the same amount. Although Sid and Ed did not see eye to eye about comedy, Sid learned a lot from Ed, the most important thing being to stay solo, never to team up with anyone. There was a young double act in the show that went under the name of Court and Bold. They always seemed to be shouting at or blaming each other if things did not get a good enough laugh, and Ed never missed an opportunity to mix it between them.

Sid's name on the bill was just a shade smaller than 'Printed By'. One day Sid asked the funniest-looking chorus girl for a date the next morning and a coffee, purely and simply because, although she had a slightly funny look, a small cast in her left eye and slightly protruding teeth, she had a figure that made Lana Turner's look like a man's. This girl's figure was perfect. Sid thought, I could always get her to look the other way. But she said 'No' to the date. Sid knew why. Ed was using her in a couple of his 'pull your pants down' sketches. Sid suspected that by next mid-June her figure was not going to be the sensation it now was.

Sid spoke to her nicely. 'Hello, Lavinia.' He never heard what they called her for short. 'Fancy a coffee in the morning and maybe a drink afterwards?'

'No thanks, Sid,' she said in a full, nasal, northern accent.

'Why not?' he asked, slightly offended.

'Mr Low might not like it.'

He was liking it all right, Sid thought. He'd be a berk if he wasn't. 'What's it got to do with him anyway?' he asked aloud.

'Well, yer see, he doesn't like anyone working in his sketches mixing with too many people in the same company. He sez it's bad for the show's image.' Her 'Bugs Bunny' teeth flashed.

Sod yer, Sid thought, although he said, 'Oh, okay, er ... Have you heard about Ed?'

'Heard what?'

All chorus girls love gossip, even the kind Sid was about to deliver made up. He thought he would have a little fun.

'Well, it's only a rumour,' he said.

At the word 'rumour', her Bugs Bunnies flashed again and her ears almost stood up.

'Well,' Sid continued, 'and I am only telling you this in secret because somebody told me in secret and that somebody was someone outside show business.'

Her big blue eyes looked like organ-stops except, of course, for the slight cast. 'Yes?' she said excitedly.

'Well, this particular someone saw him in Boots.' Sid waited.

Lavinia looked at him. 'Boots?' she echoed.

'Yes, Boots – the chemist, not the cobbler's.'

'Go on.'

'Well, he was talking ... to a girl ... behind the counter. Now, listen to this bit. He was, or, so this fellow said, he was actually ... smiling!'

'How d'yer mean?' she asked, thinking the least he had done was flash himself.

'Now, this stranger was asked if Ed had showed his teeth, and the stranger said, "The smile happened so quickly it was over in four and a half seconds." So the stranger said that he, personally, did not see them and the reporter from the local press asked the girl behind the counter the same question but she had fainted.'

Sid stopped abruptly. Lavinia just kept looking at him, nodding her head, waiting for him to continue.

'Well?' she finally said.

'That's it. Ed smiled!' Sid replied.

After about ten seconds' wait and several more nods she said, 'Yer daft bugger,' and walked away.

There were two other girls on the bill who were acrobats, with pretty faces, nice boobs – and legs like male Russian shot-putters. They would run to the front of the stage from the back in their act, and people nine rows away shook in their seats. The first three rows were always covered in a thin film of dust, and the cymbals on the drums played of their own accord. Children cried and an old man had a heart attack one first house. He was sitting in the middle of the third row and everybody thought he had stayed for the second house. Nothing was suspected until a lady arrived with the same numbered ticket. She thought he was being rude and ignoring her so she told an usherette, a dear old lady of over sixty-five, who shone a torch on him that was stronger than the spotlight for the show. She had to disturb the whole row to get to him. As soon as she realized he was a gonner, she faint'd over his legs, pulling him down to the floor with her. Her torch hit the ground and went out. He landed on top of her and this poor old usherette actually fainted six more times before the interval. The manager brought the ice-cream down but he could not find her so he had to sell the ices himself in his dress-suit. She eventually managed to roll down past the front two rows, while the boys, Court and Bold, were doing their soft shoe dance to 'Home in Pasadena'. She arrived at the curtain partition that separated the audience from the band. She rolled through and the musical director, who was standing up conducting, disappeared very quickly from the audience's view. The usherette stood up in his place and shouted to the audience, 'He's dead.' They thought she was talking about the conductor. Everybody in the band stopped playing except the drummer, who was extremely deaf and permanently drunk. The band and the front row all got up to look and to see the conductor's body but he was only knocked out by the edge of the piano. The old usherette ran up the aisle and out of the theatre and was never seen again. Court and Bold carried on. Well, Bold did. Court ran off. The drummer kept going, and the manager of that particular theatre still holds the record for selling the most ice-creams.

Sid met Carrie while he was appearing in summer season at the Wellington Pier, Yarmouth. Although she would never admit it, and he would never refer to it, she had let him pick her up. She was twenty and he was twenty-four.

Poor Sid – no birds. They had all been taken up and by the end of June each girl in the show had her own fella. During the last week in June, Sid came out of the stagedoor – no mail, as usual; even his mother and father had not written. Well, they had, but had misunderstood and thought he had said Dartmoor, so they had been writing to Sid Lewis, c/o Wellington Pier, Dartmoor. His agent had now got a phone but only took incoming calls. As Sid walked down the few steps from the stagedoor on to the planks of the pier itself he looked to the left, as he always did. It was a great view – one enormous expanse of water. It was his favourite view because you could not see Yarmouth at all. Leaning on the rail this particular morning, looking out to sea, was a young woman with long brown hair. She wore a dress, and that was all it was – a dress, a cheap, thin, cotton dress. It was a bright day and with any luck he would be able to see through it, but alas – no – she was wearing a slip. She turned and saw him and as they looked at each other she moved away quickly, sending her ice-cream scoop flying into the sea. She was left holding an empty cone.

Sid walked over, smiling, and in his young, sophisticated way said, 'Well, it's better than being left holding the bag.'

She went the colour of strawberry ripple.

'Can I get you another one?' he asked.

'No thank you. It wasn't your fault. It was loose.'

'A coffee?'

'I don't like coffee ice-cream.'

'Are you on holiday?'

'Yes, thank you.' She had toned down a little in colour from strawberry ripple to raspberry explosion.

'Alone?' he pursued.

'No.'

'Oh?' He waited. Nothing more came from her. 'Right. Well, I'm sorry to have troubled you. I'll leave you to your empty cone.'

He started to walk away. After he had gone no more than four paces he turned round to do his Gary Cooper wave. He saw her trying to force the heel of her shoe into the division between the planks. She did not see him turn towards her so he turned away quickly.

'Oh,' she screamed.

Sid turned back again. 'What is it? Has your ice-cream jumped back?'

'It's ... er ... my shoes. One of them is stuck.'

'Allow me to take it out. But first you must take it off.'

Sid bent down and gently took hold of her calf. She started to tremble a little and had to steady herself by putting her hands on his back. He undid her shoe, took her foot out but held it in his hand. The shoe was not really stuck but Sid acted as if it was very difficult to get out. Finally he freed it. He put it back on her foot and fastened it.

'Thank you very much, Mr ... er ...'

'Lewis. Sid Lewis.'

'Mr Lewis.'

'I'm appearing here.' This threw her. She obviously did not know that there was a theatre on the pier.

'Yes?' Strawberry Ripple said.

'Here. I appear here. I'm a theatrical.'

'What?'

'A theatrical. Show biz. Like people in films.'

'Laurence Olivier?'

'Well – in a way. Come and have a coffee.'

'I can't, Mr Laurence.'

'Lewis.'

'Mr Lewis.'

'Well, why not? I'm not going to harm you. Just a coffee, as I feel partly responsible for the lost ice-cream. You know, just a coffee. No touches. No footsies under the table.'

She was now sunset red.

'A coffee,' Sid urged. 'A tea. Sit there with an empty cup. Look, the café's full and you'll be quite safe.'

A little boy of about four years of age stood at the end of the pier next to them and peed into the sea. She almost fainted. 'All right,' she gasped, and ran towards the café.

Sid followed her shouting, 'And get one for me, two sugars.'

She slowed down and he caught up with her. 'I mustn't stay long,' she said. 'I'm supposed to meet my mother at twelve outside the hotel opposite the pier.'

'Are you staying there then?'

'Good Lord, no. We're at the holiday camp, and very nice it is. It's just Mummy and I. Dad's working.'

'How long are you here for? Two coffees, please. I mean – how long are you here in Yarmouth?'

'Two weeks. This is our third day.'

'Oh. Would you like to see the show I'm in?'

'No thank you. We can see them free at the camp.'

'Well, I meant ... I thought I'd get you a couple of comps.'

'Comps?'

'Complimentaries.'

'No, don't please go to any trouble. Mum and I go to the camp dance every night.'

'You dance?'

'Yes. Mum leads.'

The waitress brought the two coffees. 'One and six, please.'

Sid flipped two bob. 'Keep the change, sweetheart.' He felt like Humphrey Bogart in *The Maltese Falcon*.

They sipped their milky, non-coffee tasting coffee and kept silent for a while. After a couple of minutes Sid said, 'I'll take you over to your mother.' Coffee went everywhere from her mouth. A new colour came to her face – deep Smith's Crisp, Sid called it.

'Sorry. Oh, I'm so sorry,' she said to everyone. 'I'll be all right. Please don't.'

He saw that she was more frightened than worried. 'Well, can I maybe see you tomorrow?' he asked.

'No. Er ... no. Oh dear. Yes, I'd like to but I can't. This is the first time I've been alone since I've been here and look at me. I get into all this trouble.'

'Trouble? What trouble?'

'This.' She spread her arms. She was almost in tears.

'Listen.' Sid spoke quietly. 'I come here every morning between ten-forty-five and eleven. I hang about the pier and at about one pm I go back to my digs for lunch. Digs, you know, where I stay, and after lunch I maybe go to the flicks, or if it's a nice day, to rollerskate.'

She looked at her watch. 'I must go.'

'Well, if you're here any morning, I'll see you.'

'Yes. Please can I go?'

'Of course you can. What's your name?'

'Carrie.'

'Okay, Carrie, off you go.'

He watched her leave the café and slowly got up, feeling in his pocket for a threepenny bit to leave as a tip, which he did. He had reached the door, when he suddenly realized he had already done the Bogart bit, so he went back for the coin but within those four seconds it had gone. He looked through the window of the café as Carrie crossed the road. He saw her meet a woman and remembered saying to himself, Thank God, she must take after her father.

On the morning of 5 November, 1954, Sid jumped out of his hotel bed, washed, shaved, and dressed, before his breakfast. It was his wedding day. He was going to marry Carrie. In five more hours, at eleven o'clock, that very morning. At six-thirty am he knocked on my door, opposite his. I was hard and fast asleep – well into dreamland. In my dream I was appearing at The Dunes Hotel, Las Vegas, to the biggest crowd they had ever had and to the biggest laughs they had ever heard. What was so amazing in my dream was the ease with which the laughs came. I only had to walk on stage wearing a string vest and a large cap, shouting, 'I love you all.'

In my dream I had received the keys to the city and was being made an honorary Indian chief (Cherokee) by a topless squaw with the biggest knockers I'd ever seen. I remember saying, 'Those knockers, those knockers,' when, as the dream faded and reality stepped in, I was actually saying, 'Who's knocking? Who's knocking?'

A distant voice said, 'It's me, Sid.'

Not knowing for the minute where I really was – I was still taking bows at The Dunes – I sprang out of bed in the darkness, hitting the wall the side of my bed was up against. Although I did not leave the bed, I very quickly left The Dunes.

'Open up. It's Sid.'

'Aren't you well?'

'Great.'

'Just a minute.' I had slow recall coming through. I swung to the other side of the bed and, with a sigh, put my bare feet on to the freezing oilcloth of a hotel in Luton. Once out of bed it took only one step to reach the door and from the darkness of my room I looked out to see Sid in his dark suit – a flower in his buttonhole, a smile on his face, just waiting to say, 'I do.' He stood there in the most dimly lit corridor it has ever been my pleasure to almost see. I am sure the light bulb was the one Edison threw out shouting, 'Another failure, mum.'

'Come in,' I said.

He did and looked at me. 'Aren't you ready?' He looked perturbed.

'Sid, it's only twenty-five to seven.' He stood there and grinned.

'So. I once played the Old Black's Regal, Gateshead, and it's always twenty-five to seven there, even at a quarter-to-four it's twenty-five to seven in Gateshead.'

I said, 'If you carry on like this you'll be asleep at the wedding.'

'Put some light on,' he replied.

I switched the wall light-switch down, up again, almost sideways, and back down again. Suddenly the whole room was plunged into a little less darkness. I closed the door and felt my way back to the bed. It was still invitingly warm.

'You're not going back to bed, are you?' Sid said.

'Keep your voice down a bit,' I whispered.

'What for? There's only you and me staying here. There's only two rooms and we've got them. Didn't you notice when we came in last night they took the "Vacancy" sign down, turned it over and it said "No Vacancies" upsidedown.' He glanced around. 'I've never seen such a dark place.' He found a standard lamp by knocking it over. He picked it up and lit it. The shade leaned to one side like Frankie Vaughan's top hat. The shade was made out of imitation, imitation parchment. It also had a big burn mark on it.

Sid sat on the edge of the bed.

'You shouldn't sit there,' I said. 'You'll get bits of fluff over your suit and you do your act in that suit, don't you?'

He nodded as he went to sit in the easy chair. This chair also leaned to one side like Frankie Vaughan's top hat. As I looked at him sitting there, he gave the impression he was turning for home and base in a Spitfire.

'What's the time, Eric?' he asked.

'Twenty-to-seven.'

A pause.

'That was a great party last night.'

'Good.'

'Yep. My stag night – my bachelor party – last time out with the lads as a single fella. I know there was only you and me there, but we don't know anyone here, do we?'

'No.'

'You're not annoyed are you? I mean, with me being here early?'

'No. I'm asleep.'

'Well, I couldn't tell in this light. For all I know there could be a girl in that bed with you.'

'I'll check when the sun comes up.'

'Anyway, I enjoyed last night. That was a good speech you made, when you said, "I'll get the bill." That was the best part.' He smiled.

'What's the weather doing?' I asked.

'It's pouring down.'

'Pity. It might clear up.'

'So might a leopard's spots.'

That answer was followed by some seconds of silence. I could hear the rain. I remember thinking it could spoil the kids' bonfire night. I had heard they were going to set fire to the town hall.

'Am I doing the right thing?' Sid asked.

'You're certainly not doing the right joke. It might clear up – so might a leopard's spots. Bloody hell!'

'I mean ... am I doing the right thing ... getting married?' He stopped talking and made a nervous twitch with his mouth.

'Well, four hours four minutes from now, you'll know,' I told him, trying to keep the conversation light.

'I'm serious,' he said.

'Are you getting cold feet? Who's getting cold feet then? I thought it was only the girl who got cold feet.'

'Look, I want to know. Am I doing the right thing?'

'Will you please keep your voice down,' I hissed. 'How the hell do I know if you're doing the right thing? I'm your best man, not a clairvoyant. If you don't know how do you expect me to know? I mean ... I don't know, do I?'

'I love her. I'm almost sure. Yes, yes, I love her very much. She's the best thing that's happened to me in my whole life, but I have this nagging thought at the back of my mind. Am I doing the right thing?'

I thought, Here we are, two kids – him and me, in this scratty hotel in Luton, and one of us – him, is all dressed up to take the biggest plunge since Blondin fell off his tightrope. I couldn't help him. I mean ... what could I do? I was almost as bad as him. I had got up twice during the night to make sure I hadn't lost the ring. I did the only thing I do well. I said a few stupid remarks, like, 'It'll all turn up in the wash. It's all my eye and Betty Martin and Jerry Lewis. He who hesitates supports Fulham.' And finishing with, 'He who laughs last wears false teeth.'

I looked at him sitting in Frankie Vaughan's hat. 'Sid,' I said, 'I don't know what you mean when you say, "Am I doing the right thing?" You know, I mean, if you love the girl and you're sure, then you're doing the right thing. That's it, isn't it?'

'What a bloody stupid statement that is!'

I had to agree.

He took the carnation out of his buttonhole. It was beginning to look a little jaded. He had bought his, and mine, the day before, knowing he would not get one from Carrie's mother. She would never forgive him for marrying Carrie if she lived to be a hundred. According to Sid, the old trout was past that age already.

'I'm not going to leave show business,' he said, unwrapping the silver paper from his white carnation. I looked over to my carnation, perched in a plastic beaker of water. It was now brown. It had been white the night before. Probably the tap-water. I must remember not to drink it. I could end up with 'Luton Liver'.

'I get the impression Carrie wants me to leave the business,' Sid was continuing. 'I know she wants me to get a normal job. She gives me subtle hints like she only lets me kiss her goodnight outside the Vauxhall factory.' He laughed and so did I. He went on, 'But it's true, Eric. It does worry me. I know she doesn't understand show business and I'm adamant that I won't leave it.'

The silver paper was now on the floor surrounded by a few carnation petals. My carnation was almost black and the water it was in seemed to be bubbling. The water from the tap was probably coming direct from the Okefenokee swamp. It was exactly like the water you see monsters slowly sink into at the pictures. I was fascinated watching it trying to eat the carnation.

Sid moved to the other side of Frankie's hat.

'Have you got much work lined up?' I asked.

'No. I've got three weeks arranged after the Salford panto.'

'What about summer season?'

'Nothing yet.'

'Well, Ed Low'll see you right, won't he?' I said.

'No chance. He wouldn't touch me with an Airwick on the end of a twenty-foot barge pole.'

'Why not?'

'Well, he found out what I'd been saying about him in Yarmouth.' Sid shrugged. 'From that toothy bird. What's her name? Lavinia. So my chances of working with him have been well and truly Friar Tucked.'

'What Lavinia?'

'That girl I told you about with the buck teeth. The raver with a great body. Anyway, she's four months gone.'

'Really?'

'So I was told. It happens every summer season with Ed. He's known as joke 'em and poke 'em. Good God, there's more Lows in our business than impressionists of Al Jolson.'

I looked at my watch on the bedside beer box and waved goodbye to my carnation as it sank slowly in the mess. It was half-past seven. 'Something'll turn up.'

'Yeh, her mother saying "I told you so".'

'Well, the way I see it is, you've got three and a half hours to make up your mind. Nobody, but nobody, can do that for you. That's for sure, and if you're going to run, run now, because –'

'You sound like James Stewart in *Mr Smith Goes to Washington*.'

'If you run now,' I went on, 'you'll make Carrie unhappy and her mother happy. If you stay, you'll make Carrie happy and her mother unhappy.'

'I'll stay – just to make her mother unhappy.'

'Good. I will now arise, shave, wash, check on the ring, so there will be no jokes at the church. You nip downstairs and tell our land-lord, Wild Bill Hickock, I'm in town and waiting by the breakfast table. It's to be hot, buttered rolls at forty paces.'

The pub where we were staying was called The Dog and Badger, which, I am sure, was what I had for breakfast that morning. Neither Sid nor I ever saw the landlady, only the landlord. Sid did say he heard moaning coming from an upstairs attic very similar to Mrs Rochester in that film of *Jane Eyre*, but, knowing Sid, it could have been a joke, although, having seen the landlord, it could also have been true.

Sid slowly climbed out of Frankie's hat. 'I'll get a paper,' he said.

'Get me the *Sketch* or the *News Chronicle*,' I shouted.

The water was now over the rim of the beaker.

Not being there, and having to go on what Carrie said, her wedding morning went something like this.

At seven-thirty the alarm bell went. Not the alarm clock, the alarm bell. Carrie's mother pounded into her bedroom in their council house in Baden Powell Street. She was wearing an old, grey, heavy material dressing-gown that reached the floor. She weighed a good fourteen stone and always, when she wore that dressing-gown, reminded Carrie of a barrage balloon. A cup of tea in one hand and a saucer in the other, she landed near Carrie's bed. Carrie was already wide awake. She took the tea from her unsmiling Mum, who then put the saucer in her dressing-gown pocket.

'Thank you, Mum. What's the weather like?'

'Pouring down,' she answered darkly.

'Never mind. It might clear up by eleven o'clock,' Carrie said happily.

'No it won't. You've still got time to cancel everything. I'll ring the vicar and The Dog and Badger.' Her mother looked at her with unblinking and expectant eyes. 'Think about it, Carrie. Think about what I am saying. It's for your own good, dear.'

Carrie calmly sipped her tea.

'Me and your Dad only want what's best for you. We only have your interests at heart. We could keep the presents until you marry someone else. No one would mind. Your Dad's very upset but he's not the type to tell you.'

'Oh, Mother.' Carrie looked up. 'He doesn't even know which church I'm getting married in and by eleven-thirty he'll be drunk. That's all he cares about.'

'That's not true,' her mother snapped. 'You don't seem to care what you say anymore since you've gone around with that fellow. I wish I'd never taken you to Yarmouth. I hate Yarmouth.'

'You always said you loved Yarmouth.'

'I used to.' She was getting desperate. 'I mean ... look what happened to your Auntie May.'

'What happened?'

'He left her. Her husband left her.'

'He had to, Mum. He died.'

'Ah, yes, but had he lived he'd still have left her.' This was said as if that bit of information was a family secret.

Carrie's Mum slowly lowered herself on to the bed. Carrie heard the springs in the mattress fight back and quickly give in. 'My dear little girl,' she said. A new ploy, thought Carrie.

'Did I ever tell you about your father's sister's cousin, Rene?'

'No.'

'Well, she married into show business.'

'Really?'

'Yes, well, it was almost show business. He was a salesman for women's under things.' Carrie's Mum looked around the room with slight embarrassment.

'Yes?' Carrie questioned.

'He thought like ... er ... er ...'

'Sid,' Carrie helped.

'Yes , he thought he was funny too. He used to say selling corsets was living off the fat of the land. Well, Rene used to laugh until one day she found him living *with* one of the fat of the land. So anyway, she left him.'

There was a short, sharp silence.

'And you're saying Sid will do the same with other women?' Carrie asked.

'It's written all over him. He's got thick eyebrows.'

'Well, Mum, if he does, it might be my fault. Maybe because I'm not good enough for him in bed.'

'Carrie!' Carrie's Mum almost screamed.

'Well, tell me this, Mum. When did you and Dad last make love?'

The springs in the mattress wailed in sympathy.

'I'm going to tell you something you don't know, young lady,' Carrie's mother said. She was almost in a state of shock. 'Thank the Lord, and you will thank the Lord, that when *they* reach the age of about thirty-eight they lose interest.'

71

No wonder Dad drinks, thought Carrie. She said, 'Why don't you like Sid?'

'Who?'

'Sid, the man I'm going to marry.'

'What makes you think I don't like him?'

'Who, Mum?'

'Him.'

'Sid?'

'Yes.'

The situation was saved by Carrie's Dad walking into the bedroom. 'Hello, my precious,' he said, 'and how's my little princess this special morning?'

Carrie's Dad was the opposite of Carrie's Mum, small framed and thin. He was the kind of man who had a size fourteen and a half neck but always wore a fifteen and half collar around it. Together they were the image of the Bamforth's Seaside Saucy Cartoons.

'Hello, Dad.' Carrie smiled. 'It's a pity about the weather.'

'Well, never mind. This time tomorrow you'll have had it.'

Carrie's Mum turned the same colour as the always-damp mat under the sink – puce. Carrie's Dad had not realized that he had said anything remotely naughty.

'Do you like Sid, Dad?' Carrie asked.

'Sid who?'

'The man I'm going to marry this morning.'

'Oh, a nice boy, I'm sure.' He looked at Carrie's Mum to see if he had done the right thing. He noticed her colour. 'Having a hot flush, dear?'

'Get out.'

'Yes, dear. See you later, Carrie,' he said.

'Yes, Daddy.'

As he left she climbed out of bed. Carrie's Mum watched her. There's no doubt, she thought. She's got a lovely, young body. (Carrie stretched herself.) And a lovely, young face to go with it, and it's all going to waste on that idiot. What can she see in him? Oh, God, why didn't you hear my prayers? She could have done so much better for herself.

Carrie had now slipped into her dressing-gown. Her Mum was still sitting on the edge of the bed, staring at nothing, one of her curlers hanging loose on the back of her head, still thinking: only six doors down that Frankie Priest, a lovely boy, he's down in Newmarket now learning to be a jockey. I know she's six inches taller than him and a stone heavier, but he might win the Derby one day. Billy Lee. His father is a manager of one of those Freeman, Hardy and Willis shoe-shops, and his spots would eventually go. Roddy Margerison . . .

'Mum, Mum, what time is it?'

'Eh? What? Oh, it's nearly eight o'clock. There's plenty of time. Go and have a long soak in the bath. I've told your Dad to stay out of there this morning. He's using next-door's. You know what it's like in there after him. It's worse now since he painted the bathroom and we can't open the window anymore.'

'Poor Daddy,' Carrie mused.

'It'll be poor Mummy and Daddy if you marry this Rodney.'

'Sidney.'

'Yes, him. He'll take us for everything we've got.'

'Mother, we've got nothing.'

'We might have nothing but it's a damn sight more than what he's got. Is he Jewish?'

'I don't think so. I don't think Lewis is a Jewish name.'

'Aren't you sure?'

'I think he's Welsh.'

'They're as bad.'

This was the story Carrie told me six months after the wedding.

Mr and Mrs Sid Lewis waved goodbye from the reception room of the Bricklayer's Arms in Thomas Road. Carrie kissed her mother on the cheek and her father on the floor. Sid and Carrie's Mum touched gloves. He kissed his own mother, stepped over Carrie's father and shook hands with his own Dad. All the guests waved and cheered and Aunt Hilda's dog, Toffee, was getting too excited and barked at everybody. Aunt Hilda was crying and Toffee now began grabbing guests' legs in such a manner that his name should have been Crumpet.

The taxi arrived to whisk the honeymooners off on their journey of love and gentleness. London was to be the venue, Paddington the area and the Alma Hotel the location. Sid gave the driver the destination from the back of the cigarette-smoke-saturated car.

'The first Greenline bus-stop going towards London, please.'

'Wha?' asked an astonished driver.

'The first Greenline bus-stop going towards London, please, and we've got ten minutes to find one. The bus leaves Luton at two-fifty and it's now two-forty so hurry up!'

'But your mother said we were going from the railway station,' Carrie said.

'Not my mother.'

'That would be my mother,' Carrie uttered faintly.

'Awrigh, your mother. First Greenline bus-stop going towards London,' Sid resumed, over-sweetly.

'But I've probably lost a fare thinking I was going to the station,' said the driver.

'That's better than two or three teeth,' Sid answered impassively. He was beginning to lose his cool with this man.

Carrie grabbed him by the arm and pulled him back fully into his seat. 'Don't be like that,' she whispered discreetly.

Sid kept looking at the driver through the rear-view mirror. Every time the driver looked in his mirror, Sid was looking straight into his eyes. The driver, a man of at least seventy with a touch of asthma – his breath sounded like car tyres on a gravel path – was now intently looking for a Greenline bus-stop. He saw one and stopped. They had been in the car no longer than five minutes.

'What number is the Greenline bus, darling?' Sid asked, without taking his eyes off the driver.

'Seven-fourteen,' Carrie and the driver both said together.

Sid helped Carrie out of the car and then walked round to the boot, opened it and took out his three cases. The driver stayed where he was and lit a nipped cigarette. The driving side window was open just enough to drop money through. Sid had the luggage out on the pavement and walked round to the driver's window. He leaned down towards the small opening.

'How much?'

The driver looked nervously everywhere except at Sid and coughed out, 'Twenty-seven and six.' He then wound the window up an inch more. Sid looked at him and continued to look at him as he slowly took out his wallet. The driver relaxed a little thinking he had made it.

'Twenty-seven and six. Not bad for five minutes' driving,' said Sid. 'Here's ten bob and that includes the tip. Your bloody car isn't worth twenty-seven and six.'

They looked hard at each other like an Australian fast bowler looks at an English opening bat. Then the driver snatched the note quickly and professionally, and drove off, winding the window down and giving them a reversed Churchillian sign.

Carrie and Sid were soon joined at the bus-stop by a small, drunken one-man-band. He slowly walked round the corner carrying all his equipment. He was a small man of a well-used sixty, wearing an old, long, gabardine, flasher-type raincoat. On his back was fastened a Salvation Army bass-drum with a picture of the prime minister on it. On his elbows, tied with rope, were two large drum sticks. Projecting from his chest was a piece of piping with a mouthorgan welded to the end of it, just resting maybe a quarter of an inch from his mouth, so close, in fact, that every time he breathed you were treated to a musical wheeze. Sewn to the shoulders of the raincoat, one each side, were two Morris Dancers' handbells that played with a minimum of movement. Nestling under his left armpit was an old fashioned klaxon motor-horn, tied by string to his upper arm. Under his right armpit was securely fastened a bagpipe, with a mouthpiece stuck through the buttonhole of his raincoat to stop it from going into his eye. Around his waist was a steel clamp similar to a stave round a beer barrel. This was holding a washboard with the legs cut off. On every one of his fingers were thimbles. Hanging by a length of string from a button was a penny whistle. In between his legs, at knee height, were two small cymbals. This gave him the appearance of being bow-legged. His shoes were tied with red ribbons from a chocolate box. One of the ribbons still had 'Black Magic' written on it. On his head was jammed a top hat with the words 'Mr Music' written on a card resting in the hatband. He had so many musical instruments attached to him Joe Loss could have conducted him. He weaved up to Sid and Carrie and stood next to them. Sid looked at him. Carrie looked the other way, rather embarrassed. He took a half full or a half empty (depending on whether you are an optimist or a pessimist) bottle of Scotch out of his greasy raincoat pocket and took a long swig – the movement causing his attachments to move giving out a chord in B Flat. He looked up at Sid. Sid looked down at him. Mr Music took another swig in B Flat.

Sid smiled at him and said, 'Do you play requests?'

Mr Music squeezed his left arm and a rather damp, rude noise came from the motor horn, via his sleeve. Carrie tried to pull Sid gently away, her face going quite red. She looked away from both of them and saw the Greenline 714 coming towards them.

'The bus is here, Sid.'

After a third swig, Mr Music shook himself quite hard. It sounded like the Midland Light Orchestra tuning up.

Sid picked up his cases, one in each hand and one under his arm. When the bus stopped he stood in front of Mr Music and nodded to Carrie to get aboard. Sid followed her. Mr Music tried to get on the bus. The conductor tried to stop him, but the Midland Light Orchestra had both his feet on the step and was holding tightly to the rails. The engine of the bus was still running and shaking a fugue out of Mr M.

The conductor barred the man with his arm. 'You're not coming on my bus with that lot, mate.'

Mr M ignored him as he tried to get further into the bus.

'Mate, you're not coming on my bus with all that stuff,' repeated the conductor.

'Why not, eh? Why the bloody hell not? Tell me that. What for, eh? Come on, why not? Why the bloody hell not?'

'Because we haven't got a music licence.'

The conductor pushed the old man and the bell at the same time. The bus moved, the old man lost his balance with the weight of the bass-drum so he had to step backwards as the bus moved away.

Sid looked back to see the old Mr Music waving his arms and shouting filthy abuse at the bus in a drunken rage. The conductor looked at Sid and asked, 'What the hell was that?'

'I think it's the 1812 Overture.'

'Pity,' smiled the conductor. 'We could have dropped him off at the Albert Hall.'

7

Many, many years later, more than I care to remember, I went to
see The Right Reverend Martin Laureston Watson-Tucker DD,
OBE. He officiated at Sid and Carrie's wedding. Over the years we
have all vaguely kept in touch with him. He told me how well he
remembered the wedding – it being his first wedding followed by
his first funeral. 'I remember it well, indeed I do.' He spoke and
looked exactly like the late, and very much missed, Margaret
Rutherford dressed as a man.

'I was highly nervous, Erik.' He always sounded my name as if
it was spelt with a 'k' instead of with a 'c' – very crisp and with
a lot of chin movement. He was a good man. He gave much of his
time to charity and the young. He was now a bishop and being
spoken of as a future archbishop, and to think that it all started in
Luton.

'Highly nervous with it being my first wedding *and* my first
funeral.' He sat back suddenly in his chair and clasped his hands
at the back of his white head as if he had just solved an Agatha
Christie murder. I remained silent in my chair opposite. He then
shot forward, almost leaving his chair; so fast and violent was the
movement that the ash in the open fire swirled up the chimney with
a small hiss.

'They were late arriving at the church, what?' He went back to
a more normal chair position. 'Forty-five minutes late to be precise,
what?' A pause. 'If it hadn't been for you, Erik, Sidney wouldn't
have been there at all, what, what?'

'That's true, Martin. It had reached ten o'clock and he wasn't
anywhere to be found so I borrowed the landlord's bike and went
looking for him. I had the feeling he would run.'

77

'What, what?' He found a new position in the chair, leaning back with one little, fat gaitered leg over the arm of the chair and the other one tucked under him. 'I don't think I'll ever forget you riding towards the church in the pouring rain with Sidney sitting on the cross-bar, Carrie crying, her father lying asleep along one of the pews, what? Her mother was the only one who seemed to be smiling, but even she burst into tears when she saw you both on the bicycle, what, what? You know I had a feeling about that wedding. I felt something would go wrong. You see I'd never met theatricals before I met Sidney. I asked him what hymn he would like sung by our choir, Mr and Mrs Freebody, and he said, "The one about a bear whose eyes were crossed and bear's name was Gladly." It took Mr and Mrs Freebody and myself four hours to work out the hymn he meant. It was that beautiful hymn, "Gladly the cross I'd bear".'

He moved again in his chair. He was now sitting cross-legged. 'The wedding service went well but it was only minutes before the funeral was due. Sherry, Erik, what, what, what, what?' The 'what whats' were coming thick and fast.

'Not for me, Martin. I'm fine, thanks.'

He rose from his chair and stood with his religious bum pointing towards the roaring fire. I felt like Mr Tutman in the presence of Mr Pickwick. I said, 'I always thought it was nice of Carrie to follow your ... er ... career.'

He looked at me with soft, blue eyes – watery would be a better phrase. 'What, eh, what, oh, yes. A lovely woman – always came to see me when she came back to Luton. I think that's too sweet, don't you?'

'She's a nice lady.'

There was a pause. 'I meant my sherry.' He walked towards the sideboard, poured another sherry and swigged it straight down, then poured one for the glass. All this was done with his back towards me, rather like a conjurer setting up his tricks. He came back to his chair and sat down. His body was facing me and both his legs were over the arm of the chair like a ventriloquist's dummy.

'Carrie was on time at the church, eh ... what, eh ... what, what?' It was now the more sherries, the more 'whats'.

'Yes,' I murmured.

'It was you and Sidney, you naughty boys.'

Here I was at fifty-two years old being told I was a naughty boy. 'Sid had lost his nerve,' I explained.

'Her mother was a funny colour,' Martin said. 'I thought she was going to die.' He took another drink. 'I'm sure it was that that made me go wrong in the service, eh, eh?'

'Really?' I was genuinely surprised.

'Ashes to ashes is not supposed to be said in the wedding service, what? But what's the difference, the amount the people listen, eh, what? The Generation Game could use that one, eh, what?'

What the Generation Game could use I couldn't figure out.

'Another small one, Erik?'

'No, honestly.'

'Quite right,' he said as he glided back to the sideboard.

'I thought the funniest ...'

'Are you sure?' he asked from the sideboard.

'Positive.'

'Not even a small one?'

'No, really.'

He went back to his conjuring act.

I continued, 'The funniest thing was when we all made our way up the aisle to leave, and what with being that bit late.'

'Forty-five minutes, eh, what? Eh, what?'

'... and the rain, the coffin and the mourners, coming down at the same time, and Carrie and Sid having to go in single file to get by the coffin and the bier running over Carrie's Mum's corns –'

'Her screams still live with me.'

'But when she tried to take her shoe off to rub her foot and she bent down they kept going and she was almost run over. When she got up she had a wreath hanging round her neck. She looked like the winner of Le Mans.'

Martin emptied his glass. 'What ever happened to Carrie's mother?' he inquired.

'Nothing.'

'Pity.'

'Pardon?'

'Nothing, you say.'

'No. Carrie's folks live in Hampshire in a cottage in the Wallops, for which they pay a small rent to Sid.'

'Would you like another drink, eh, what?' He asked me as if I had kept up with him. I had not had one yet. 'A tiny one, Martin, really,' I said.

'Of course.' He poured a small sherry for me and a large one for himself. He looked more like a conjurer than ever. He was almost into self-levitation and he was certainly making the sherry disappear. He rejoined me by the fire, sitting in his easy chair quite normally. He leaned back looking towards the ceiling.

'She was a bitch,' he mused. I thought I heard a slight slur in his speech.

'Well?' I said, leaving him space to elaborate.

'Are you doing a Christmas thing this year on the telly?'

'A Christmas show? Yes.'

'Good. I shall miss it as usual but I watch the "returns", eh, what, what, what?'

'Yes.'

'I saw part of your last Christmas thing, last May. Quite nice. Do you make it all up as you go along?'

'No, it's written and rehearsed.'

'Is it really?' It was his turn to sound surprised.

'Yes, at least two to three weeks.'

'Good Lord.'

'And we get paid.' I was used to this kind of conversation.

'Really? I see you have a Rolls Royce. What do you earn? A fortune, I presume. Something like £120 a week, what? That's what the miners are after, you know. They deserve it, don't you think, eh, what? Eh, what?'

'Well, I suppose . . .'

'A real bitch, a viper. She didn't want that marriage to take place. She would have stopped it. She had no love for Sidney. I remember saying to my wife, Carla . . .'

'Carla?'

'Yes, Carla.' He sounded a trifle irritable.

'Only I never met your wife, Martin.'

'No, er . . . well, we . . . She . . . You see, early on in our marriage. She . . . wanted to do God's work, so she went abroad to help the less fortunate.'

'Where?'

'What?'

'Where abroad?'

'Monaco,' he almost whispered, followed by a loud 'Ahem,' and a dry, embarrassed cough.

'Monaco? I didn't think there would be needy . . .'

'Oh, yes. The French are a very needy race,' he said quickly, then threw a log on the fire with such venom that for maybe a full minute he was covered by a shower of sparks. I brushed one or two off that had landed on me. I only hoped that the smell of burning cloth was from the man of the same. He was regaining his composure. I thought it time I left.

'Well, Martin,' I said, 'I must be going. It's quite late and you've been so kind.' I started to rise.

'Eh, what? No.'

'It's getting late and I have to drive back to London, Martin. It really has been lovely seeing you again.'

'Listen, sit down. Have another drink.' He almost ran to his conjuring box. He poured two very large sherries. I put my hand out as if to say no. He put both drinks on his little table by the chair. He sat down cross-legged on the chair, leaning his head on his fist, and resting his elbow on the arm of the chair.

'She came to me before the wedding and told me Sidney was already married, and that if I went through with the ceremony I would be a party to bigamy, what? Do you like Monty Python?'

'Who doesn't?'

'Me.'

The door leading from the hall then opened. I would like to tell you that John Cleese walked in. In his place came a beautiful woman bearing gifts of coffee, cheese, biscuits, celery, thin brown bread, butter and Marmite. She was tall and about thirty-five. No wedding ring, I noticed. Her tights, shoes and dress were black. Her hair was beautiful, the softest of auburn. She had large green eyes that looked directly at you without the slightest sign of embarrassment.

'Allow me,' I mumbled, trying to help.

'Please sit down, Mr Morecambe. I'll manage. You can't be any more difficult than an archbishop or a dean. We had the Dean of Westminster here last week.'

'I knew the Dean's brother, Dixie.' Right away I knew, wrong joke, wrong place, wrong time. I felt ashamed.

'Would you like a brandy, Bishop?' She looked at him with a kind of look that would have got a round of applause from an audience watching *Emmanuelle One*, *Two*, *Three* and *Four*!

'Yes, please. You haven't met my housekeeper, Mrs Clapp, have you, Erik?'

I was deflated. How could such a beautiful body and face have a name like Clapp attached to it?

'You know who this chap is, Amanda?' asked Martin.

Good God, I thought, Amanda Clapp. It sounded like something you hear of other men getting. I can't come out at the moment, I've got a touch of the Amanda Clapp.

'Are you doing a Christmas show this year?' she inquired.

'Yes.' I squirmed.

'Good. I'll miss it. I'll see the repeat. I saw your last Christmas Show last May. It's very good the way you make it all up so quickly.' I did not bother to argue. She poured Martin's brandy and my coffee. 'If there's anything else, please ring.'

As she left the room I remembered thinking, Somebody's prayers have been answered.

Martin and I sat and ate in silence. After a while Martin said, 'Two years.'

'What? What?' I said. I thought, Good God, I'm doing it now.

'She's been with me for two years. A widow. Her husband died, of natural causes. He was run over by a car.'

'Really?' I tried to appear disinterested.

He picked up his glass of brandy. Amanda must have poured four doubles in it. Then he sipped and talked for the next half hour, before falling asleep. He was still asleep when I later thanked Mrs Clapp for having me. She said, 'It was a pleasure,' and I left.

8

AUGUST 1976

The group rapped out a chord and Sid walked out on stage.

'Hello eeeevvveeery-boooody ... May I, the late and great Sid Leweeeeis, welcome you to Al and Manny's ding-dong at the ...' Sid waved his arms to get them to shout the name of the club ... Nothing. 'Welcome to Al and Manny's party at the ... Come on, you berks, you're not drunk enough yet not to know where you are. If you don't answer this time you'll have to pay for your own booze. At the ...' Everybody shouted at least six different names. 'Okay you bastards,' Sid grinned. 'Al and Manny want you to have a good time and, as always, they will foot the bill. At least that's what it sounded like.' Sid looked round the room. 'And if anyone wants to entertain their peers, no comments please, they have our permission as long as they and the audience are drunk. Now, everybody, *daaaance.*'

Another chord and Sid jumped into the arms of waiting friends and left the stage. The group played some easy-to-dance-to music and the party started to glow. Sid was in his element, hopping from table to table, knowing everyone, smiling, talking, gagging, drinking.

'Hello, Sid. How's the wife?'

'Fine.'

'And the kid?'

'A lot better.'

In the background there was a raucous laugh, followed by, 'It's the way I tell em ...'

More noise.

'Hello, Sid.'

'Hello, Jeff.'

'Hello, Sid.'

'Hello, Arthur. How's your mum?'

'She's doing fine. She comes out next week.'

'Hospital or prison?'

'Prison hospital.'

Arthur and Sid laughed together.

'By the way, Sid.'

'Yes?'

'If you see Chick, don't ask after his wife.'

'After his wife's what?'

'Oh, don't joke, Sid.'

'Why not?'

'She's er ... You know, she's got the er ...' His voice dropped to a whisper. 'The big one. Terminal.'

'Good God.'

'Yes, the big "C".' He looked around. 'She doesn't know.'

'Oh, that's terrible.'

Arthur looked around again. 'He's only told me so keep it quiet, Sid. I'm telling you in confidence because it was told to me in confidence.'

'But she can't be that old. I mean, she's what?'

'Thirty-seven.'

'Jesus.'

'Had most of her stomach taken away last year.'

'I remember that.'

'Anyway, Chick's very cheerful about it.'

'What about Rita?'

'She doesn't know.'

Arthur moved away and Sid moved on. Poor Rita, thought Sid. He was walking round and through groups of people, actors, comics, singers, and hearing snatches of conversation.

'... I told him straight. I said, don't call me a pouff ... I wouldn't have minded but we were almost back at the park and I thought, "Oh, Jimmy, Jesus, I wonder if he's a policeman." He was ever so tall ...'

Over to the left '... It's the way I tell 'em.'

'... A Rolls.'

'What year?'

'Oh.'

'... about back at your place ...'

'Naw.'

'Why not?'

'You'll try to do me.'

'Of course I won't.'

'Well, then there's no point is there? I mean if you don't fancy me, what's the use?'

'Of course I fancy you, you stupid, beautiful thing.'

'Well you just said you wouldn't do me.'

'How would you feel if I said I might ...?'

'Sid, Sid, over here ... Hello, Sid.'

'Hello, Al.' Sid shook Al's hand, probably because it was a non-working day. 'Is Manny here?' he asked.

'No. Manny's ill. He's not well. You know how it is, Sid, we're brothers. Always have been. Have you heard about Rita?'

In the background, 'It's the way I tell 'em.'

'Yes,' Sid answered.

'Who told you?'

'Arthur.'

'Chick told me. He told me not to tell anybody else.'

'It's very sad.'

'Very sad. She's such a lovely woman. We've got Yarwood on the third of September.'

'He's great.'

'I only hope that while he's here Heath and Wilson stay alive.' Al looked at the party going on around him. 'Come to the office, Sid,' he invited. He put his arm around Sid's shoulder and steered him towards the office.

One wall of Al's office was covered in pictures of every star who had appeared at the club. The thing that made Sid smile was the fact that every picture was the same. Every one was taken at the same place – Number One dressing-room – with the star in the middle, Al and Manny on either side of him, her, them or it, and with the same expression on both their faces in every picture – a stiff smile caused from fear!

'Scotch?' Al asked.

'Fine.'

'Ice?'

'Please.'

Al poured two stiff ones. 'Do you know how much these "do's" cost Manny and me?' he said. 'Two grand.'

'I thought it came out of the –'

'Two bleeding grand, Sid.'

'It's a lot of money.'

'How's Clare?'

'Carrie's fine.'

'And Elizabeth?'

'Elspeth's fine too, but it's going to take a while –'

'Cliff's coming at the end of September.'

'Great.' Sid sipped his drink. 'The doctor says the marks on her face will –'

'Do you like Serina?'

'How do you mean?' Sid took a larger sip.

'Is she any good?'

'... Good? Any good ...? I would say, er, she seems to be doing fine ... Fine. I think they like her.' Sid felt Al's eyes asking all the questions. He now knew how Jerry felt when Tom had him over a boiling-hot frying-pan.

'Do you think she's got hot pants?'

'Hot what, Manny? I mean, Al ...'

'You know, do you think she's crumpet?'

'No.'

'No?'

'No.'

'Oh.'

'How long are you staying tonight, Al?' Sid said.

'She's a pretty girl. She's Jewish like me. I'm Jewish, did you know?'

'Yes, I know.'

'You're not, are you?'

'Not really. Only if my job depends on it. Then I would be, just a little bit.'

Al smiled. 'Which bit?'

'The bit the rabbi threw away.'

'It's the way you tell 'em,' Al said and laughed out loud. 'I don't think Manny likes her.'

'No?'

'Another Scotch?'

'No thanks, Al.'

'Is she here tonight?'

'Who?'

'Serina.'

'Er ... I think so, although I haven't seen her.'

'Pretty kid. Keeps up with the fashion. The women punters like that. She came on stage last week wearing glasses on the back of her head. That's what I call style. Nobody saw till she turned round and walked off –' There was a knock at the door. 'Yes?'

'Benny.'

'Come in, Benny,' Al invited. Benny was the bouncer, built like the side of Windsor Castle and thicker.

'Sorry, guv. It's the police.'

'What about them?'

'Well, there's only one and it's pissing down outside so I fought, should I give 'im a drink, you know. I fink it's a good fing to keep in wiv the law, like.'

'Bring him into the club, Benny, and give him anything he wants.'

'Right, guv.' Benny left.

'Well,' said Sid, 'I think I'd better go and motivate with your guests, Al.' Sid made for the door. 'Give my regards to Manny when you see him.'

'Thanks, Sid, and if you see ...'

'Yes?'

'Nothing.'

Sid closed the office door and left. The first people he saw were Joyce and Lionel. They had their backs to him so he walked quietly towards them and said, 'Will somebody introduce me to Marge and Gower Champion?'

Joyce turned and flung her arms around Sid and hugged him tightly like the old friend he was, while Lionel stepped back and did a dance routine for three seconds that would have taken anyone else a chorus and a half. Joyce asked about Carrie and Elspeth, while Lionel just let what was the brownest face in the club wrinkle into more wrinkles. He shook his head six times quite hard to prove that his hair was real and said, 'Sid, you don't look a day older. You couldn't.' The three of them laughed as Sid guided them to a table.

The office door opened a little and Al Keppleman squeezed his way out and walked around the dark side of the club to the dressing-rooms. As Sid settled Joyce and Lionel at the table there was a fellow being helped out by a couple of friends. Sid did not see who it was, but he never heard 'It's the way I tell 'em' again that evening.

Serina was in her dressing-room, putting the finishing touches to her make-up for the third time in the last half hour. On the dressing-table, under the cups of her spare bra, were a bottle of Scotch and a bottle of gin almost completely hidden. Next to them was a pair of thick-rimmed glasses.

As Al stole slowly along the dark side of the club, trying to keep his presence and his destination a secret from everyone, he watched the entertainers performing, albeit for free, and thought, Some of these people shouldn't be allowed in my club, or any other club for that matter. He looked at them as he walked silently along, performing, eating, drinking, and later on complaining.

Why do they always complain? he thought. Pros complain at anything. It doesn't matter how good it is, how expensive, or how cheap, or how free: they complain. They are born complainers. They complain the beer's cold, the beer's warm, the beer's perfect but the glass is chipped. What do you mean we have to go to the bar and get it ourselves? I know the food's free – it will be the leftovers from last night. No they have a firm in to do it ... Who? I think it's Benyalls – worst catering firm in the whole of London, the complaining pro says as he stamps out his cigarette on the carpet as if he was at home.

Al was making his way to the door that led from the auditorium to backstage. At the moment there was a woman soprano singing on the stage with no music. She was singing something from *Madame Butterfly*. She was terrible and looked old enough to remember Madame Butterfly as a caterpillar.

He reached the door without once being seen or spoken to. He put out his hand and casually turned the handle. Oh, hell, it was locked. Why was it locked? What berk had locked it? Al couldn't go up on stage to get backstage. Everybody would see him and they would all know he was going to see Serina for a little bit of naughty ... That's what Al thought, anyway. If he took his glasses off and his jacket and walked quickly across the stage with a limp, no one would recognize him. He did and no one recognized him – except Benny, who was already backstage showing the Law around the club.

''Ello, boss. Just showing the Law around the club, guv.'

'Yes, of course, good,' said Al. 'Well done, Benny. I'm er ... just having a look around too. You know, just to see if everything is running smoothly. I've just come from the office. Who locked the intercommunicating door?' His eyes flashed.

'Wot, guv?'

'The intercom – The door leading backstage.'

'I did,' Benny said proudly.

'Why?' Al asked with controlled temper.

'You said to, guv. You said to keep that door locked because we don't want everybody using the dressing-rooms for a bit of nookey. That's what you said, guv.'

'Yes. You're right, of course, I did, and you were right, Benny. I was just asking who'd locked it because whoever it was had done a great job on locking it. You see what happens, constable. Entertainers are known for that kind of thing ... Er ... right, off you go, Benny, and lock my office door, there's a good lad. I'll be back in a few minutes, so stay close to the office, okay, Benny?'

'Yes, guv. Come on, 'Enry.' Benny and Henry left backstage. Al, who was perspiring quite freely, looked around, then made his way towards Serina's dressing-room. As Benny and Henry were walking across the stage and while the same woman was now singing some song from *The Barber of Seville*, Benny said, 'Mr Keppleman's a good boss. He's going to give Miss Serina one now. Mind you, he's dropped a bit lucky. He almost bumped into his brother.'

'His brother?'

'They're both giving her one but neither of them know,' Benny explained. He and Henry walked towards the noise and the crowd.

'Hello, Benny,' said Sid, strolling up.

'Hello, Sid.'

'I haven't seen you all evening.'

'You saw me inside the office when I said about the Law. Well, this is 'im, 'Enry. 'Enry – Sid. Sid – 'Enry.' Nods were exchanged. 'Sid's our compère.'

'Is he looking after the law, the way the law should be looked after ...?' Sid asked.

'Well, my coat and helmet are in the cloakroom,' said 'Enry.

'Coat and helmet? Sounds like a German double act.' Benny thought for a second and then guffawed. Sid, thinking he had a captive audience, carried on, 'My brother-in-law was in the police.'

'Was he really?' The perfect feed line, given quite genuinely.

'Yeh. He was no good though. He couldn't catch his pants on a nail. He went to a robbery once and the thief had been wearing calf-skinned gloves and my brother-in-law arrested a cow in Shropshire.' Benny didn't laugh this time and Henry smiled a policeman's smile, the one that makes you realize that they know you're taking the hit and miss out of them.

'We gotta go now,' said Benny. 'I've gotta lock up the office.'

'Why? Has Al gone?'

'Yeah ... He's gone to see his little bird, ain't he?'

'Who, Benny? What little bird?'

'Well, wiv any luck right now he'll be going it wiv Miss Serina, won't he?'

Sid gave nothing away. If the copper had been Sherlock Holmes looking at him through a magnifying glass, he wouldn't have seen a flicker or a twitch, but if Sherlock had had a stethoscope he would have heard Sid's heart miss a couple of beats.

'Surely not before her big number?' Sid said sharply.

'Nah! Before her big mirror.' Benny laughed till tears rolled down his face. Henry was completely out of his depth, not quite sure what it was all about. 'Come on, 'Enry,' Benny said, wiping the tears away with the back of his hand, then taking out his hankie and wiping his hands on it.

Henry smiled. 'Nice meeting you, Sid, and thanks for the laughs.'

'Pleasure. You can get 'em all in a good joke book. Take care. I know Benny don't speak proper and he's built like a brick cooling tower, but watch out, he's a poofta as well ... Give us a kiss and I'll prove it.'

'There's some funny people about,' Henry said, as he walked away.

'I hope that includes me,' Sid shouted back.

The smoke and the noise of the party coupled with the Al and Serina news started to irritate Sid. But so what, he thought. I mean, if she wants to keep her job, why not? She's sitting on a fortune so good luck to her. Hell fire, she can't really sing. I mean, she couldn't hold a tune if it had handles on it. He walked towards the bar thinking, I wonder if I should go backstage, knock on Serina's door and frighten the Eartha Kitt out of Al. He almost laughed out loud. He arrived at the bar and ordered a whiskey.

Sid was still smiling when he was joined by Jimmy Parker. Jimmy was an actor in his late thirties, good-looking but going to seed: drink was beginning to win through, though he was still an excellent television and stage actor. He seemed always to be in a play on television or in the West End. Straight or comedy, he could play both with surprising ease. Tonight his dress was the actor's outfit – faded jeans, Kickers on his feet, a Rugby shirt covered by an old sweater and round his neck, Snoopy on a gold chain. By the look of him, he'd had quite a few 'wets' that evening. His hair wasn't in all the right places but the girl he was with was right in all the best places. Sid thought, Where does he find these girls? I don't see a looker like that more than twice a year. Yet this under-dressed, over-drunk actor can have a gem like this one by his side. Where do they find them? There must be an agency for them. The Great Chicks Agency.

Jim said to the barman, 'Same for me, a large one, and a Baby-cham.'

'Hello, Jim,' said Sid.

'Sid. Er, have you met ...? What's your name, kid?'

She held out her hand and said, 'Estelle.' She didn't seem to mind Jimmy being drunk, untidy or rude.

'Hello, Estelle, are you enjoying yourself?' asked Sid.

'Yes, thank you, it's a very good party and a very nice place,' she said easily.

Jim had his drink in his hand, leaving Estelle's Babycham on the bar. Sid did his duty and handed her the Babycham.

'Thank you,' she smiled.

Jim was leaning with his back to the bar in between Sid and Estelle. People were milling around them, trying to get to the bar.

'What are you doing at the moment, Jim?' Sid asked loudly.

'Her,' he shouted back louder and laughed. Estelle's eyes never moved from Sid's. There was no reaction to Jim-lad's comment, nor did she seem hurt or embarrassed by it. Sid tried to make room for someone to get to the bar. He was now next to Estelle.

'Are you an actress? Are you in the business?' he said.

'Her? Jesus wept!' Jim laughed out loud. At least it moved him from the bar. 'Her leg was in a cast once. The nearest she gets to a theatre is when she tries to pick up the doorman.' Sid felt un-comfortable for Estelle but her eyes never left his. Maybe she's deaf, he thought.

'Blue movies, Sid,' Jim went on. 'Blue movies, old boy. Tell Sid the films you've played the lead in, kid. Go on, tell 'im,' he ordered. 'She makes more money in three months than I make in a year, just for flashing it, Sid.' He gulped the whiskey. 'A film about every four weeks. That's right, isn't it, kid?' One or two people were be-ginning to listen as Sid tried to move them away from the bar. As Sid stepped back, Jim came towards him, still talking: 'Private parties a hundred quid a night. Exhibitions, one twenty-five a night, Sid, and most of it in cash. You know, old man – loose, the readies, the Nelson Eddies ... Buy me a drink,' he hissed at her.

'It's free tonight, Jim. Well, at least, till midnight. Then you buy your own.' Sid was trying to sound happy.

'Make her pay for it like she makes other people pay for it. Give the money to the barman.' Jim thrust a fiver into the top of Estelle's small handbag. She never looked at him once; her eyes were cool, still looking at Sid, as if to challenge him to believe what he'd heard. Jim took the small handbag from her, took his fiver back, and put it in his pocket. Then he opened her bag and started to rummage in it. Sid went forward to stop him, but felt her hand holding his arm. Jim took out a tenner and went back towards the bar, forcing his way through. 'Hey,' he shouted to a barman. 'Hey, you, spotty. Two large whiskies and a Babycham and keep the change.' The drinks were in his hand before you could say, 'And still going strong,' and the tenner had disappeared before the Queen could blink at the light.

Jim turned back to Sid and Estelle with a triumphant grin on his face. He gave Estelle her bag back and handed Sid his Scotch, then started to drink his own as Sid went back to the bar and picked up Estelle's Babycham. When Sid rejoined them, Jim began talking loudly again. Sid took Estelle's arm and guided her to a less crowded place away from the bar, followed by Jim.

'She's done some great films. *Estelle in a Harem* – great, that one. *Estelle Takes a Donkey Ride* – oh, a classic that one, a knock-out that one.'

'I don't think I'm bothered, Jim,' Sid said slowly.

'They're great, Sid. Run about thirty minutes. Sixteen mil sound and colour. She's a star in the Middle East. Two hundred and fifty quid each to buy. Didn't you see her in *Black Is Big and Beautiful*? She makes Linda Lovelace look like Mary Whitehouse.'

Sid took his eyes away from Estelle's. 'So I was right,' he said. 'She is in show business.' A slight nod of her head thanked him.

Jim finished his drink and was now trying to get the barman's attention again.

'I've got a bottle in my room,' Sid said, thinking Jim was going to get another tenner out of Estelle's bag.

'A full one?'

'Full enough.'

'Okay. Let's go to your room,' he urged.

'I'm sorry, there's no Babycham.'

'Don't worry, I hardly drink anyway,' Estelle said.

Sid led the way up the steps on to the stage to get backstage to his room, followed by Estelle and Jim Parker. Jim walked over to the mike and said in a low, drunken voice, over the music, 'Don't forget to see Miss Estelle Fuller in her latest film, *The Hand-Embroidered Jockstrap*. Ha, ha, ha. I'm the support.' No one heard him as he had, in his drunken state, switched the mike off.

Sid quickly walked over to Jim and whispered in his ear, 'The whiskey's poured and waiting.'

Jim allowed himself to be led away to the dressing-room. As the three walked single-file down the corridor to Sid's room, Serina's door opened and out came Al. As soon as Al saw Sid he quickly turned and went back into Serina's room and closed the door. Sid laughed, saying to himself, I did frighten the Eartha Kitt out of him.

Jim was following Estelle and Sid, bringing up the rear. He was knocking on all the doors and trying to open them. He arrived at Serina's door, knocked and opened it. Inside, Serina stood in front of her mirror. Al was in the corner with his face to the wall. Serina was putting her bra on.

'Don't cover them up, darling,' Jim said. 'Let me do it for you.' He tried to get into the tiny room but Serina was having none of that. She picked up a box of white powder and hurled it at Jim. The blow hit him on the head and all the powder settled over his hair and face. Serina pushed him out of her room and locked the door. Through the locked door she shouted all the names she could lay her tongue to, while Al tried to claw his way out of the room with his bare hands.

Sid was almost at the door at his own room. He looked back at all the noise and saw Jim covered in white powder, in his eyes, up his nose and in his mouth. He was now coughing as if he had just lit his first cigarette of the morning. Sid walked back to try and get Jim to his room. Estelle looked at Jim and laughed out loud for the first time that evening. If Jim could have seen her he would have hit her. As it was he lashed out with his right arm, but Sid caught it in mid-air and dragged Jim to his room, followed by a laughing Estelle, while Serina was shouting her lungs out and telling Al not to worry, nobody had seen him.

Sid explained to Estelle where the drink was and, while Sid was pouring hot water into the sink, Estelle was pouring cold scotch into a glass. She looked at Sid as if to say, 'Say when.' Sid told her with a glance to give Jim a lot. Jim was cursing and swearing that he was going to kill people. His clothes were now covered in powder. He cupped his hand in the water and drank and gargled and then spat it out. It cleared his throat and his mouth. Estelle handed him a very large scotch. She poured Sid a small one and gave it to him.

'Thanks,' he said, gratefully.

'Who was the bitch? Eh? Who was she?'

'It doesn't matter,' Sid said softly. 'Drink up.'

Jim gulped the whiskey. 'If I ever see her again, I'll belt her in the mouth,' he swore. 'I'd recognize her by the size of her knockers. Did you see them?'

'Yes,' Sid lied. 'You don't get many of those to the pound.'

Jim sat down as Estelle started to repair her own make-up. 'What are you doing?' he asked in his usual tone.

'I'm repairing my make-up,' she said sweetly.

'If you ask for any powder, I'll kill you.'

Sid heard Al leave Serina's room and the door lock again. Poor Al. Unbeknown to him, his brother – who was supposed to be ill – had been there before him. Benny, by now, had told all the staff. Sid had seen him in the room; Al had seen Sid see him in the room. In the excitement of the love-making and the powder-throwing, and being seen by almost everyone in the club, Al in the ensuing confusion picked up Sid's glasses by mistake and was now bumping into things and people. Could it be right after all? he wondered. Did it make you go blind?

He walked back to his office muttering, 'Oh no, never again. That's the last time for sure. That's definitely the last time.' He also thought of his brother, Manny. I must ring him to find out if he's any better, he thought. What's the time now? Nine-thirty. He'll probably be watching TV.

Al got back to his office to find Benny standing outside the door with Henry. 'Let me in, Benny,' Al said hurriedly.

Benny grinned and said, 'Right, glove,' and then swayed a little. 'Eh?' Al demanded.

'Right, guv,' Benny said, slowly this time.

After a couple of minutes spent looking for the key, Al was let into his office. He told Benny to get Manny on the phone, while he went to the loo. Benny sat behind the desk and rang Al's brother in Golders Green. Al came back and took the phone from Benny and waved him out.

The phone was ringing as Manny came in the front door. He ran up the stairs and in a voice completely out of breath said, 'Hello.'

'Hello, Manny.'

'Manny who?' Manny said.

'No, you're Manny, I'm Al.'

'Hello, Al.'

'Are you all right? You sound bad.'

'I am bad. Wouldn't you be bad if you'd just run up a whole flight – Run up a frightening temperature.'

'What is it?'

'You rang me, so I say what is it.'

'What's your temperature?'

'I don't know. Maybe a hundred and eighty.'

'A hundred and four is very dangerous.'

'So, it's starting to drop a little.'

'Try some chicken soup.'

'How's the party, Al?' Manny tried to sound low and miserable.

'Great. Everybody says thanks and where's Manny? One drunk thought he'd seen you leave the club through one of the fire exits. Ha, ha, ha, ha. He *must* have been drunk.'

'Drunk? What drunk?' Manny rasped.

'Some drunk.'

'Was he one of our drunks?'

'What do you mean, one of our drunks? Anyway, my eyes are bad. You know that and they're worse tonight.'

'Does the drunk work for us?'

'No, I think he was a juggler.'

'A drunken juggler? Won't his balls be all over the place?'

'He isn't working for us, Manny. He's just here at the party. Are you in bed?'

'Of course I'm in bed. I'm almost dying. Has Serina been on yet?'

'Serina?'

'Yes.'

'Why?'

'I'm asking, that's why enough.'

'I haven't seen her all evening.'

'Well, if you do ...'

'Yes?'

'Just remember me to her.'

'Why?'

'Because I'm asking you to. Is there any reason why you shouldn't? I'm not asking you to go out of your way. I just said if you see her, remember me to her. What's wrong with that?'

'Nothing. Okay, I'll give her your regards, but only if I see her.'

'Al, you're getting more like Granpa Bengie every day. And Al ...'

'Yes?'

'Thanks for ringing. I'm getting tired now. I think I'll take a pill and sleep. So don't ring me back, I'll be asleep. I'll see you sometime tomorrow at the office, in the afternoon. Oh, and yes, I don't think we should have that photo taken with the chimp next week. Bye.'

Manny put the phone down, went to his desk, flicked a telephone pad open, memorized a number, came back to the phone and dialled.

'Hello, Manny here ... Fine. You? ... Good. How about supper at your place tonight? Great ... Chinese? ... Okay, I'll get it on the way over. One day I'm going to open a Jewish take-away. I'll be over in about forty minutes. Anything special you want? I mean Chinese food ... Pancake roll. Okay. By the way, where's wonder boy? ... Manchester? You're sure? ... He's just phoned you? ... A cousin's wedding ... Two days .... Well if I'm not too tired after tonight, I might take you out tomorrow for dinner ... Well, to be on the safe side, the other side of Watford ... Yes, leave it to me. See you soon. Bye, bye, Shelley.'

Manny put the phone down and rubbed his podgy little hands together, went into the bathroom and got out the Old Spice.

Al put the phone down after speaking to Manny and from his inside pocket took out a little address book, found the page he wanted and held it open. He couldn't focus properly on the phone numbers in the book unless he put it down on the desk and stood up. Now he could see the numbers in the book and on the phone itself, but he was so far away he couldn't reach the phone to dial. He took off the glasses and knew by the feel of them they weren't his own. He sat down to think. I must have picked these up in Serina's dressing-room and left mine there, he pondered, but whose are these then? He put them slowly into his top pocket. He couldn't see with them and could hardly see without them. He walked to the mirror in the loo, looked at himself without the glasses and saw a blurred Manny looking back at him. He then put the glasses on, looked again and saw a much smaller blurred Manny looking back at him. He went back to the phone and picked it up, held it very close to his eyes, picked up the little address book, held that very close to his eyes, and dialled the number he wanted with great difficulty.

'Hello. Al ... Fine. You? ... Good. Nice to hear you. Sorry you're not at the party. Yes, I know ... Has it gone down? ... Completely.

Oh good. Er ... is anyone there with you? ... What's he doing in Manchester? ... A cousin's wedding. When will he be back? ... Two days ... Oh. Er, Manny's not too well ... No, I think it's nerves and frustration. His breathing's bad. He should have a friend like you to help him keep fit. Look, this "do" tonight goes on till about two-thirty, so I thought, seeing as you can't come to the party, how's about if I brought some Chinese take-away back to your place? One of these days I'm going to open a real Jewish take-away ... Of course I will, a bottle of your favourite ... Yes, advocaat. I can be at your place at about one-thirty. I'll leave here before the end. I'll see you later ... What? ... No food ... You're on a diet. Oh, okay. See you later. Bye and thanks, Shelley.'

Back in Sid's room the Scotch was almost gone. Jim looked quite grotesque, sitting in the chair and still covered in now blotchy powder marks. His eyes were closed and he was snoring loudly. He had obviously passed out. Estelle looked at him and said, 'Thank God for that.'

'What made you come with him?'

'I didn't come with him, he came with me. I'm keeping him at the moment. He's spent every penny he earned. He's in so much trouble with the tax people. He owes more than he earns and every penny he gets goes to paying his tax bill, so at the moment I'm having to keep him and pay for everything. The only thing he pays for is booze and I think he takes the money out of my handbag for that.'

'Jesus, you're a cool one,' Sid said quietly.

'Most of what he told you was true, you know. I am in flesh flicks. I make a very good living at it and you know who got me the job in the first place? Jimbo there.' She pointed to the brewery snoring in the chair. 'But he was wrong about two things.'

'What?'

'The money is twice as much as he thinks.'

'And?'

'Whether he believes it or not, I *am* an actress. Maybe not in the Glenda Jackson class, but even in skin flicks, you have to act a little bit. I do what they ask me to do in these films and look at the camera as if it's the greatest lover in the world, while some idiot watching thinks it's him turning me on. It's just for the money, Sid, strictly for the money. In my own world I'm a big star. Bigger than that lump in the chair. Do you know, there isn't a sheik who wouldn't give me a fortune just to spend one night with him.'

'But surely you could have got on as a legitimate actress?'

'Maybe, but the great Jim O'Toole didn't seem to think so, or bother.' Sid burst out laughing at the name. 'Don't laugh,' she said. 'That's his real name and he tries to live up to it.' Sid put out his glass towards her and she poured the rest of the bottle in it, maybe half a measure. 'Don't drink it neat,' she said. 'It's not too bad for you in moderation with water, but whisky on its own can be a killer. My dad told me. He was a doctor.'

'Was?'

'Yes, drank himself to death, and so will he.' She glanced at the slumbering body, who hadn't moved in the last quarter of an hour, and his breathing was about once every minute.

'So what happened when you met the mighty O'Toole?' Sid asked.

'The usual. He tried to get me into bed as quickly as possible. I'll give him his due. He persevered for five months. He thought he was the greatest lover in the world and he gave me a soon-to-be-forgotten performance. He still thinks he's great but he gets worried now because he doesn't know if I'm acting or not.' She laughed. 'He did try and get me into a film with him, but it didn't work out. He – well, I say he; it was his agent – Jim put some pressure on his agent so I got a commercial, where I was a half-naked girl lying on a water bed exhausted and out of focus in the background, while some fellow told the world that nuts were full of protein!'

'What are you going to do about him tonight?'

'Leave him here if you don't mind.'

Sid looked at Jim. 'Well, I don't think he's going to move again for a long time so, sure, leave him here, I don't mind.'

'When he wakes up, he'll get a cab and make his way home.'

'I'm working later on tonight,' Sid said. 'I'm trying out a new act. It's a little thing that I've had in mind for a long time now. If it goes well with this crowd here tonight I'll have a new bit to work on, and if it doesn't go well it doesn't matter. Stay and watch it if you want. You might like it. I'm calling the character "Mr Lonely".'

'No thanks, Sid,' Estelle answered. 'Not that I don't want to see you work, but I have to work early in the morning.' She leaned over Jim and shouted in his ear, 'Another day, another two grand.' Then slapped his face as hard as she could. He didn't waken.

'You needed that,' Sid grinned. 'Will he make his own way back to your place if he ever wakes up?'

'We don't live together, Sid. I live with my mum, but she doesn't know about my way of earning a living. She thinks I'm a very private secretary to someone high up in the government, who has to work all hours and can't discuss her job. You see, like all mums, she's dumb when it comes to her kids. Lovely, but dumb. She honestly does think I'm a private secretary with the government.'

'Can I ring you sometime?'

'If you want my phone number, I will give it you with pleasure and I hope one day with all the pleasure you like.' She wrote out a number and handed it to him saying, 'Thanks for all your kindness, Sid.' She found her car keys and left with a, 'Good luck with the new act.'

Sid looked at the still sleeping Jim Parker. He washed the glasses in the sink and dried them on the towel. As he left the room he turned out the light and in the darkness he heard, 'You didn't believe any·of that crap, did you?' Sid switched the light back on. 'I'll watch your new act later on,' Jim said, with still-closed eyes. 'And that phone number is the Battersea Dogs' Home. Close the door when you leave.'

Sid did as he was told and made his way to the phone. On the wall was the oldest telephone directory in the world. It was the one with God's phone number in it. Many pages were missing and what pages there were were well and truly written on. He checked to see if the Bs were still intact. They were. He thumbed through till he found Battersea Dogs' Home. He looked at the paper Estelle had given him. The Bitch! he thought.

I was lucky enough to see Sid the first time he ever appeared as 'Mr Lonely', at the club on the night of the party. He walked out after being introduced by another comedian, who was too drunk to do or say anything coherent or remotely funny. He did a couple of gags and slurred into the introduction of 'Mr Lonely'. It was badly done. As Sid heard the name 'Mr Lonely' he cued the band and they played a fanfare of loud separate chords to get the crowd to look at what was going on. Then the club went into complete darkness. A few women gave out tentative screams and one or two jumped up as a few male hands made their way towards female breasts and thighs. A spotlight hit the side of the stage and Sid walked into it. The whole audience looked as Sid walked slowly down to the stage, dressed in his now famous garb. The audience went quiet and gave Sid their full attention. He did about ten minutes, got some very good laughs, handled a few hecklers with simple ease, and left the stage to excellent applause. He was, as he said later, a small hit. It was the birth of the wonderful Mr Lonely.

He changed back into his dress-suit in the dressing-room as quietly as he could, trying not to disturb Jimmy Parker, and then headed for a table out front. He sat with a few of his fellow pros and listened to congratulations on his new bit. He was on his second drink when a small man, about forty years old, dressed in a blue safari outfit, with an orange neckerchief tied loosely around his neck, pranced over to his table. He was as queer as the government's policies. He also had a soft-centred name, Ivor Nolan. Sid asked him to sit down.

'Darling, I'd love to but I can't. I'm with friends,' he lisped. 'I only came over to say how much I enjoyed your little act. It really was very sweet. Have you ever done it on TV?' Sid shook his head. 'Well, dearie, here's my card. Please ring me and we can have a little chat.' He handed a card to Sid and left.

One of Sid's friends said, 'You play that card right and you're in there.' They all laughed.

Sid looked at the card, then put it in his pocket. He noticed BBC on it.

9

Having been told by two almost armed guards that, 'No way are you going to get in the BBC precinct with your car,' Sid parked opposite, on a cindered, home-made car park, full of potholes, old bangers, and rather sad-looking empty caravans. The price to park there would have made an oil sheikh shudder. He walked back towards the BBC entrance, was stopped, checked, and then allowed in. He walked up to the main building and, after leaving the reception area, found his way to the lifts. He was still on time for his appointment, having left his home early, to allow for traffic he never encountered. In the lift with him were two stars and a tea lady with a trolley full of buns, rolls and biscuits. Urns contained tea or coffee and you had to guess which you got after the first sip. Out of twenty people that morning, five coffees were right, and five teas were right, there were eight don't knows and two abstained. The stars in the lift only looked and spoke to each other. The tea lady just blankly looked ahead. Sid pressed for the fourth floor, the lift doors closed on an old lady character actress, who walked as if she was permanently late. The two stars looked at Sid as if he'd just strangled a baby. They were all destined for the fourth floor.

At exit time, Sid asked the tea lady if she knew which was Mr Nolan's office. She told him. He made his way there. It was his first time in the BBC television centre. His previous work on television had been with the other side in a talent show, in which he came last. The winner got 92 out of a possible 100; Sid got 11. The winner was a complete amateur, a crippled piano accordionist. He played 'We'll Meet Again' and 'Bless This House'. Two weeks after winning, he was dead. He went exactly the same way as he got his accordion; fell off a lorry.

Sid was now at the door he should have been at, and on time. After a quiet, nervous knock, to which there was no reply, he knocked louder, but there was still no response. He knew that people were in the room; he could hear Mr Nolan on the phone and a typewriter being hammered heavily. He turned the handle quietly, as if he was going to rob the place. It was locked. He had one more ace up his sleeve. He got as close to the door with his mouth as he could, looked along the corridor to check that no one else was about, and, in a high-pitched voice, shouted, 'Tea.' The bolts on the door were unbolted and the locks unlocked quicker than Houdini could have done it.

He was now looking into the face of Mr Nolan's secretary, a woman with a figure like a cornflake box, economy size. Her name was Bonnie, which she wasn't. Her hair looked like two pounds of straight candles. Her eyes observed Sid the same way a just-wakened boa constrictor looks at a fat, juicy rabbit. He felt he was standing in the way of Charles Bronson with lipstick. She was the epitome of that wonderful saying, 'She was the good time had by nobody.' She pushed Sid to one side as she looked up and down the corridor for the tea lady. 'Where's the tea lady?' she bawled. 'Who shouted "TEA"?'

'Hello, I'm looking for Mr Nolan,' said Sid.

'Who shouted "Tea", eh? Who was it? Answer me. Who shouted tea?' She came out of the office into the corridor. Sid looked into the office and saw Mr Nolan. Ivor waved a 'Come in'. He was still on the phone. Sid walked in and was immediately attacked from behind by Bonnie. She grabbed his arm in a vice-like grip and bellowed, 'What are you doing in this room?'

'I have an appointment with Mr Nolan.' Sid tried to blink away the tears as he slowly went towards the ground. He looked at her hand gripping his arm muscle. Her knuckles were whiter than a learner driver's. He tried to shake her off but she hung on like the British bulldog she resembled.

Ivor put the phone down and said 'It's all right, Bonnie.' It was as if he had said, 'Leave, leave,' to a well-trained Doberman Pinscher.

The grip was unclasped and Sid pumped his arm to keep the circulation going. At the moment the veins in his right arm were almost twice as big as the ones in his left arm.

Ivor spoke. 'Shut the door, my darling.' Sid turned and was about to make for the open door but he was too late, Bonnie was shutting it and pulling bolts closed. 'I suffer with my chest,' Ivor said. 'All these draughts. You don't know what it's like to have permanently to wear a thermal vest. Sit down please, Mr Montgomery.'

'Lewis. I'm Sid Lewis.'

'Well, sit down anyway. Oh, yes, you're Mr Lewis. Bonnie?' Sid heard an animal-like grunt. 'Who's Mr Montgomery?'

'He's next, after you've finished with him,' she said pointing to Sid.

'Oh, yes,' Ivor cooed. 'He's that impressionist.'

'Yeh,' was growled.

Ivor looked at Sid. 'Have you seen him?' he asked. 'Calls himself Monty Montgomery – the eyes, ears, nose and throat of them all. He's brilliant. He's the only one I've ever seen do an impression of Mike Yarwood.'

'Oh, yes?' Sid said, putting his head on one side quizzically.

Ivor started to make a few notes on a scribbling pad. This gave Sid time to take stock of the man who sat opposite him. Today Ivor was dressed in a purple silk Russian blouse with a collared neck, and one of his ears sported a round, gold ear-ring. He put the pencil down and looked straight into the eyes of a rather nervous Sid. He spoke: 'I'm going to Covent Garden tonight.'

Sid thought, I hope you get back. He said, 'Oh, great.'

'Yes, ballet, the Russian ballet.' Sid watched his eyes light up at the mere thought of watching those great big male Russian dancers prancing about in their tights. 'Do you like ballet?' Ivor asked Sid.

'No, not particularly. I mean, instead of getting all those dancers to stand on their toes, why don't they just get taller people?' Sid beamed. Ivor looked shocked, hurt and frightened. From behind him Sid heard Bonnie snort like a dragon spitting flames. He thought, The best thing to do is to ignore her and if she touches me, I'll kick her in the groin, and if I break a leg that's my hard luck.

'Tea!' was heard outside the door.

The quickness of Bonnie's movement to the door actually made Sid jump. The door to Fort Knox was opened and Sid's tea lady was there.

'Russian tea for me, Bonnie ... Sid?'

'Eh, nothing for me, thank you,' Sid said without turning round.

'Did it take you long to get here?' Ivor asked.

'Forty-six years,' Sid answered.

'Pardon?'

'Half an hour.'

'Parked all right?'

'Well, Butch Cassidy and the Sundance Kid wouldn't let me in the BBC car park.'

'Oh?' Ivor simpered.

'Here's your tea, Ivor,' Bonnie roared. She leaned over the desk and put a plastic cup of black fluid with almost half a lemon floating in it on to a batch of never-to-be-read scripts. This gave Sid a chance to cast a sideways glance at the incredible bulk; fourteen stone at least, and wearing a dress that gave the impression her legs parted below the knees. In her hand she held a cardboard plate with six sugar lumps on it, as well as two doughnuts, two currant cakes, a cheese roll and a brightly wrapped chocolate biscuit. She left his vision and he heard the door close and lock.

'Well, Sid, I'm glad you phoned and more than glad to see you here.' Sid nodded, not knowing how to answer. Ivor took a black Russian cigarette from a tortoise-shell case, put it in a nine-inch amber holder and lit it with a slim, gold, Dunhill lighter. The room was starting to smell like a Turkish brothel.

'They're a lovely smell, Ivor,' the beast said to the beauty.

'Thanks.' He turned to Sid. 'I enjoyed your show. Very clever, and the party was fun too. Bonnie, remind me to write and thank the Kepplemans.' The noise of chomping food stopped and the sound of a reminder being written took over.

'Have you seen any of the shows I've produced on TV?' Ivor asked.

'I'm sure, I must have,' Sid lied.

'Saturday nights mostly, sit-coms, variety and, of course, the specials.'

'Ah, well. I work while your shows are showing. I'm at the club so there's not much chance to watch TV, and there's only one television backstage and that's in the star's room.'

Ivor's face became longer and longer as the conversation went on. 'I sometimes have a show on Sunday nights,' he said. 'Two weeks ago ... What was it called, Bonnie?'

Bonnie put the chocolate biscuit down and put a pencil in her mouth as she thought. '"The Drum Beat Parade",' she said at last. She picked up her biscuit again. 'The one with all those soldiers.'

'Oh, yes.' Ivor beamed.

'Four weeks ago it was Bell Bottoms Up,' she went on.

'Yes, yes. That was the one with all those sailors,' Ivor said excitedly.

104

'And next month you do that one about the rag trade – "Puff the Magic Dralon".' She went back to her eating again. Ivor looked at Sid inquisitively.

'On Sundays Mr Nolan –' Sid began.

'Ivor.'

'Ivor.' Sid carried on. 'On Sundays I do concerts and one or two extra bits with my own act up and down the country – you know, for the extra money.'

'So you've never seen my work then?' Ivor almost sighed. Sid shook his head. 'Pity. Oh, well, never mind . . . Now, the idea I had in mind for you, Sid, was first of all a pilot show. That's a show we make and if it's good we put it out. If it's not, it's scrapped. But it gives us all an idea if we're going in the right direction. Now, I think your character, Mr Lonely, is ideal for television. It's visual as well as verbal. He can be put into almost any situation and the part I like is, he's topical. By that, I mean politically topical. How long have you been playing him?'

'That was the first time I did it.'

'Really?' Ivor sounded genuinely amazed. 'I must say that pleases me. That means no one except the people who were there that night have seen it.'

'That's right,' Sid replied.

'So we're dealing with something new. Oh, good, that's a challenge. We like a challenge, don't we, Bonnie?' He put his hands together as if about to pray. He sat there for a full minute, then sprang up, to reveal he was wearing Russian boots with his pants tucked in them. Sid looked towards the back of the door to see if a big, furry hat was hanging there.

Ivor came round and sat on the edge of his desk. 'Listen. I've had a word with them up there,' he said pointing upwards. Sid didn't know if he meant God or the people in the rooms above him. 'They listen to me. If I think I've found a new talent they let me have a go.' He turned to Sid. 'Thank God, darling, we're not bothered about ratings here at the Beeb.' He floated about the room like Isadora Duncan.

No wonder they lock the doors, Sid mused.

The hitting of typewriter keys started at the back of Sid with a ferocity and speed he didn't think possible. Maybe she's just typing anything, he thought. Not real words, just rubbish. Sid looked at Attila the Hun and she looked as if she was really doing it.

'I'll try and get the show organized for a Sunday,' Ivor said. 'The audiences are better on Sundays. They have nowhere else to go ... before or after.'

The typing stopped abruptly as Ivor sat down. Maybe she was playing for him to do his dance to, Sid thought.

Suddenly Bonnie clumped towards the door, unlocked it and left the room. 'I'll get these copied,' she rasped.

'Now, Siddles, about—'

'May I ask you something, Ivor?'

'My darling, ask away.'

'That girl ...'

'Bonnie?'

'Yes. Will she be on the show? I mean will she be connected in any way?'

'Of course. She's devoted to me.'

'I can see that but—'

'I think she might even kill for me. Bonnie's been with me for six years. Of course, her name isn't Bonnie. It's Ann.'

'Ann?'

'Yes, her name is Ann Clyde, so that's why I call her Bonnie. You get it? Bonnie – Ann Clyde.' He giggled. 'Isn't that clever?'

'Yes, very,' Sid said slowly.

'She's quite harmless really. Now then, my darling. Writers. Have you anyone in mind?'

'Writers?'

'Now, I think we're in luck. I have two boys I think might be able to do it. I've had my eye on them for months. University types. Very smart dialogue. Political satire, witty and crisp. I'm sure they could write for your Mr Lonely. I took them out of radio. They wrote twenty-six of their own series. That political show – Guy Fawlkes, MP for Uppminster. Big hit it was.' He put his hand in his desk drawer, brought out a perfume spray and wafted it around himself, giving Sid a little squirt. Sid gave him a quick sharp look that would haunt a normal person. 'Their names are Troughton and Davis. Edmund and Hilary.'

'But do you think I need class writers?' Sid asked. 'I do gags, Irish jokes and the like.'

'Not on my show you don't, duckie.'

'Oh?' Sid was slightly taken aback at the venom Ivor used.

'What you don't seem to understand is what we've got,' Ivor went on forcefully. 'I'll stake my reputation that with God and the writers' help, I'll make Mr Lonely into a national figure.

106

What we have could be dynamite in television and comic terms,' he enthused.

'You mean that little thing I did in the club?'

'Yes, my pretty one. That little thing you did in the club. A year from now, who knows? I mean, I've got a feeling, that's all.'

Sid was starting to smile. He was beginning to pick up the vibes this middle-aged poofta was pushing out. 'Well, I must say that I think it's very clever of you to spot anything in what I did,' he smarmed. 'I've never done anything like that before. I thought of it in twenty minutes.'

'Good.' Ivor bounced. 'The great things, most of them, have been spur-of-the-moment things. Look at Noel's songs – thought of within seconds.'

'Really?'

'Of course. Now off you go. I have to see a Mr –' He looked at his notes.

'Mr Montgomery,' Sid reminded.

'Good memory. I hope that you can remember your words as well.'

Bonnie hurled herself back in the room. Sid stood up to go and Bonnie gave him an almost-smile.

'Have we got his number, Bonners darling?' Ivor asked.

'No,' she growled.

Sid gave it to them, said his thanks and left with a very light heart. On his way towards the lifts he looked around to see if he was alone again. He was. He shouted, 'Tea,' at the top of his voice and five doors opened, including Bonnie's.

10

The television show came out one Wednesday night, fairly early in the evening. This was more by accident than anything planned. But it was great for the show because the youngsters saw it – kids between the ages of seven and fifteen, who, had the show been later, would probably have missed it because of homework, having a bath or some even being in bed. But the BBC, in its infinite wisdom, put it on at the completely awkward time of 6.40 to 7.10. It worked beautifully. Sid was happy with it and saw new possibilities not seen at rehearsals. Carrie quite liked it, although she had really never liked anything he had done before, so to Sid this was a step in the right direction. Carrie's mum missed it. She went out to Bingo. Most of the people who saw it loved it. There was nothing to dislike about it. In particular, the kids thought it was great. Thousands of them wrote to the BBC demanding to see it again. It was a rarity in the fact that for once the whole family could sit down and watch a show together without wondering, 'Am I going to be embarrassed?' or the children asking, 'What did he mean, Mummy?'

It's not easy to explain why Mr Lonely became so big with the public. He had the gentle approach of the late Arthur Haynes, yet, at times, the coarseness and strength of Jimmy Wheeler. He would walk on to the screen alone, talk to you for a couple of minutes about life in general and soon have you laughing. Then he would introduce a guest singer or musician to you, leaving you to enjoy them. They would finish and back he would stroll and entertain you for a while without speaking, with things like putting up an umbrella, or taking it down. His gift was that he was able to make you laugh by doing the same things you yourself had done. He was soft but never a fool. That's why children loved him. At other times he was sharp

108

and penetrating, especially with his political routines. That's when adults loved him. And always at the end of his show he would sing his famous Mr Lonely song, with the same sad appeal as the wonderful Bud Flanagan. The camera would slowly zoom out, leaving this tiny, incongruous figure standing there, while you at home would wait for him to fade from your screens. What can I say about Sid Lewis? Genius? Yes, that's what I'll say. Genius.

Ivor had done his job very well, being an extremely astute producer. He knew the character of Mr Lonely better than anyone. He kept the whole of the production light and simple. He wasn't out to show how clever he was, yet through the simplicity and speed of production he showed everybody how clever he was. The BBC were cock-a-hoop and naturally wanted to set up a series and a deal for the autumn. Sid's agent didn't know what had hit him. He went out to lunch with – and was never off the phone to people who were in charge of the negotiating side of that vast organization. Leslie realized, without understanding, that he was into something big. He made a deal for Sid that Sid thought was impossible. He signed a contract for more money than he thought was ever in the vaults of banks. After the first series, Sid Lewis became a major star.

He left the Starlight Rooms with mixed emotions. He had loved working there. He had never been a real success there, but Al and Manny had kept him in work at reasonable money. He was well into his third year there, but the future now beckoned. Leslie, Sid, Al and Manny had a lunch together and talked Sid's contract out with a promise to Al and Manny that once a year Sid would work their club at reasonable money. Sid and Leslie gave their word. The first time he worked the club as Mr Lonely he broke all existing records. He was now paying more in tax than he'd earned the year before. Whether that's a good thing or not I don't know, but it's the nearest thing Sid had ever had to a status symbol. Twelve months before he was doing his own tax. At most it used to take him two to three hours on a Sunday afternoon. Now he had a firm of auditors called by a very fancy name – Crawford, Adam and Foiley.

11

MAY 1978

Yeah, I see you going down the street in your big Cadillac,
You got girls in the front and girls in the back,
Yeah, way in the back you got money in a sack,
Both hands on the wheel and your shoulders right back.

Roger Miller

Sid, the new star, paid the driver of the taxi and entered the Euston
Television Studios. The faces of the staff and even other show business people smiled. Sid had a gift for making people who didn't
know him happy. People he had only just met felt happy at having
done so. Harry Secombe has the same gift. If you don't like Harry,
you don't like people. Only a few are given this gift and none of
them realizes the happiness they give to others.

That afternoon Sid was doing a television programme, albeit an
interview. He was wearing his best dark suit, a blue shirt and a plain
tie. He could never understand how other performers went on any
type of programme at all wearing a check shirt, jeans and what often
looked like running shoes. In his mind you had to look smart. If
he was run over by a steamroller, he would turn on his side to keep
the crease in his trousers. His mother used to tell him, 'A crease in
your pants, a clean collar, well polished shoes and you'll get the job.'

He walked towards the reception desk. The lady who was in
charge of the desk, phone and any person who was in a radius of
her was an attractive lady, one who would give you no trouble but
was the complete boss of her three yards. If she said, 'I'm sorry,
Mr So-and-so is out,' and you saw him there sitting on her lap,
you would say, 'Well, when he comes back, would you mind telling
him I called.'

'Good afternoon, Mr Lewis. Miss Gamerlingay's secretary will be with you in a few moments,' she said to him. She then continued with her phone conversation, while at the same time told someone else how to get to Mr Ashley Broad's office.

'I'm a little early,' Sid said to her.

'Believe me, around here that's as rare as Willie Hamilton going to Buckingham Palace and asking the Queen if he could take the corgis for a walk.' She beamed. 'Ah, here's Miss Gamerlingay's secretary now. Hello, Bobbers, this is Mr Lewis.'

'Hello, I'm Sid Lewis. I think I'm expected.' Sid tried to keep the conversation low.

'Hello, Mr Lewis. I'm Roberta Moor-Roberton, known to everyone here as Bobbers. I'm sorry you've been kept waiting.'

'No, I haven't. I'm a little early. I've been here no more than two minutes.' He turned to nod his thanks to the receptionist. She smiled her thanks, while at the same time keeping half a star under control.

'If you'll follow me, Mr Lewis, I'll take you to the hospitality room,' said Bobbers. 'Miss Gamerlingay is there, and Dr Magnus Pyke – he's on time too. It's nice to know that both your stars are already here ...' She saw a small look of surprise on Sid's face when Dr Pyke's name was mentioned. 'You get on all right with Dr Pyke, don't you?' She held the swing door open for him.

'I don't know,' said Sid. 'I've never met him. I didn't know that he was also on the show, but I'm a great fan and he works like one, so I'm sure everything will be fine.'

Bobbers was one of the most attractive women Sid had seen in hours. She was wearing a man's white shirt and black jeans. He had never seen jeans so tight. She could not live alone. She would have to have someone to help her get them on and off. Maybe they were sprayed on? He watched her walk as he followed her. Her movements were a sensation. Sid thought, And some people get a thrill watching Kevin Keegan. This girl walks like a pigeon on a hot pavement.

'First door on the left, Mr Lewis,' she said. This time he held the door open. She was obviously pleased by this. He followed her into the room. A small table was on the left hand side and that was being used as the bar. Three armchairs were in the room and two television sets; one was in colour and one didn't work. Just behind the door, four hooks were strategically placed for twelve overcoats. What it meant was, that in the winter you could not open the door for overcoats, and in the summer you could not open the door for overcoats either. As Sid looked around he thought, Well at least there's ice. It's in a cup but it's ice.

To be honest, Euston Studios were mainly offices, with little television output, apart from the odd show like this. As Bobbers and Sid entered the room the seven people in it turned towards them with typical British enthusiasm. Four of them looked away, while the other three ignored them completely. Sid smiled at everyone in the room with his now famous 'Share that amongst you' smile. In a way he felt like a man who had been accidentally invited to a Tupperware morning, and not only had he arrived late but had brought a bottle of Scotch. The secretary and Sid looked at each other for a second. They didn't speak. They were now joined by Miss Gamerlingay.

'Sid, how nice to see you.' She shook his hand firmly.

'It's nice to meet you, Miss Gamerlingay.'

'Henrietta – Henrietta Sarah Gamerlingay. It's a terrible name, I know, but I tell everybody as soon as I meet them and that gets it out of the way early on. My friends, and I'm sure we are going to be, call me Henry.'

'Henry?'

'Henry,' she repeated as she straightened her bow tie and pulled down the points of her waistcoat. 'Have you met Knickers?'

'Pardon?'

'Knickers – Mavis – Mavis Nicholson. We call her Knickers, you see. Nicholson – Knickers. Henrietta – Henry ...'

'Yes. We did meet once but in all probability she wouldn't remember when.'

'*Knickers,*' Henry shouted. Mavis looked across the room at Henry and with a smile excused herself from the tall, thin man to whom she was talking. This was the thinnest man Sid had ever seen. You could only see him from the front. He was the original chinless wonder. Twenty years ago, if he had been convicted of murder and sentenced to hang, they would have had to put the rope under his arms. Mavis made her way towards them. Henry stood there waiting with a half pint of beer in one hand and the other hand stuck in her pants pocket. Mavis was wearing a plain, very nice, feminine dress. Sid thought, How feminine she looks. He also thought that, next to Henry, so did he.

Mavis joined them and in her soft, Welsh voice said, 'Hello, Sid, how are you?'

'Hello, Mavis,' Sid replied. 'I was just saying to Henriet – er, Henry, that we've only ever met once before.'

Mavis frowned, trying to think where, while Henry began to light a small cigar, which was stuck in a pipe-shaped cigarette holder. 'Wasn't it at some charity or other?' she asked.

'It was at the Lord's Taverners Ball, two years ago. In the private room, where all the people who have done anything get a couple of free drinks, before they go downstairs and start paying for them.'

'Have you met Maggers?' asked Henry.

'Who's Maggers?' Sid asked.

'Magnus – Maggers – or Pykers – whichever,' said Henry.

Bloody hell, Sid thought. Maggers, Pykers, Knickers. I suppose I'll be known as Sidders, but Sidders wouldn't mind some crumpers with that seccers Bobbers.

Mavis beckoned Maggers to join them. He was at the far end of the room and crossed it very much like Tarzan crossing the jungle, except Maggers' vines were invisible. Maggers, Sidders and Knickers were talking to each other nineteen to the dozen, when Bobbers appeared and gave Sidders a whiskers and waters. She tried to give Maggers a ginners and tonners but he was moving his arms so much she gave up the idea and drank it herself. Sid thought that Maggers must get his drinks intravenously. He probably had a fellow who called at his home late at night, came in through the window, stuck the needle in his arm, gave him a large gin and tonic while he was asleep and left.

Unfortunately for Sid, Bobbers left the room. However, within a few minutes he was asked to go to makeup and from there into the studio for a run-through for voice level and cameras. The run-through only took a few seconds and so as not to lose any spontaneity, the questions for the show were to be different from the questions for the run-through. There were three cameras in the studio, but they might only use two. If so, they would take the third camera and put it at the back of the studio. To Sid there was nothing more sad than a dead camera with its long lens pointing to the floor as if it would never rise again, rather like a naked eighty-year-old man.

On this type of show – an afternoon show – there would be no audience; although there were forty or fifty seats in the studio, they were all empty. The working area consisted of two chairs, one for the guest and one for Mavis. The microphone was attached to your tie, or it was on a stand between the interviewer and the interviewee, or it might be a boom mike. That type of mike is controlled by a very long retractable arm which the boom operator works backwards and forwards, and the mike head can also be worked from side to side. But the boom mike would probably not be used on Mavis's show. It was the type of mike that would be used in a play, where they have rehearsed with the artists and know when and where the performer is to speak. It was not for a show like this, where there would be no definite pattern of dialogue. Anyway there were Maggers' arms to think of. One quick sentence could knock an inexperienced boom operator from Euston Studios straight into the BBC. Both the artists and the tech boys preferred the tieclip mike. For the tech boys the fun came when they had to fix one on to the dress of someone like Raquel Welsh or Sophia Loren. The man who had that job would pray for a go-slow or better still work to rule.

The idea was that as soon as Mavis had finished with her guest, she would then be given a close-up and the first guest would be dragged from the chair and the second guest transplanted into it. This was, of course, unseen by the viewer. It was always thought to be better to be the second guest as you had the advantage of getting a warm seat. In a soft accent the viewer would see and hear Mavis say, 'That was Magnus Pyke, ladies and gentlemen. Now my next . . . Well, what can I say about my next guest that hasn't been said before? Let's find out. Ladies and gentlemen, will you say Good Afternoon to Mr Sid Lewis.'

It was at this stage that the nerves came. How many times have you watched a person on television who was not in the least bit nervous until he realized the camera was on him and on him alone? He doesn't believe that the camera is on him, he's fine if he thinks it is on anyone else, but when he looks slightly to the left or right and sees the camera is making its way towards him with a red light on it, lit up, you will see the strongest of men go a funny colour. (That's if you have colour: or go a funny black and white if you only have black and white.) This is the time when the nerves creep up upon you. This is the time you start to feel like an oyster at low tide, or a turkey in November. But this is only an unrehearsed chat show – no sweat. 'Come on,' you say to yourself. 'It's not like doing your own show with twenty million people watching.' Now that's when you get the real nerves. That's when your heart starts to thump – the kind of thump you would get if Sophia Loren walked naked into your bedroom and said, 'Hello, Sid. Carlo's had to go back to Italy for a few days. Move over.' But this is a show with no studio audience, a relaxed question-and-answer show. Still, Sid felt a certain amount of deep-breath tension. Yet it soon passed when he started to talk.

'May I say good day, Mr Lewis,' Mavis began. 'One of the first things –'

'It's a pleasure to be here.'

'Thank you –'

'Because you may –'

'First thing I feel I would like to know, Mr Lewis –'

'Sid.'

'Sid.' She smiled. 'First – is the name Lewis. Are you a Welshman, Mr Lewis?'

'No, I –'

'You see, the reason I'm asking you is I'm Welsh and Lewis to me is a Welsh name.'

'No, I'm not a Welshman, although there might have been a Welsh connection in the past. There's no mention of it in my family. I'm a Cockney, born within the sound of Bow Bells.'

'How wonderful. Where were you born?'

'Potters Bar.'

'Pot – but Potters Bar surely isn't within the sound of Bow Bells? I mean you can't hear Bow Bells in Potters Bar.'

'I have excellent hearing.'

She said, 'You must have.'

'Pardon?' he smiled. 'I was deaf for six months you know, completely deaf. My mother took me to a specialist.'

'Did you have an aid?'

'Yes. Only a cheap one. It was a card with "Speak Up" written on it. That was my father's idea. But everything worked out fine, all by accident. My mother put some olive oil in my ear one night as she put me to bed and the very next morning I heard from my sister in Luton. She used to ring up every time Luton Football Club won. Sometimes she would ring up twice a year –'

Mavis was quick to realize that if she wasn't careful, she would end up as his straight-woman and she didn't want that. She began again. 'Your success came to you, if I may say so, rather late in life.'

'Yes,' Sid answered. 'I suppose it did really, but I was making a good living ...'

'How old are you?'

'Could you make that question a little more direct?'

'How old are you? You must be ... what? Forty-nine? Fifty?'

'Forty-six.' She set the trap and I fell in, Sid thought.

'And your wife?' Mavis was going on.

'Oh, yes?'

'Oh, yes, what?'

'She was a child bride,' Sid said.

'A lot of women don't like to tell their real age. Why do you think that is? I mean your wife, what was her first name?'

'Carrie.'

'Carol.'

'Carrie.'

'Carrie.'

'Yes.'

'Does she object to anyone knowing her right age? I mean if a woman is forty, she'll usually tell you she's thirty-eight. A woman of forty-three would say thirty-nine ... fifty – forty-seven ... until they get to about eighty-five, then they tell you they're past ninety. Maybe you think I'm talking rubbish, but haven't you noticed that most women take a few years off? Does your wife object to telling anyone her right age? I find that most men tell the truth or as near as doesn't matter. Does your wife?'

Sid said, 'I don't ... I, er, honestly ...' He thought, Carrie always takes a couple of years off except in her passport and that picture makes her look ten years older anyway. He spoke again: 'You see, Mavis, age is a funny thing, and I wish I was right now.'

'How old is Carrie?'

It was like somebody saying, 'Check,' and you'd lost your queen early in the game. Think Sid and think quick.

'Your age?' Sid castled.

'Forty-three.'

Check again and your bishop's gone, he thought. Aloud, he said, 'Yes, she's thirty-nine.' Checkmate! They both grinned.

'Are you happily married?' she persevered.

'Very much so,' he answered, a shade too quickly and definitely too automatically. 'But you could soon put a stop to that,' he said, wishing like hell he hadn't.

'Why? Are you a ladies' man then?' Two pairs, Jacks and Kings.

'Of course, my wife's a lady.' Three deuces.

'Does your wife mind you being a sex image?'

'It's better than a sex change.'

Mavis ignored him beautifully. 'It's rare for a comedian to have a sex image. You have. Does Carrie mind?' Seventeens pay eighteen or over.

'What sex image?' Twenty-three – bust.

'Well, you must know you are not disliked by your female fans. Ninety per cent of the letters that have arrived at the studios this week, after telling the viewers that you were going to be my guest this week, are from women.' Nineteen pay twenties or over.

'But that's because more women than men watch this kind of programme, surely?' Twenty.

'Yes, but a lot of young women watch this programme. They are not all over ninety.' Pay pontoons and five cards only. 'So what would you do if a woman wrote you a sexy fan letter?'

'How old is she supposed to be?'

'Let's say, she's forty.'

'I'd swop her for two twenties.' Ace, two, three, four, five in hearts.

'Are you a religious person?'

'Good God.'

'With that answer you must be.' Solo.

'Well, I don't read the Bible every day, but when I get to about sixty-five I'll start reading it more. As I get older I'll start reading it every day.'

'Why?'

'Well, you could say I'll be cramming for my finals.' Misere.

'In your act you do religious jokes, don't you? And even anti-religious jokes.'

'Well, a joke is a joke is a joke.'

'Tell me a funny religious joke.' Abundance.

'Oh? Well, er let's see ... Yes. A man phoned his priest and said, "Could you come over right away, my wife is dying and would like –" And the priest said, "Your wife? But I buried her three years ago." "Well," said the man, "I married again." "Oh," said the priest, "congratulations."' Abundance in trumps.

'You have a daughter, haven't you? Elspeth.'

'Yes.'

'Is she the only child?'

'Yes, she is.'

'Were you an only child?'

'Yes, I was, apart from my brothers.'

'Now I ... Are you serious? I thought you were an only child.'

'I am. It was a bit of a joke. Only a little bit. Yes, I am an only child.'

'... because I was going to say, looking at you, I would never have said you were an only child. I would have said you had lots of sisters. It's just an impression you seem to give.'

'I don't know why, but I am an only child, according to my mother. My dad never says much anyway, and he also has a bad stammer. If it hadn't been for the stammer I could have been two years older.'

'And you were born in Potters Bar?'

'Yes. In the saloon bar, to be exact.' Sid thought, All these little gems are being ignored. Do they want a serious talk, or do I get in what I can?

'Did you go or did your parents take you to see many shows as a child? You know, live entertainment?'

'Well, there was always panto, and variety, at the Hippodrome, Golders Green.'

'Anywhere else?'

'The Palladium pantos, a few music halls here and there, but most of the theatres were closing. If you wanted to see any of the big shows with big names when I was a kid, I mean names no longer with us, Sid Fields, George Formby, Will Fyffe ...'

'When I first came to London to work I used to see the plays in the West End every week. I never went to a music hall. I knew they existed but I never went. I would only go to the Palladium to see a big American star, like Danny Kaye or Judy Garland.'

'Didn't you ever see Max Miller, or the Crazy Gang, or Gracie Fields? They were just as good as any American star, you know?'

'What do you think killed music hall?' Mavis asked.

'Well, you for a start ...' Two cherries and a lemon.

'Only because it didn't appeal to me. Surely you can't force me to go, can you?' Three plums. 'And I used to go to a play a week.'

'How many do you go to now?'

'Well, er, um ... I still manage ...'

'Come on, Mavis, how many a year?'

She smiled. 'Maybe two a year.'

'Did you go to the Palladium the last time a big American star was there?'

'No.'

'Well, I'll take you there some time.' Three sevens.

'With Carol?'

'Carrie can't stand shows.'

'I don't think I should go with you alone.' Jackpot. 'When I was a little girl in Swansea there were the Empire and the Playhouse theatres, but Dada used to come to London once a month. It was part of his job, and when he got back he would tell me all about the shows he had seen and the places he'd stayed at. One of his favourite places was right in the middle of the West End, the Mapleton Hotel. He would stop at the Mapleton Hotel – '

'When my father came to London he would stop at nothing.'

'Well, it's been a great pleasure and I'd like to thank you for spending your afternoon with me.'

'It's been a plea –'

'And, of course, to the lovely Magnus Pyke. Next week I will be talking to an American doctor who says he can prove that cigarette smoking can be good for the health, and my other guest will be Mr John Junkin, scriptwriter to the stars, telling us what some of them are really like and why he now lives in Jersey as a tax exile. So from me – good afternoon.'

The camera made Sidders and Knickers into shadows on the screen. The sound was taken out and an organ played some unknown melody. The mikes were the first things to be taken off and the fellow with the earphones said, 'That's it. Thank you, everybody.' The studio manager and the three performers all looked at each other as if to say, 'How was it?' But really nobody knows. You hear words like, 'Great', 'Fantastic', or 'That's the best for the last few weeks,' or, 'You were super, darling.' But really nobody knows. Only the viewer. They are the only ones because they saw it and they are the ones you are trying to entertain.

Carrie was sitting at home watching the television, waiting for Sid's afternoon show to come on. She had eaten a snack lunch, poured herself a second cup and had just switched on the television as the phone rang in the hall. It was her mother, phoning from Nether Wallop, near Stockbridge. Her mother phoned every now and again; a complaining lady. When she phoned it was as if she had saved up two or three weeks' worth of bad news. She never phoned in the cheap rate because she hated Sid and she thought he would be out in the afternoons, and if she phoned in the evening he might answer the phone. When he did answer the phone she always said 'Sorry, I've got the wrong number,' and put the phone down.

'Hello,' Carrie said.

'Hello, Carrie, this is your mother.'

'Oh. Hello, Mum.'

'Hello, Carrie. Sid there?'

'No.'

'Good.'

'He's working. He's –'

'You can't call what he does work.'

'Well, he's on television this after –'

'His last show was terrible. I can't go out shopping here now. I have to go into Middle Wallop for my shopping.'

'As a matter of fact he's on "Good Afternoon".'

'He should get a real job. Your father says it's only nancy boys go into television.'

'How is Dad?'

'By the way the doctor avoids him now, I don't think he's got long left with me.'

'Oh, dear.' Seven years she'd been saying this.

'Last week the undertaker bought him a drink in The Swan ... a pint.'

'Mum, Sid's on television this afternoon. Why don't you watch it and I'll ring you back?'

'What time is it on?'

'Now.'

'What's he doing on in the afternoon?'

'It's a chat show, you know, an interview. They ask him different questions. It's called "Good Afternoon". It's on commercial.'

'We can't get it here.'

'You can. I've watched it with you when I've come home.'

'They've altered it. It comes on earlier here than when you get it so I've missed it.'

'But it's live.'

'You see.'

'What?'

'Hello.'

'Hello?'

'Is that you, Carrie?'

'Yes, I'm still here.'

'I thought we'd been cut off. The butcher's run off with that funny maid from Windy Hills. You remember that funny maid. She entered the Sainsbury's Low Fat Yogourt Competition.'

'Sid'll be on in a minute, Mum. Mavis Nicholson is talking to Magnus Pyke.'

'He's daft. Anyway, she didn't even qualify.'

'Who?'

'The maid. The compère at the hall said, they were after low fat but not as low as that. Well, laugh, everybody did.'

'But how cruel.'

'Yes, wasn't it?'

'Look, Mum, I must go. Sid will be on any second now.'

'Roger, the policeman, thinks she's pregnant.'

'Mum . . .'

'Yer Dad says the vicar's got cancer.'

'Oh, dear.'

'And his wife had a breast off only six months ago.'

'Sid's on.'

'The left one, like Mrs Ford, the ex-American president. She had the same, at least, I think it was her. It was either her or Gracie Fields' mother. No, it couldn't have been. Yes, it was the American president, had his left one off. Carrie? Carrie?'

'Yes, Mum.'

'Are you listening?'

'Yes, Mum.' She was trying to watch Sid through the crack in the door.

'Yer Dad's got his limp back, but he's very brave about it. He never tells anybody. And the cat's died.'

'Oh, Mum, when?'

'Just now, I think. She's sitting by the fire but she doesn't seem to be breathing. Her tail's going so I suppose she must be all right.'

Carrie was watching through the crack but the sound was so low she could not hear it. 'Mum, I must go,' she said. 'I'll ring you back as soon as the programme has finished. Mum?' Silence. 'Mum?' One heavy breath. 'Are you all right, Mum?'

'Your Dad's just limped in. God, he looks pale. Would you like a word with him? I think you ought to. Hang on, I'll go and give him a hand over to the phone.' The phone was put down and Carrie could only hear muffled noises at the other end and hardly any sound on the television. She still looked through the crack of the door.

'Hello, Carrie.'

'Yes, Mum?'

'It's your Dad. He can't make it.'

'Why not?'

'It's his leg.'

'Which one?'

'Both of them.'

'Pardon?'

'The doctor says he should really have one off.'

'Can you get the phone to him?'

'Oh, look at him. He's trying again. He's trying to walk over to the phone. Hold on, Carrie. He's here.'

'Shello.'

'Hello, Dad.'

'Shat you, Carrie?'

'Yes, Dad. How's your leg?'

'Shfine.' (Belch) 'Whyshoult ... why shoultded be?'

'Dad?'

'Yesh?'

'Put Mum back.'

Carrie heard, 'She wantsa, she wantsa talk with you ... why I'll never know. She'll never getta word in.'

'Carrie, it's Mum again. Wasn't it wonderful of your father?'

'Mum, he's drunk.'

'No, dear.'

'Yes, Mum. He's as drunk as a lord, and in the afternoon, Mum.'

'Drugs. That's it, drugs. Doctor Sowerbutts has put him on drugs. It's been nice talking to you. I'll see you soon. Is your husband well?'

'He's fine.'

'Good. What's he doing at the moment. Is he in?'

'No, Mum, he's out. Goodbye, Mum.'

'Bye.'

The phones were both put down, Carrie's much quicker than her Mum's. She rushed into the room, sat on the settee opposite the television and turned the sound up. Mavis was asking if Carrie told the truth about her age. Then the front bell went, and went and went. Carrie slowly got up to answer it. At the front door was a dark-brown-skinned man with a turban.

'Good afternoon, lady,' he said. 'First, do not let me startle you. My name is Ramish and I am here selling you the wonderful table-cloths and napkins I am having here with me in my suitcase.'

'I am sorry, Mr er ...'

'Hydrobradanann,' continued Ramish Hydrobradanann.

'Well, I've bought all I can use.'

'Me too, lady. That is why I'm trying to sell you some. My wife hand-makes them and my little daughter girl makes the napkins. All beautiful embroidery. I've been selling here in North Finchley now for many, many years and my father before him. Let me show you please, lady. Let me show you the beautiful work in all of them.' He snapped open the suitcase and had three flying tablecloths in the air. 'Feel them, lady. I am wanting you to feel them, please.'

'I honestly don't need any.' She tried to be nice.

'How about a carpet, please? I could get you some from the van.'

'No, thank you. I have all the carpets I need.'

'Persian carpets?'

'Yes,' she lied.

'Very well, lady, I will not interfere with you any more. A few hankies maybe?'

'Look, Mr Hilowbaddin. At the moment my husband is on the television.'

'Then maybe you would like some chairs. I go get them from the van.'

'No, please. Nothing at all, thank you.' She closed the door in his face and in a heated state went back to where the television was blaring out. Mavis was just saying, 'And John Junkin, scriptwriter to the stars, will be telling you what some of them are really like and why he now lives as a tax exile in Jersey. So from me – good afternoon.' The commercial followed. It was from Allied Carpets.

Sid, with the others, was being ushered back to the hospitality room for a couple – or three if you wished – drinks, crisps, and nuts.

'Great. Liked the part where you ...'

'Yes, but when you put your arms out ...'

'Really? I thought it was ...'

'One of the best that's ever been ...'

'Goodbye, Magnus.'

'Goodbye, Sid. It was a pleasure working with you. When I told my kids you were going to be on this show with me they were very envious.'

'Obviously very intelligent children,' Sid said and everybody laughed.

Magnus spent several minutes waving goodbye. Sid thought, I bet he could dislocate his shoulder saying hello.

Mavis was talking to her producer. Sid was looking for the

secretary, but at the moment was talking to the stage manager. 'Well, that's very kind,' Sid smarmed.

'No, it's true. We all think you're bloody great.'

'Thank you.'

'You don't believe me, do you?'

'Yes, I do.'

'Well, we do.' The stage manager picked up his third, or was it his fourth, G and T. 'You're a lucky bastard, 'cos the lads like you, all the scene lads like you. It gets around, you know, those who are nice to work with and those who are not.'

'Yes. Well, I suppose it does,' Sid said, trying to look interested. He thought, How the hell does Prince Philip do it? I wish that secretary would come in.

'You see, we've seen 'em all here. You should see some of the crap we've seen who've made it big. Pass the nuts, just at the back of you.' Sid did and watched him take a handful, put them all in his mouth, swig his drink down and say, 'Now I know I shouldn't tell comedians a joke, but this is a belter. You can use this in one of your sketches. A wife is in ... no that's not, oh yes ... her husband comes home early from work.' The stage manager laughed. 'And he finds his husb ... I mean, his wife, in bed, you see, having it off with this fella, so he says ... the husband says, "Hey, what's the meaning of this?"'

'I'm sorry, Sid, that I couldn't come over before,' Mavis said as she walked into the middle of the conversation.

The stage manager snarled, 'Oh, Christ, Mavis, I was half-way through a bloody joke.'

'Oh, I'm sorry, Colin.'

'Where was I?'

Sid said, 'The husband. "What's the meaning of this," the husband said.' '... meaning of this, and the wife said, rolling over, "That seems a fair question. What is your name?"' Ha, ha, ha, ha. Oh, dear, ha, ha, ha, ha. You could use that one, Sid.'

'Yes, but not under my own name,' Sid answered.

Mavis led him away from the stage manager, who had moved to another group and had picked up someone else's drink and was again stuffing his face with nuts and crisps. She said: 'I would really like to say thank you for doing my show, Sid. I know it's only an afternoon programme, but it gets very good figures.'

'Not as good as yours, I bet.' Her black eyes flashed.

'Anyway love, you know what I'm trying to say. Just a special

124

thanks, that's all.' She kissed his cheek and walked towards the door. "Bye, everyone. See most of you tomorrow. Thanks again.'

The stage manager came back to Sid and almost in tears said, 'I'm sorry, Sid.'

'What for?'

'About that joke.'

'Forget it.'

'No, I told it wrong. I left a bit out. The husband said, "What's the meaning of this? Who is this man?" I left out, "Who is this man?" you see. And the wife said, "I think that's a fair question. What is your name?" Ha, ha, ha. "What is your name?" Ha, ha, ha.'

Tears were starting to roll down the stage manager's face. Sid suspected that drink was coming out of the right one and crisps and nuts out of the left one. He thought, it's time I left. The secretary won't be coming now, so I'll fade.

He made his way towards the door saying his thank yous and goodbyes when a voice from the back of the room shouted, 'Sid. Sid. Just a minute.' The stage manager ran across the room, pushing a couple of people aside. 'Goodbye, Sid. You were great, great.'

'Thank you, and thanks for all you did.'

'Yeah. A fella knocked on this house . . . the door . . . of this house . . . and said to the lovely young woman who answered the door, "Do you use Vaseline in your household?" "Yes," said the woman. "We use Vaseline when me and my old man have it off. We put it on the door knobs so the kids can't get in the bedroom." Ha, ha, ha.'

Sid grinned and left. As he closed the door, the lift door opened and out came the secretary. 'Are you leaving, Mr Lewis?' she asked.

'Well, er, yes. I was just waiting.'

'Oh, well, goodbye and thank you. I'm sure it was a good show.' With that she went into the room he'd just left. As she opened the door, he heard, '. . . on the door knob so the kids can't get in.'

Sod that, Sid said to himself. I'm not going back in there while he's in there. Anyway, she probably lives with one of the cameramen or some actor. So he left the building.

Sid knew you could always get a cab outside Euston Studios – well, if you held up a five pound note and had the gift of being able to convey a 'Keep the Change' look. There have been drivers who have actually shouted the number of a five pound note correctly from across the other side of the road at between twenty-five and twenty-eight miles an hour.

But where to go? It would be no good going home. That was just an evening watching television, no laughs and Carrie. I mean, he thought, why shouldn't I have a bit of fun? A few laughs. I've done my work today and finished early. What time is it? Four-fifteen, and if I go home I'll be caught up in the middle of all the traffic. No, I'll ring Carrie and ask her about the show and stay up in town for a while, till the traffic dies down.

Sid went back into the reception area. The smiling and efficient lady was still sitting behind her counter. 'Yes, Mr Lewis?' she said.

'Is it at all possible to use your phone? I'd like to –'

'Of course. What number do you want?' Sid gave her his home number. She dialled it. 'It's ringing out.' She smiled and handed him the phone. Sid automatically turned his back as Carrie said, 'Hello?'

'Hello, darling. Sid.' As if anyone else would call her darling, anyway.

'Hello, Sid. Is anything wrong?'

'No. I just rang to say I won't be home till later.'

'Oh?'

'Yes.'

'Right.'

'Yes ...' What excuse? 'It's the traffic. If I left now I wouldn't be home till sevenish. Well, between six-thirty and seven. I'm calling from the studio.' He whispered as people walked around him, and he had to turn away from them. If you could have set it to music it would have been a dance routine. 'And I still have to get to Marble Arch underground car park to get my car, and at this time of day, cabs are impossible to get. I mean, looking out now there's at least six people waiting to get a cab.' Sid looked out. It was as empty as an old maid's bed in the afternoon. 'And it looks a bit like rain.'

'It's lovely here.'

'Yes, you'll probably miss it.'

'Most likely.'

'Did you see the show?'

'No, I'm sorry but I missed it.'

'Pardon?'

'Well, I sat down to watch it, but I had the BBC. I thought it was on BBC. So by the time I'd realized, it was too late. I switched over just in time to see "Produced by Rita Gamble".'

'Gamerlingay.'

'Pardon?'

126

'Rita Gamerlingay.'

'Yes.'

'Did anyone ring after the show?'

'Well, I don't know, Sid. Elspeth had left the phone upstairs off the hook. It must have been like that since she went out. I'd only just put it back and you rang,' she lied. Sid could not shout or lose his temper, where he was, so Carrie took the easy way.

'Oh, okay then. Anyway, I'll be home between seven-thirty and eight.'

'I thought you said six-thirty to seven.'

'No, darling. Seven-thirty to eight. Okay. 'Bye, sweetheart.'

'Oh, Sid?' she almost shouted.

'Yes?'

'An Indian gentleman called this afternoon with some tablecloths and things.'

'An Indian?'

'Yes.'

'You didn't buy anything, did you?'

'No.'

'Good. It was probably Spike Milligan anyway.'

'Really?'

'Goodbye, love. I won't want anything to eat.' Sid put the phone down, thanked the receptionist and once more left the building. He was standing outside wondering what to do and where to go, when Miss Roberta Moor-Roberton also came outside carrying a brief-case.

'Hello, Mr Lewis,' she said.

Sid turned quickly, his face brightened. 'Hello, er ... I'm sorry I can't bring your name to mind.'

She smiled. 'Moor-Roberton.'

'No, not your second name, your first,' he lied.

'Roberta.'

'Of course. Roberta.'

'Bobbers. Are you waiting for a taxi?' she asked.

To Sid she had what he thought was the Swedish look. Blonde hair to her shoulders, dark blue eyes, full lips and very white teeth, tallish, around five foot eight, a great figure, and age-wise twenty-six or twenty-eight. 'Yes,' he said. 'I'm wondering what to do. I have a few hours to kill and I was wondering what to do with them.' He held his hand over his eyes to shade them from the sun. It was a beautiful day, not a cloud in the sky and no chance of rain. He thought, I hope Carrie doesn't see any pictures on the news taken in London, or worse still see the weather forecast with some idiot saying, 'Well, haven't we had a beautiful day, especially in London?'

'You're lucky, having to wonder what to do,' Bobbers was saying. 'I always seem to have something to do. I've got to get these scripts to Henry Sullivan.'

'The writer?'

'Yes. Do you know him?'

'Good Lord, no. Only of him. He's written some great TV plays. He's won more awards than Ronnie Barker and Glenda Jackson put together.' Sid didn't want to lose her. 'If I get a cab,' he continued, 'I could give you a lift to his place.'

'There's no need. I have my own car.'

They all have their own bloody cars nowadays, he thought.

'But if you like I could drop you off some place,' she offered. 'I've only got these to deliver.' She pointed to the briefcase. 'Then I'm off home. Evidently there's a problem in the second act and he has to sort it out.' She gave him a Swedish grin. 'And my car's underneath, in the car park. I'm going to his place first, in Green Street, and then home.'

'Where's home?' Sid asked, as if it was a question he asked everybody he met.

'I have a flat.'

'I'd like to mend it for you some time.' A thought seemed to pass through her mind and a lot passed through Sid's.

'I'll get the car and pick you up here. I'll be about five minutes.' She left and made her way to the underground car park. Sid quickly went back to the receptionist. There were three or four people queueing for her help. Sid got her attention and mimed to use the phone again. She mimed back, 'The same number?' He nodded. She dialled and handed him the phone.

'Hello?' Carrie answered.

'Hello, Carrie.'

'Who is it?'

'It's me, Sid.'

'Oh, hello, Sid. Is there something wrong?'

'No, but I've just been invited to a party. I think I should go because I think it would be good for me to be seen around. It's good from a business point of view.'

'Yes.'

'It's in the West End and lots of names will be there.'

'Oh, yes.'

'Yes. There's talk of Cary Grant being there and Lee Marvin. Would you like to come?'

'What time does it start?'

Oh, Christ, I've ruined it, he thought. I'd have given a hundred to one she'd have said 'No'. He said, 'It starts early, so that it's over before midnight or thereabouts, because Cary and Lee are going back to the States tomorrow, and when I say the West End, it's the other side of the river. It starts about five-thirty to six.'

'Oh, well, I'd never find the place anyway.'

'No, dear. I wouldn't like you driving to a strange place. I'd have to come home and pick you up.'

'Oh, well, I won't bother. Is it all right if I don't wait up?'

'Yes. No. Don't wait up. Get an early night in. I won't be that late.' Sid glanced out towards the street but there was no Swedish type blonde honking her hooter yet. 'So I'll see you later. Should I give Cary and Lee your love?' He laughed.

'What's the weather like?' Carrie asked.

'It's absolutely gorgeous, but er ... there's a storm brewing in the distance. I've heard a couple of claps of thunder.'

'You should have taken your raincoat.'

'Yes, I should. I'll see you later,' he rushed. 'Goodnight, dear, and give Elspeth a kiss for me.'

'She's staying with your mother in Potter's Bar.'

'Oh, yes. Well you can have the kiss then. 'Bye.' Sid put the phone down.

Carrie put her finger on the phone button and waited for the burring sound telling her she had a clear line. She dialled a number from memory. A girl's voice answered, 'Crawford, Adam and Foiley.'

'Mr Crawford, please.'

'Who's calling?'

'Mrs Dexter.'

A few clicks later. 'You're through.'

A short silence.

'Hello, darling.'

'Hello, Daniel. I'm free tonight till midnight at the earliest.'

Once more Sid left the Euston Studios building and stood by the kerb. Within seconds a white Stag with the hood down and a beautiful woman at the wheel came to a halt beside him.

Before he could get into the car, an old lady shouted, 'Hello, Sid,' and laughed – well, cackled more than laughed. 'Come on, dearie, give us yer autograph, you're my biggest fan.' She cackled again, as she handed Sid a piece of brown paper torn off an old paper bag from her basket. 'To Seward,' she instructed.

'Stewart?'

'No.' She thumped him. 'It's for my grandson, Seward.'

'Seward? S-e-w-a-r-d?'

'Seward, dearie. My grandson.'

Sid wrote it out and gave her back the scrappy old piece of brown paper and his pen, which she took. 'Thank you,' he said. There was not a word from the old lady. Sid got into the car. 'Sorry about that,' he said.

'Funny old dear,' commented Bobbers.

'Yes. She looked the type who used to knit whilst they chopped off heads during the French Revolution.'

'Have you made up your mind where you want to go to?'

'Oh, yes,' Sid smiled.

They drove away, heading towards Park Lane first, and then home.

'These are great cars,' he said.

'It's not mine.'

'Oh?'

'It's Daddy's.'

'Daddy's?'

'He lets me use it through the week, while I'm in the flat. He uses the firm's car.'

'And Mummy?'

'Mummy uses her own.'

'How d'you park all these cars outside your flat?'

'We don't.' She smiled. 'You see, Sid – you don't mind if I call you Sid, do you? I have a flat of my own, and Mummy and Daddy live in the country. Long Parish in Hampshire. I go there most weekends.' She drove beautifully. Normally Sid would be nervous being driven by a woman.

Twenty minutes later she got back into the driving-seat and said, 'Thanks for staying with the car.'

'You weren't away that long,' Sid replied. 'How come he let you get away that quickly?'

'One of the reasons could be he wears more make-up than I do, and smells sweeter.'

'Make-up maybe, sweeter never.' He fastened his seat belt as she drove off.

'Well?' she asked.

'Well, I've been giving it a lot of thought, or I could ask you if you'd like to have dinner with me. I know a quiet restaurant that's a knockout and not a soul would recognize me.'

'Where?'

'Off Fifty-Second Street and Madison Avenue.'

'If you're sincere about taking me out to dinner, Sid,' she answered, 'the answer's yes, but I'll have to go home, bathe and change.' She joined the traffic. Then carried on, 'One thing, Sid. What about your wife?'

'A lot of people say that.'

A hotel room with two people in the single bed. A handsome man in his late forties, a woman with happiness in her eyes and her body, smiling to herself. Oh, Sid, she thought, I wonder who you are with and if it's raining ...

'What a beautiful ... You can't call it a flat. An apartment is a better word. And in Mayfair, too.'

'I'm glad you like it. Where do you live, Sid?'

'On the outskirts of my salary. I hope I'm not being rude but is this place really yours?'

'No, it actually belongs to Mummy and Daddy. They know I'm not a little girl and always ring before they arrive.'

'The phone or the door?'

'Mostly the phone.'

Sid looked around the room he was in. The last time he'd seen anything as lavish as this was in a film about Cleopatra. He said, 'How often does the Queen pop in?'

'Never, but Princess Margaret's next visit will be her third.' Bobbers said it as if it was true, and as far as Sid was concerned he believed it.

'So how long have you been a Socialist then?'

'All day at work. Would you like a drink?' she offered.

'I'd love one.'

'Well, the bar is over there. Help yourself, and I'll have a Campari and soda.'

Sid walked over to the white leather bar with four stools around it, found the drinks and put them on the bar top. 'Have you ever been to LA?' he asked.

'Los Angeles?'

'No, Luton Airport ... You know, Campari and soda.' While he was looking for the glasses, he asked, 'Are you married?'

'No, but if you're interested, I'm engaged, and if you're really interested there's a picture of him on the piano. The one in the plain gold frame. Let me get it for you.' All this she did with a touch of humour. She had eyes that looked into you and a mobile mouth that always looked as if she was going to burst into laughter. She handed Sid a photograph. It was a picture of a very serious City-type man in his thirties, with thinning hair, cut away collar, a white shirt, and a small, knotted, plain tie. The words written at the side of the dark jacket were, 'With affection, Robin.'

'Well, do you like him?' she asked.

'Do you want the truth?'

'Oh, yes.'

'He looks like he's been stuffed by a very good taxidermist.'

In no way was she offended. Sid thought, she will probably end up marrying him, but carrying on as she obviously does now. I can't be the first.

Bobbers put the picture back on the piano. 'Pour mine out,' she said. 'I'll have it in the bathroom.'

Sid watched her open one of the doors and disappear. He took a sip of his own drink and grimaced at hers. Carrie will be watching the news now, he thought, and he walked over to the window. It was starting to rain.

'It's starting to rain, Carrie,' Daniel said.

'That's all right, darling. I brought a raincoat.' Carrie smiled from the bed.

'I would never have thought it would rain today.'

'I did.' She was laughing.

'Where are you?' Sid shouted with the two glasses in his hands.

'Keep coming.'

'A man of my age could find that difficult.' He followed the sound of the laugh. He entered the bathroom with its sunken bath, gold taps and mirrors which made it look as if there were six more people in the room with him.

'Put the drink down on the table, please.' Bobbers was now in a bright red towelling dressing-gown and a bath hat that looked wonderfully comical on her head. It was also red. Sid sat down on one of the chairs by the table and put his drink next to hers. She joined him on the other chair.

'Cheers,' he said. 'Bottoms up, if you'll pardon the expression. May I ask you one more thing?'

'Why am I a secretary at Thames Television when I have a flat – sorry, apartment – like this? Yes. Go ahead and ask.'

'Why are you a secretary at Thames Television when you have an apartment like this? In my bathroom at home, to sit down and drink like this, we'd both have to sit on the lavatory seat. This bathroom is bigger than my dining-room.'

'The answer to that is simple – convert your dining-room into a bathroom and eat out,' she replied.

'You're very quick with answers, aren't you?'

'Not at all. It's just that I'm used to the same questions. I'm sorry ... Look, I come from a rich family. I'm an only child. My father is Sir Henry Moor-Roberton. He's very big in property. He's very rich. He's more or less retired now and he works mostly from home.'

'Hampshire. I remember.'

'The only time Mummy and Daddy come to town is to see a show now and again. I didn't want to do nothing, or just have my picture taken at some Hunt Ball for the *Tatler*. I want to go forward. I love my job and if you want to know, I'd like to produce on television. This flat belongs to my family and the way you're looking and talking, I should have a little pad in Camden Town.' She finished her drink and turned the taps off. 'Now, young man, go and watch the news on TV in the lounge. I'm sorry to have to tell you this. It's a colour set with a thirty inch screen. Help yourself to another drink and think where you could take me for dinner. Probably some café.' She looked at him for a few seconds.

Sid said: 'Thank you, but before I go could I try your hat on? It would get a big laugh for me on TV.' She pointed to the door and he made his way towards it. 'That fellow in the picture? Do you love him? Are you going to marry him?'

'In three weeks' time.'

'So what am I doing in your bathroom?'

133

'Leaving.'
Sid left.

'Would you like to go out to eat, Carrie? We could go to the restaurant here, if you like, or we could go somewhere special and expensive. If we eat here we wouldn't have to waste time travelling back here, would we?'

'Daniel, why don't you go to the Chinese take-away and bring some food back here?'

'The hotel wouldn't be very happy about bringing food into the rooms, and what about the plates and things? No, we'll eat here, downstairs in the restaurant, okay?'

'Yes, fine. It's just that I want to be alone with you as long as possible. I honestly don't want to share you, even with the waiters.' She put her arms around him and said, 'I need you as often as I can have you.' She kissed him gently and slowly and smiled down at him, then jumped out of bed with no embarrassment at her own nakedness. Standing by the single bed, she said, 'I could do with a drink. I'll have a Cinzano Bianco. You're like Sid, aren't you? You're a whiskey man.' She snatched up the eiderdown from their bed, wrapped it around herself and made for the bathroom. She threw Daniel a towel to wrap around himself. He put the towel round his waist, went to the wardrobe, took his trousers off the hanger, found some change and put it in the drinks machine. A miniature bottle of Cinzano and a miniature Bell's Scotch fell into the trough at the bottom of the machine. Carrie left the door into the bathroom open, Daniel took the two miniatures into the bathroom and took the glass out of its holder by the washbasin, poured Carrie's drink into it and handed it to her, put the lid of the toilet down, sat on it and sat Carrie on his knee. Carrie said, 'Our bathroom at home isn't much bigger than this. Cheers!'

'Bottoms up!'

12

'So with that in mind I'll play for you and you alone, Mrs Carmichael, Bing Crosby singing "The Folks Who Live on the Hill",' DJ Tony Brandon said.

'What time is it?' Sid yawned.

'Mmm?' Bobbers mmmed.

'Time is it?' He was almost asleep again.

'Six-thirty.'

'Eight-thirty?'

'Six-thirty.'

'Six-thirty?'

'Mmm.'

'Why is Bing Crosby in bed with us?'

'It's Tony Brandon.'

'Okay, why is Tony Brandon in bed with us?'

'It's the radio. It's set to wake you up at six-thirty.'

'You've got everything, haven't you?'

'You thought so last night.'

Sid put a hand out and tapped her bare tummy under the sheet, then sprang out of bed. His feet landed quite firmly on a soft sheepskin rug. He stood there as the early morning and Bing Crosby filtered through to his brain. He was swaying. He took a deep breath and almost passed out. There was only wine in his legs, champagne in his stomach and about four large brandies in his head. His mouth tasted like a brewery smells. He sat down on the edge of the bed, hoping to stop the room from disappearing completely. Crosby was on his last few bars, while Sid thought he was on his last few minutes.

Through a music centre that would have made Bang say to

Olufsen, 'We should have one of these,' came the voice of Tony Brandon: 'What a great voice he had, they don't make 'em like that any more, when he was born they threw away the mould –'

'Shut up.'

'Pardon?' mumbled Bobbers.

'Shut up,' Sid said to the music centre. 'How do you turn this thing off for God's sake?'

'An old George Harrison song,' the music centre said, and Shirley Bassey sang the words, 'Something in the way you move,' which upset Sid because at that particular moment he couldn't.

Bobbers leaned on one elbow and stretched over to turn it off. 'Are you all right?' she asked.

'If dead is all right, then I'm all right.'

'How about some breakfast?' she suggested.

Sid heard his head turn towards her. Bobbers saw two red eyes look at her. They were unfocussed. 'Breakfast? Breakfast? Good God, woman, look at me. I can't move.'

'I told you you were drinking too much.'

'Shut up ... We are not married, so don't sound as if we are. That's the same thing Carrie would have said, so please ...' His voice faded away into a rasping bronchial coughing eruption. It was nature's way of making him blink. 'Oh God,' he tried to bellow, but it came out as a death rattle.

'That's one hell of a hangover. Are you working today?'

'I am, but my body isn't.'

'At the studios, or are you only rehearsing?'

'Studios. I'm on cameras this morning at nine-thirty.'

'It's almost seven now.'

'How far away are we from Shepherd's Bush?'

'Half an hour. Depends what time you're leaving.'

'I'd like to get there for about nine.'

'Well, that's right in the middle of the start of the rush hour.'

'God, that's Irish ... and female ... How can you be in the middle of the start of the rush hour?'

'Well you know what I mean.' She lay back on the pillow. Sid tried to raise himself from the sitting position he was in. He was concentrating so hard that Carrie could have walked in and he wouldn't have seen her. Bobbers opened her eyes and looked at the darkness of his suntanned back and legs but laughed at the whiteness of his bum. 'Where did you get that tan?' she asked.

'States.'

'Florida?'

'Vegas.'

'Vegas?'

'Yes.' He was now standing up, on his own, unaided, and not swaying – sinking a little, but not swaying. 'I went to have a look at the MGM Grand Hotel, and to see what they like over there without anybody knowing. I was only there about five days.'

'Are you going to work there then?'

'Around Xmas.'

'Really?'

'They want me to do a week or two just before Xmas. It's the worst time of the year for business so they won't be taking too much of a gamble with someone who's unknown over there. But the money is ridiculous.'

'That's good, isn't it? You know, working Vegas.'

'Good – it's great.'

'I've never been to Vegas.'

'I have.' Sid tried to smile, but found it too difficult.

'Are you taking Carrie?' she asked, sitting up.

'If she wants to go.' He was slowly trying to move some of his limbs.

'Well, if she doesn't and you want someone to carry your bags ...'

'And I suppose your husband'll carry my music.'

'Oh yes ... I forgot I'm getting married.'

'I could talk Carrie out of going,' Sid said, putting one foot in front of the other with about as much confidence as a drunken baby.

'What's Vegas like at Xmas, darling?'

'I'm told it's fantastic.'

Bobbers got out of the bed and quickly put on a négligé. She caught up with Sid who was slowly walking towards the bathroom rather like a young geriatric. 'Sid, help me to think,' she said. 'I mean there must be a way for you to take me to Vegas with you!'

'There is,' he said in a dark brown voice. 'Tell your husband-to-be that you want to go there for your honeymoon. He'll do any-thing for you, that's what you told me.'

'Sid, you are a genius. That's a fantastic idea.'

'Sweetheart, that's not an idea, it's a plan.' He had reached the bathroom door and looked at himself in the full-length mirror. 'How could you love anything like that?' he coughed.

'I don't. But he could force me into telling lies when we get to Vegas.'

Sid left her for the bright lights of the bathroom. Bobbers made her way to the kitchen and started to make some strong black coffee. She then sat down at the table to wait and think. Getting her husband to agree was easy, and by the look of it Sid could go without his wife. And with him being a star, he must have connections over there, so he would be able to get them a hotel room and things like theatre tickets. Oh, it was going to be terrific, with all that lovely weather and all those shops ... She felt a tremendous excitement at the thought of having her husband and a lover with her on her honeymoon.

When Sid walked into the kitchen she was on her second cup of coffee and had mentally packed three suitcases to take with her. Sid was dressed in yesterday's suit; it had lain on the floor all night.

'You okay now, darling?' she purred.

'Coffee,' he snarled. He was losing his avocado colour as there was a little bit of red creeping in to his face. At the moment he had the look of a cut-out pumpkin on Hallowe'en, with his eyes as the two burning candles. His movement was more relaxed now and less like a surfboard with legs. She poured him a mug of hot black coffee and he gripped it in his hands like a cowboy next to his camp-fire. He sipped the steaming hot liquid. The only sound in the kitchen was his quick slurps.

'Darling?'

'Yes,' he whispered hoarsely.

'If I get Robin to take me to Vegas for our honeymoon, when would you be going? It would be nice to stay at the same hotel. Maybe you could fix it, I mean a room for Robin and me.' She refilled his mug.

'That would be easy,' he croaked. He ahemed twice and his left eye winked out of control while his right eye just looked unblinkingly ahead. 'Baby,' he muttered.

'Yes, darling.'

'What did I have to drink last night?'

'Well, there was a couple of whiskeys here, apart from those at the studios, half a bottle of ouzo –'

'Ouzo ... What's ouzo?'

'Ouzo, my lamb, is a Greek drink of very high spirit content, which, when you pour water on to it, goes a cloudy white and has a flavour of aniseed. The Greeks drink it very slowly and with a lot

138

of water. Last night you insisted neat was the right way, and you drank half a bottle, quickly. That was followed by a bottle of red wine, a very good Beaujolais to be exact, of which I had a glass – full, I admit – but one glass. You managed the rest, plus two large Kümmels, then back here you had a bottle of champagne and four large brandies, and that was while I was with you. Then we went to bed.' She smiled.

He noticed the smile; it was the smile of reminiscence. 'I was good, eh?'

'Well, I don't know. I was asleep before you got into bed. The last time I saw you, before I fell asleep, you were trying to get your trousers off over your head. Looking at you this morning, I would say you made it.' She finished her coffee.

'You mean,' he said, with genuine surprise in his voice, 'you're still a virgin?'

'As far as you're concerned I am,' she laughed. 'But personally, I'm not a fanatic about it ...'

'What's the time now?' He tried to do an attractive leer.

'It's too late or too early. Besides, look at the state you're in. I don't want your TV producer here surrounded by Scotland Yard men looking down at your dead body. Have a little – and I hate to say the word – breakfast. It will do you the world of good. Then phone for a cab to take you to the BBC.' She got up to put her cup on the draining board, adding, 'Not that I care about your wife, Marie –'

'Carrie.'

'Carrie, but, you know, what about you being out all last night? What will she say?'

'I rang her last night and told her I was staying at a hotel as the car had been locked in the underground garage and the attendant had gone home with the keys by mistake.'

'She would believe that?' Bobbers asked, unbelieving.

'Why not?' Sid said. 'Wouldn't you?'

'Sid, if she believed that rubbish, she deserves you. She's probably got a lover of her own.'

Sid roared with laughter even though it hurt. 'Carrie, a lover?'

'Why not?'

'Do me a favour.'

'Come on, Sid. Why not? Is there something wrong with her? Has she got bolts sticking out of the back of her neck?'

'There's nothing wrong with her,' he said quickly and

defensively. 'As a matter of fact, she's a knockout. She's still got a great figure and lovely soft skin, and not a mark on her legs. There's nothing wrong with her.'

'So wouldn't or couldn't somebody else think that?'

'If I found out, I'd kill him.'

'That's typical that is. If I found out, I'd kill him. So chauvinistic, so bloody typical.'

'Could I have some more coffee?' Sid asked.

'Get it, you know where it is,' she snapped.

He had obviously touched on a very sore little nerve. She was glaring at him. He still didn't feel too well and the small but powerful confrontation hadn't done his hangover much good. 'Is there a loo close by?' he whimpered. He looked very rough.

'There's the cloakroom one, by the front door,' she answered. He rose. 'But don't you dare be sick in there,' she shouted to a retreating figure. She was still angry with him, still wanting to get at and irritate him. 'Would you like a nice greasy bacon sandwich,' she yelled. The groan was heard four streets away.

Sid arrived at the studios in a taxi, feeling slightly better but still not super fit. The taxi was stopped at the main gate by a uniformed man.

'Yes?'

'Mr Sid Lewis,' the driver said nervously, pointing to the back of the cab with his thumb.

The uniformed man peered into the darkness of the cab. 'Who?' he demanded.

'Mr Lewis, Sid Lewis.'

The name meant nothing to the BBC-employed uniformed man. He was joined by another uniformed man who asked, 'Trouble, Len?'

'Sez he's Lewis – Sid.'

The second man peered into the cab, then said, 'I'll check.' He went slowly into an office while the first man peered once more into the cab. The second man came just as slowly back and peered again into the cab. He straightened up, rocked on his heels, looked up into the sky, gave the taxi driver a smile that could freeze the Thames in August and said, 'Charlie says it's okay.'

If Charlie said it was okay, you were in. Charlie was the blind chief car park attendant, thought by some to be richer than most of the stars, thanks to astute handling of four or five spaces for cars of the stars. Some stars who didn't tip were known to have to walk half a mile to the studios – but only when it rained.

The driver of the taxi stalled the car and left it in gear as he tried to start it again. 'Hurry up; there are others waiting to come in. Come along now,' said the first uniformed man, followed by the second uniformed man saying, 'Get this bleeding lump of junk out of 'ere. Can you 'ear me? Get it out of 'ere, you funny little man.'

Obviously an ex-sergeant-major.

At last the car moved and took Sid up to the front of the BBC. Sid had not interfered because he knew it was useless. He paid the cabbie the right money and began to look in another pocket for some change to tip him with, but as soon as the driver had been given his fare he drove off without waiting for a tip.

Once inside the BBC Television Centre, you see a long reception desk manned by three ladies. No matter which one you go to, you will always pick the one who is just going for her coffee break. So you have to ask the lady next to her for your dressing-room key, but she is usually dealing with a messenger with a parcel. So it was when Sid entered that morning.

'Look, I don't know. I'm only the messenger. I was told to deliver this parcel to the BBC for a Mr Ammonds.'

'What does Mr Ammonds do?'

'I don't know!'

'Well, there's no Mr Ammonds in my book of names. There's a Mr Hammond ... If I'm not mistaken, that Mr Ammonds defected.'

'Eh?'

'Mr Ammonds. I think he defected. I think he went to another company – you know, went to the other side.'

'Well, I'm sorry, love, but it does say BBC and this is the BBC, isn't it?'

'Oh, yes.'

'Well in that case the responsibility is now yours. As far as I'm concerned, you can sod Mr Ammonds.' The messenger then bent down, rezipped the leathers on his legs and left.

'Cheeky devil,' the lady snarled. 'Gerda, did you hear that?'

'Could I have my key to green six, please,' Sid asked via a thick head and dry lips.

'What?' Gerda shouted back.

'That bloody messenger.'

'Six green, please,' Sid whined.

'No, what?'

'Didn't you hear him? How rude he was?'

'Number six green.'

'They're all rude. You would think we were here for their benefit.'

'Yes, sir. What number, please?'

'Green six.'

'Has Karen come back from coffee break yet?'

'She's here now,' Gerda said.

'She'll look after you,' the upset young lady said as Karen took her place on the stool. 'It's my coffee break now.'

'Yes?' Karen asked.

'Six green.'

'Name?'

'Lewis, Sid Lewis.'

'Ah! Mr Lewis, I didn't recognize you. Aren't you well?'

'Fine,' he belched, as she handed him the key for six red.

'Thank you.' He walked away and then looked at the key. 'This is six red, love,' he shivered.

'Yes.'

'Six green is the one I asked for.'

'Green?'

'Green.'

She looked very quickly through the keys. 'It's gone,' she said finally.

'Gone?'

'Gone.'

'How?'

'Your dresser's probably taken it.'

'Did he sign for it?'

'What's his name?'

'I only know him as Butch. He's very thin, about sixty years of age, wears eye make-up and ear-rings.'

'Butch what?' Sid was asked.

'I don't know, but look, don't worry, I'll find him myself. Now, if I find him, should I send him to you to tell you that I've found him, or should I come back and tell you he's been found, or should we both come back and tell you that we've found each other? It's up to you. What do you think?'

'Oh yes,' was the reply.

Sid didn't know if she meant it or whether she was funnier than him. To keep himself on an even keel he decided she meant it. After all, when they are as pretty as she was and funnier than him, that was the time to worry.

He weaved his way towards the swing doors leading to the dressing-room area. This is a maze of rooms and corridors that were specifically designed to make you permanently late. After a few wrong turns and a long conversation with another lost comedian, Sid found the colour of area he was supposed to be in. Now he only had to find the dressing room. After about five more minutes he found a room that he took to be his, all things being equal. It had a number six on the door. Thinking Butch was in there, he walked in, only to find a fading female singing star and a new young comic in the middle of a routine that will never be seen on television.

'Sorry, sorry. I'm really sorry.' Sid tried to sound casual, as if he expected to be in this situation.

'Jesus! Don't you ever knock?' the fading star said calmly. The new young comic just stood there and grinned at Sid.

'Why should I knock to come into my own room?' Sid remonstrated.

'This is my room,' the fading star answered sharply.

'No, it's mine. Number six green.'

'Number six red, this is number six red,' she told him as she started to comb her hair.

Sid put his head outside the corridor to check. The number on the door was six, but it was on a small red background, not a small green one. He swallowed hard. 'Ah,' he cried, 'forgive me. I am truly sorry. Yes, you are right. I should be in green – I must have somehow got ... Er, you haven't seen Butch anywhere, have you? I'm looking ...' His voice faded.

'I suppose this will be all over the studios now,' she wept.

'Why?' Sid asked. 'You're not going to mention it are you, son?' he said to the still-grinning new comic.

'Not me. Can I have your autograph, Mr Lewis? No, I mean, when I tell the wife I've seen you she'll be knocked out. She thinks you're great. So do I. Bloody great.' Walking over to his trousers, he fished out a scrap of paper. 'I based the whole of my act on yours. I copy everything you do,' he grinned.

'Thanks,' Sid said.

'You never told me you were married,' the female voice said. 'How dare you ... Get out of my room, you creep!' The grinning new comic was looking for some of his clothes.

143

'Who do I make this out to? What's your wife's name?' Sid asked.

'Elsie,' the grin replied, adjusting his pants and tucking his shirt in. Sid gave him his bit of paper, the new, young, grinning comic looked at it, nodded his head, said, 'Thanks,' and left the room. It was now very quiet. The only sound that could be heard was the static coming from the fading star's hair as it was still being combed.

'Well, I'll be going now, I'm late for rehearsals as it is.' Sid made for the door.

'Sid, sit down a minute,' she said.

'I'm late already,'

'Please Sid,' she begged. 'I'm so confused.'

Sid sat on the arm of the settee. He was a star and being a few minutes late was really no sweat. 'You're confused about what?' he asked.

'That horrible little man.' She looked at Sid through the mirror as she sat down. 'I didn't know he was married, honest,' she purred. 'You know me, Sid. I mean, how long have we known each other now, Sid? Good God, you got one of your big breaks on one of my shows, didn't you, dear?' Sid nodded. 'Well, they've asked me if I'd use that little squirt on my new special. Well, I mean, I had to say yes. They want us to do a dance routine together and a couple of songs, and they want me to do one of his sketches. He works like you, but he's nowhere near you, Sid.' She got up and took a cigarette from her handbag. 'I happened to meet him in reception and he asked if he could carry one of my bags.' Sid just made the appropriate noises. 'I mean, I never knew he was going to attack me. It was a good job you came in when you did, darling.' She lit the cigarette and drew an enormous amount of smoke down into her lungs. 'You won't tell anybody will you, Sid? You won't, will you, darling?' She looked at him directly for the first time since he had stumbled into the room.

'Of course not,' he said. 'What do you take me for?'

She smiled a thankful smile and took another drag of smoke in. 'Haven't you been well, darling?' she asked, looking at him as she walked nervously around the room.

'Food-poisoning,' he lied.

'Oh'. She was over by the door. She turned the key and took it out of the lock, looked at him and threw the key on to the dressing-table close to him.

Sid rose from the arm of the settee and walked past her towards the door, key in hand. He checked that it was locked this time, switched out the lights and heard the sound of clothes being discarded. He slowly and quietly unlocked the door and walked out. As he walked along the corridor he heard a female voice shout a word that his father would definitely deny.

13

Sid had seen some beautiful women in his time – and his time was usually between nine-thirty pm and one-thirty am. Now being a star, he went around in the social circle to receptions or, as they were called in his youth, parties. He was very popular at these receptions and luncheons, and often he would be invited to a small private dinner of six to twelve up-market people. He was a star. 'Lord and Lady Up-market request the pleasure of Mr and Mrs Sid Lewis', 'Sir Henry and Lady Beatrice . . .', 'The Right Honourable . . .', 'The Russian Embassy', and so on and so on. Mrs Lewis rarely went. This was known within the circle, so a lone female guest was often invited.

Carrie went to only one function Sid could remember – a Foyle's Luncheon. Sid stood up to speak. It was very warm and Carrie fainted as Sid said, 'Ladies and gentlemen, first of all let me say how . . .' Sid looked along the table to where the noise was coming from. He was standing next to a sat-down Anna Ford, sitting next to a sat-down Jack Higgins, sitting down next to a face-down Carrie Lewis. The toast-master in his red jacket, wearing a row of six military medals – five of which there had never been a war for – dashed to help Carrie. He tripped over the lead of the microphone Sid was speaking into and the mike left the table faster than a good tip. The toast-master and three waiters lifted her over the low top table into the audience. Sid picked up the mike and put it back into its socket. He tried valiantly to carry on as Carrie was carried out. The microphone was fortunately still in working order. He hopefully tried a few ad libs like, 'I told her not to eat here,' or, 'She does this when I speak at home,' but all these pearls of wit were drowned by shouts of, 'Give her air,' 'Undo her dress' (which one

146

Italian waiter tried to do). Sid finished his speech in mid-stream and left with only one consolation – the next speaker after him was an unknown singer called Mr Desmond O'Connor. Sid took Carrie home and as far as he could remember it was Carrie's last outing with him professionally. Carrie had made up her mind never to go out to one of those 'do's' again, while Sid had made up his mind never to ask her.

All the mail that came to their home was opened by Sid, except anything that was specifically addressed to Mrs Lewis. Her mail was usually from her mother, addressed to her in her maiden name, or from Elspeth. Sid's mail was mostly to do with his business: contracts, fêtes, police stag nights, luncheon receptions and now and again, small dinner parties – 8.00 for 8.45; black tie; RSVP; Sir and Lady Dunkirk-Beaches, Belgravia ...; Lord and Lady Oliver Newton-John ...; carriages at ...; theme of dress – favourite murderers; decorations will be worn. The scribbled note on the back of the card: 'Looking forward to seeing you again. You don't have to do anything, just be there.'

But one card stood out in particular. On the back it just said, 'Found her as promised, Henry.' That's the one I've got to go to, Sid thought. He looked at his diary. It meant cancelling work, but, if Henry was right and the young lord usually was, it mustn't be missed. 26 June, 8.00 for 8.45.

Sid shouted, 'Carrie.' No answer. Louder, 'Carrie.' No answer. Upstairs? 'Carrie.' She must be out shopping, Sid thought. I'll phone Henry now. He dialled the number from memory.

Wilson, Lord Henry's man, answered the phone – a man who had never had anything at all to do with women or a joke.

'Yes.'

'Lord Henry, please.'

'Who's speakin'?'

'Well, you were when you said, "Who's speakin'".'

'Pardon? Hello? Who are you?'

'Oh, hello, my lord.'

'This is not Lord Henry speakin'.' Wilson spoke like Jim Laker – left all his gs off anything ending with -ing.

'Look, are you Wilson?' Sid asked.

'Yes.'

'Well, Harold, will you let me speak to his lordship?'

'Ah, I know that voice. You're Mr Lewis, aren't you?'

'Yes, I am. How are you, Arthur?'

'Fine, sir. Very well. His lordship is dinin' at his club.'

'But it's only ten-thirty. He hasn't gone there yet, has he?'

'No, sir, at the moment he's bathin'.'

'Oh.'

'But not to worry, sir. I'll tell him to ring you the second he's dry.'

'Hurry him up, Arthur.'

'I'm going up there now, sir.'

'Thanks. Goodbye.'

'Goodbye, sir.'

Arthur didn't let Sid down. Within twenty minutes Lord Henry was on the phone. 'Sid,' he exclaimed.

'Henry, you feel much cleaner now?'

'Arthur helped,' Henry lisped.

'You dirty old devil.'

'Not old, Sid.'

'I saw a late film on TV about you the other night, *The Picture of Dorian Gray.*'

'I should be so lucky.'

'Sod your sex life, for the minute.'

'I should still be so lucky.'

'I've got your card for the twenty-sixth,' Sid persevered. 'I'm on, Henry. Who is she?'

'Well, she's supposed to be with me, but that's a little white lie. Anyway, my darling, there's twelve of us, if you know what I mean. I'm alone, but she's coming with Mountfort.'

'Who?'

'You know, Lord Hamlyn St John Laurent Mountfort. My dear, he's making a fortune at the moment. One of the biggest, and apart from that, the money is rolling in from his import business. He's the biggest dealer of Ginseng in the world. Most people get theirs from Korea or Siberia, but Hamlyn's been so clever –'

'What about the girl?'

'– he gets his from the New Forest. It's an aphrodisiac from the root of a tree. Well, love, his thought was, surely one root tastes like another. So, if you titivate the bottle ... Have you seen the bottle?'

'No.'

'Well, it's so phallic in shape and the pills themselves look a trifle grubby, but psychologically it works. He's making a fortune. He's thinking of selling the castle and going to live in or buy Bermuda.'

'The girl, Henry.'

'Oh yes. You know Mountfort's gay?'

'Yes.'

'He makes Oscar Wilde look like a navvy.'

'Henry . . .'

'The girl is divine. He's bringing her for you, and she's bringing him for me.'

'Who else is going to be there?'

'Frankly, I don't give a damn, as long as Mountfort is, and Louise, of course.'

'Louise?'

'Lady Louise Susan Webb.'

'No.'

'Yes. Well, you know how beautiful she is. I think you'd better knock a few years off your age. Make yourself about fortyish, even if you have to use make-up. You can borrow some of mine.'

'How old is she then?'

'Whatever she tells you. See you on the twenty-sixth, fully made up. Ciao. Unless you want to speak to Wilson again?'

'Cobblers,' said Sid.

'I should be so lucky.'

'Hey, before you slam the phone down, what kind of a party is it?'

'Just a few friends. One or two people I owe.'

'Your set or mine?'

'Both, I would say. Look, Sid, we've known each other on and off for years. You've been to quite a few of my parties before. Why suddenly all the questions? It may be eight, ten or twelve people for dinner. You either want to come or you don't. There's a partner for you and a partner for me. It's that simple. I'm not asking you because you're a big star. I'm asking you because you're a good friend. You've no need to bring your music, you know.'

'I'm sorry, Henry. I'm sorry if I sounded off. But I've had one or two problems lately with the show and one of the writers, so I'm a wee bit uptight. I'd love to come. It should do me good.'

'Good. And I thought your show was great the other night.'

'Thanks.'

'So did all my relatives. You're very popular with my cousin Elizabeth and her husband Philip. And my Aunt Elizabeth.'

'Great. By the way, how's business for you?'

'As a matter of fact, it's doing very well. I'm coming out with a new line in jeans next month. The shirts did fab, and I'm working on a new thing for men's underwear – iridescent underpants. I think it should be a big seller. Anyway, cherub, I must go. So I'll see you on the twenty-sixth, if not before. Oh yes, and Sid, it's black tie.'

'Thank you, Henry. You're a good friend.'

'Ciao.' And the phone went dead.

Sid looked at it for a while, thinking of Henry. Lord Henry Kerrigan Maylon-Napier. Only one of the richest men in the country, one of the nicest, one of Sid's best friends, and as queer as the British weather. Owner of a chain of clothing shops for the younger man, which he started because he was bored, and which made him another fortune. His father left him two million pounds and *he* didn't like him. Ah well, Sid thought, as the French say, *boules*, or was it *merde*? Probably both.

The twenty-sixth duly came. Sid arrived at the house in Grosvenor Square five minutes early, at seven-fifty-five, in his dress suit from Kilgour and French – four fittings – and a white shirt, so white it would have made an ad man for Dreft retire. With his sun-ray tanned face, he felt like a young Robert Redford.

Wilson opened the door. 'You are rather early, Mr Lewis.'

'Yes, I know I am, Arthur. I allowed parking time and had no trouble.'

'Won't you come in, sir?'

'It *was* eight o'clock, wasn't it, Arthur?'

'Eight, for eight-forty-five, sir. That means nobody will be here till nine-fifteen.'

'Surely Lord Henry's here?' Sid asked.

'He's bathin'.'

'All right if I go up and see him?'

'Oh I don't know, sir. I mean, his lordship is bathin'.'

'I'll nip upstairs, and I promise I won't look.'

'He'll be upset if you don't, sir.'

Sid heard Wilson creak across the hall. When he first came to the house, he thought it was Wilson's shoes that were creaking, but it wasn't. It was Wilson.

'Arthur, how many here tonight, and who?' he asked.

Wilson turned round. 'Twelve. Lord Henry and his boyfriend, you and Lady Susan Webb ...'

'You don't miss much, do you?'

'Very little,' Wilson smiled. 'And that fella from the government. Sir Cecil Bland and his wife.'

'I haven't met them,' Sid said.

'You haven't missed much, sir. He never stops talking, while she's like a frightened mouse. And she's got a twitch in her eye, so don't think it's a come-on. She can't help it.'

'Yes sir,' Sid grinned. 'Who else?'

'One of your lot ... that actor, er, you know. He's in that programme, er ...'

'What's he look like?' Sid asked.

'Tall, young, about forty, he's in that series about murder, "Nightkillers".'

'Oh, Carl Travers.'

'Yes, him. And Miss Chewing-Gum of 1977 or something.'

'I see,' said Sid.

'Then there's Mr and Mrs McCartney, coming from Scotland.'

'Paul?' Sid asked.

'No. Mr and Mrs Duncan McCartney. He runs his lordship's clothing factory near Glasgow. Nice people. And two American tennis players.'

'Men or women?'

'Most likely.' Wilson went through to the dining-room.

Sid ran up to the bathroom on the second floor. He knocked loudly on the door.

'Yes?' a voice answered.

'It's me, Sid.'

'Good God, you're early.'

'No, I'm on time,' he shouted back through the door. 'Would you like me to fetch you a drink?'

'No thank you. I've got a bottle of champagne in here. Come on in. It's unlocked.'

Sid walked into the bathroom. His lordship was covered in a chocolate towelling dressing-gown, with a hood that would have made Muhammad Ali proud. The room was enormous. There were mirrors everywhere, a sunken bath, murals on the ceiling, a chaise-longue, armchairs, a dressing-table, sinks, a door leading to the loo, and a bidet. Everything was cream and chocolate.

'Well, Sid. This being your first trip to my bathroom, how do you like it?'

Sid looked round. 'It's knockout really. It's like standing in the middle of a Mars bar.'

'Help yourself to the champagne,' Henry said.

Sid poured a drink into a toothbrush glass. 'What time will Lady

Louise be here? Should I call her my lady, your lady, your lady-ship?'

'I'll introduce her to you as Lady Louise.'

'Great.'

'That's quite a nice suit you're wearing. Yours?' Henry smirked.

'No. Moss Bros,' Sid smirked back.

'Looks like it was made for both of them.'

'Ha, ha, ha. You, young sir, are knocking five hundred pounds. Cary Grant has his suits made where I bought this.'

Henry smiled. 'Oh, I see. You're wearing one of Cary Grant's old suits.'

'Don't you like it, honestly?' Sid followed Henry into his adjoining bedroom. It was enormous. He went straight to a full-length mirror and looked at his suit. 'What's wrong with it, Henry?'

'It's too conservative.'

'How can it be too conservative? Anyway, I am a conservative.'

'Ah, that's as maybe. But you have a socialist's face.' Sid looked at himself again, and started to move from side to side. 'Sid, if you say Ju-dy, Ju-dy, Ju-dy, I'll have to ask you to leave.'

Henry's suit was laid out for him on the bed. Sid said, 'You're not wearing that suit tonight, are you?'

'And why not?'

'It would hurt my feelings if you did.'

'Why?' Henry looked slightly worried.

'Because I know the fella that was buried in it.'

'Out. Get out. Go. Out,' said Henry.

'I'll see you downstairs, then.'

'Yes, and Sid, be a dear, send Wilson up.'

'Henry, he'll never make it. It could take him a week.'

'Please, Sid.'

'Okay.'

'There's a good little boy.'

Sid left. As he walked down the stairs, which were enormous, he looked at his tiny watch. It was eight-forty. He reached halfway down the first flight when he heard Wilson creaking across the hall towards the door.

'Arthur.'

The creaking stopped. 'Yes, sir.'

'Sir wants you, I'm afraid.'

'Bathroom?'

''Fraid so.'

'Very well.' Wilson turned slowly, and with his hand on the banister, hauled himself upstairs step by step, creak by creak, and pain by pain. As he almost reached the top of the first flight, the doorbell rang. Wilson's shoulders visibly sagged.

'Arthur, you slide down the banister, and I'll deal with Henry.'

'You're very kind, sir.' He now dragged himself down the stairs, while Sid bounded up them, two at a time.

Wilson eventually got to the door, took a deep breath and opened it. 'Good evening, sir, my lady. I'm sorry I took rather a long time to get to the door. It's the legs. Please come in.' He took their coats and showed them into the drawing-room. Wilson creaked towards it, like the mast of a windjammer in a storm, while Sir Cecil and Lady Bland followed behind like two sails.

'Would you care for an aperitif?' Wilson asked.

'I see we're first,' commented Sir Cecil. 'A dry sherry for me, and a sweet one for my wife.'

Wilson looked at her and she twitched her right eye twice. He began to pour, as the bell went again. 'Excuse me,' he said. 'It's the door.' He hobbled off, leaving them to pour their own drinks.

Henry and Sid came downstairs as the creaking Wilson was almost at the door.

'Wilson,' Henry whispered loudly.

'Sir?' Wilson said, tacking slightly to the right.

'Who's here?'

'Sir Cecil and Lady Vera.'

'Thank you,' Henry said, as he and Sid walked towards the drawing-room. The door-bell rang again as Wilson shoved off towards it. Sid and Henry walked into the drawing-room.

'Hello, Vera. How lovely you look,' Henry said easily, and winked at her. She twitched back two very quick twitches. Henry leaned forward to kiss her cheek, brushing it with tightly-closed lips. It was the nearest thing she'd had to sex for ten years.

'And Cecil, how are you? You look marvellous. Government work must agree with you. Do you both know my dear friend, Sidney? Sid Lewis – Sir Cecil and Lady Vera Bland.'

Sir Cecil put a hand out to be shaken. Sid was at his urbane best, all straight-eyed, a wide smile, and an actor's genius for making them think he was looking at Paul Newman and Joanne Woodward, instead of something that David Attenborough had devoted fifty minutes to in 'The World About Us'.

'Hello,' Sid smiled. He then took Lady Vera's hand and kissed

153

it. She twitched her right eye once and her left eye twice, blushing the same colour as the back of her husband's neck which was hanging over his shirt collar.

The door creaked open. It was either the door or Wilson. Wilson stood there, blocking the way as he announced, 'Mr Carl Travers and Miss –' here he looked at a card '– Dawn Dawson.'

'Carl,' smiled Henry. 'And of course, the beautiful Dawn.' He walked over to them, leaving Sid with Cecil and Vera.

'Lucky to be here tonight,' Sir Cecil began.

'What do you do, Lady Vera,' Sid asked, 'while your husband is running the country?' He looked right into her eyes. They twitched.

'She does charity work in my constituency,' Cecil answered for her.

'Oh, I see.'

'And what do you do?' Sir Cecil asked.

It had been a long time since Sid was asked that question. He said, quite seriously, 'I'm a jockey.' Vera's eyes twitched rapidly, while Sir Cecil just looked at him with eyes that couldn't somehow focus.

'You're too tall, surely,' Sir Cecil spluttered.

'Not for the long races,' Sid said quickly. 'Will you excuse me for a moment?' He went to join Carl and his young lady, picking up a drink on the way. Wilson led in Mr and Mrs Duncan McCartney as if he was first in the America's Cup. Henry took them over for a while.

'Hello Carl, Dawn – how are you both?' Sid said.

'Fine, Sid. And you?' Carl replied.

'Never better. But I've had a bit of a shock.'

'Really?' Dawn asked.

'Well, the couple over my left shoulder – ' they both looked over Sid's left shoulder at Cecil and Vera, now meeting the McCartneys '– can you see them? They're the ones that look like a politician and his wife.'

'Got them,' Carl said.

'Now, I'm not complaining, but they've never heard of me. He actually asked what I did for a living.'

'Don't let it get you down, Sid,' Carl said. 'People like that are still talking about the Profumo affair.'

Dawn interjected with, 'They're still trying to get something good on radio.' They laughed.

154

While the McCartneys were involved in an animated conversation about horses with Sir Cecil and Vera, Duncan spotted the theatrical group and nudged his wife, but the nudge was ignored. He tried to manoeuvre her so that she would be able to see two of her favourites together. It was like watching a game of badminton without racquets, shuttles or net, and in slow motion. Eventually he had his wife in the position he had originally been in. She saw Sid and Carl across the room and almost dropped her glass, as Cecil was saying, 'So she'd broken her leg and we had to shoot her.'

To which Duncan's wife replied, not having heard Sir Cecil's last few words, 'I hope they'll be very happy ... Would you excuse us, please?'

She and her husband left Sir Cecil looking at Vera as if it was all her fault that the world was full of idiots.

Duncan spoke to Sid. 'Hallo,' he said, with the softest of Scottish accents. 'My name is Duncan McCartney, and this is my wife, Ella. She's so thrilled to see you here, Mr Lewis, and you too, Mr Travers.'

They all smiled and looked at Ella who said, 'It's true. I'm such a fan of both of you. And when Lord Henry asked Duncan to come here and then said you two would be here, well, I got so ...'

'There's been no holding her,' Duncan smiled.

'Well, I wouldn't say no to holding her,' Sid said sweetly.

'Oh, Mr Lewis,' Ella guffawed.

'May I introduce Miss Dawson,' Sid said charmingly.

'You're very beautiful,' said Ella, with a naïvety and freshness that hadn't been heard in their circle since the Flood.

'Well, thank you, Ella. I ... er ... don't know what to say. I mean, what do you say, other than, maybe you and I can go over and find a corner for a while and chat?' That, according to Carl, was the longest speech Dawn had ever made.

Wilson, the Fastnet flier, opened the door and almost held back the couple with him while he read from his card.

'Mr Kennedy P. Carradine III, Augusta, Georgia, USA, and Miss Hope Johnson Flick, New York City, New York, USA.'

'Hi!' Hope smiled to the room.

'Hi there,' Kennedy grinned.

At the door stood two handsome, suntanned Americans with more teeth between them than all the Osmonds put together. Henry ran to meet them.

'Ken, Hope,' he said. 'How lovely to see you.'

'Hi.'

'Hi there.'

'Ladies and gentlemen, this is Kennedy and Hope, who, as you all know, last year won most of the international doubles matches, and they've just flown in from Paris –'

'France,' Hope grinned.

'Yes, of course, France,' Henry mumbled, 'just to be with us tonight.'

'Hi.'

'Hi there.'

Everyone nodded towards them.

'Please help yourselves to a drink and make yourselves at home,' Henry smoothed.

'You gotta root beer?' Kennedy III grinned.

'I'll have a buttermilk,' Hope said.

'Yes,' said a flustered Henry. 'Er, please go over to the bar and help yourselves to anything you see.'

Sid looked up and saw Henry having what could be called a mild hot flush, so he excused himself to go over and meet the tennis players, and help his friend. Having worked with quite a few Americans, he could almost understand their language.

'Ken, Hope,' he began. 'My name is Sid. Sid Lewis.'

'Hi.'

'Hi there.'

'Henry, I think your . . .' Before Sid finished his sentence, Henry had split.

'Lewis,' Kennedy said. 'Now hold on thar. You wouldn't be any relation to Big Bill Buster Lewis, who beat Connors at the Fort Lauderdale tourno, would yer?'

'Er, no.'

'Cracker Lewis? Forest Lawn, New York, 1970?' Hope grinned.

'No, I'm not a tennis player.'

'Uh huh,' one of them said.

'I'm a –' It's no use saying a comic, Sid thought, that would really throw them. 'I'm a jockey,' he almost whispered.

'I have no wish to be rude, sir, but they must have big horses in this country,' Hope said.

'Yep, sure must be big,' Kennedy added.

'I'm afraid we don't have any root beer or buttermilk,' Sid said.

'Okay. That's okay. Have you got any water?'

'Of course.'

'Out of a bottle?' Hope inquired.

'Lord Hamlyn St John Laurent Mountfort and Lady Louise Susan Webb,' Wilson shouted, like Charles Laughton shouted to Clark Gable, in *Mutiny On The Bounty*.

Sid and Henry looked up at the same time. Henry almost ran to the most beautiful man Sid had ever seen – blond, six foot three, wearing a suit that made Sid think maybe his *was* one of Cary Grant's old suits, or even Cary Grant's first suit. Louise was hidden behind both Henry and Wilson. Sid had never seen Henry so flustered. For the first time, to Sid's knowledge, Henry didn't seem to care who knew he was gay. Everybody did, but for the first time you could actually see it through his excitement, rather like a little boy who had been told, 'You're not getting a train set for Christmas,' then on Christmas morning being told to go to the front room where the whole thing had been set up. Sid couldn't give a sod, as long as Henry moved out of the way so he could see Louise. He excused himself from his new-found American friends, who were still trying to sort out a drink.

'Is there any cream soda?' Ken grinned.

'Seven-up?' Hope asked.

'Coke even,' they choroused.

Wilson left the room, Henry moved to one side of Mountfort, and there she was. As was said earlier, Sid had seen some beautiful women in his time, but Louise shimmered. Henry was so thrilled with Mountfort, he forgot everyone else. Sid made his way over to Louise.

'My same is Lid, Lid Sewis.'

'My name is Louise. How do you do.'

'May I call you Louise?'

'Of course.'

'You won't call me Lid, will you? It's Sid really.' He smiled. 'A drink? Can I get you a drink?'

'You're not *the* Sid Lewis?'

'Yes, thank God,' Sid said.

'Have you met Hamlyn?' Louise asked.

'No.'

'Hamlyn?' she said, turning to Mountfort.

'Yes.'

'I'd like you to meet Mr Lewis.'

'Hello,' Hamlyn said, without looking at Sid. 'Are you one of the

Leicestershire Lewises?' he asked, looking into the distance for Henry.

'No,' Sid replied. 'I'm one of the drunken Lewises.' It had no effect on Hamlyn at all. Sid looked at Louise. She hardly flinched, apart from biting her bottom lip.

'Where's Henry?' Hamlyn pouted.

'He's just gone for my favourite drink. He'll be back,' Louise said.

'Would you excuse us?' Sid asked Hamlyn, putting his hand on Louise's elbow, to guide her away.

Hamlyn never spoke. He just stood there, this tall, handsome man, looking hurt because Henry wasn't with him. Sid and Louise made for an empty corner. Louise was looking around the room, while Sid looked around Louise. She was beautiful, quite beautiful. Her hair was black, but shiny black, the same black as a liquorice allsort. Her eyes were large and dark brown. The whites were like two perfectly-stretched hospital bedsheets. She turned to look at him. Her nose was perfect, her mouth was a dream, her neck, her shoulders ... Sid was almost in a trance.

'Do you think you could send out for a coffee? Regular,' Ken interrupted, with a grin.

'I'll settle for a malted milk,' Hope grinned.

'The best thing you can do is go into the kitchen. You'll see the man who brought you in here, a man called Wilson. He used to be one of our prime ministers. If he can't get you what you want to drink, nobody can.' It was Sid's turn to grin. Hope grinned and Kennedy III grinned.

Five minutes later, dinner was announced, a quick affair, with Lord Henry and Lord Mountfort trying to get upstairs as rapidly as thought decently possible. Sparks were coming from their knives and forks. There were two empty chairs at the table – Ken and Hope had left when Wilson asked them what the bleeding hell buttermilk was. Sid and Louise talked, ate and drank, and smiled a lot at each other. Dessert was an ice-cream with a raspberry stuck on it, like a nipple.

The meal, which wouldn't have worried Charles Forte, was over. Coffee and drinks were brought in. A conversation was started, mostly through Sir Cecil, with Sir Cecil and about Sir Cecil. The two Hs left the table individually; Sid and Louise left twenty minutes afterwards. Wilson left them to it. Everybody was merry. He took a bottle of port and a bottle of brandy to his room, and drank almost to oblivion. The last words uttered by him that night were, 'Bleeding buttermilk'.

Henry and Hamlyn could be heard upstairs, arguing about the whips and whose turn it was with the sugar tongs and the warm spoons.

As Louise and Sid walked and talked from enormous room to enormous room, on the second landing a door opened and Hamlyn, dressed exactly the same as Mia Farrow in F. Scott Fitzgerald's *The Great Gatsby*, ran out, chased by a completely naked Lord Henry – naked except for an enormous, white, Robert Redford trilby. He seemed to have a wooden spoon in his hand. Louise and Sid carried on talking, as if nothing was amiss. As if they had been married for a few weeks, they went into a room opened by Louise and locked on the inside by Sid.

'Will you sleep with me, Sid?' she asked.

'No, I'll do better than that. I'll stay awake with you.'

'You don't have to do anything, just be there.'

14

Arriving at Las Vegas Airport only twenty minutes late all the way from Heathrow, with only one change at Los Angeles, thrilled Sid. He was proud to be seen in the airport terminal carrying his British Airways bag. The fact that it was an American-built plane never entered his head. The pilot was British. He was from Coolgardie, near Kalgoorlie, Western Australia, and that was the thing to be proud of – not who made the bloody plane, but who flew it – a British pilot from Australia. To Sid, all Australians were British and proud of being so. To Sid, a pom was something a Scotsman wore on the top of his hat.

He was being met by a man he had never seen and who had never seen him. As he walked along to the luggage area a chocolate-coated voice over the Tannoy asked if a Mr Sidney Lewis from England would make his way to the United Airlines desk and make himself known. This he did and was soon joined by the man sent to meet him.

'Mr Lewis?' a transatlantic voice asked.

'Mr Hunter?' They shook hands. 'I was wondering how you were going to contact me ...'

'Is this all your luggage?'

'Yes, it is.'

'Uh, huh. Well, if you carry the small one, I'll see to the rest.'

'Good Lord, no, I'll take the big one,' Sid protested.

'Mr Lewis,' Hunter said with a condescending voice, 'I'm here to look after you while you're here in Vegas, so if you'll leave it all to me, please. I'll see you outside that door in a few minutes. Huh?' He pointed to maybe thirty glass doors. Sid nodded and made his way to the outside and the hot sun. Mr Hunter thanked the United Airlines receptionist and in return she flashed him sixty-three teeth and wished he had a nice day. Sid stood outside and waited in seventy-seven degrees of sunshine. He always felt that degrees Fahrenheit were hotter than centigrade. Mr Hunter came out with a black porter pushing a luggage trolley with all of Sid's luggage on it.

'Hi,' Hunter shouted to Sid.

Sid was not yet confident enough to do a Hi on his own, so he mimed Hi back to Mr Hunter.

'By the way, everyone around here calls me Olly. It's short for Oliver.' He lifted his arm to attract a black limousine. 'Sorry about the weather not being up to scratch.'

'Why? Did it rain this morning?' Sid asked, as Olly laughed.

'Very funny, Lew.'

'Sid. Sid Lewis.'

'Oh, yeh, of course. Geez, I'm so sorry, I really am. I mean, well geez. It's Sid. Sid. Ahh. Alrighty, yep, got it.' He hit his forehead with an open palm. 'Okay, Sid, buddy boy. In there.' He pointed to a never-ending, low-slung black limousine that had silently cruised up to where they were standing. Olly opened one of the doors for Sid to get into the car. Inside was really an air-conditioned room with an engine. Sid settled down and turned to see Olly give the black porter what must have been a very good tip, as the porter smiled a thank you bigger than the entrance to the Mersey Tunnel. Olly joined Sid in the living-room.

'Okay, driver,' Olly said and the long, black car gently drove off, seemingly without effort, noise or movement. After a few yards, Sid, out of the corner of his eye, had a long look at Olly. He was dressed in a pair of bright red slacks, white socks, and red patent shoes that matched his slacks. His top half was covered in a splash-of-green-and-white-with-a-touch-of-yellow-here-and-there shirt, that would have looked quite at home in a salad bowl. Black sunglasses covered three-quarters of his face, and what Sid could see of the remainder was suntanned to about the same shade as a bangle to help arthritis; almost golden. His hair was silver and thick. He was a very handsome-looking man. His teeth were all crowned and paper white. If you were in the dark with him you would be able to read by the glow from them.

'Have you been to Vegas before, Sid?' Olly asked.

Sid thought he heard a very slight English accent.

'No, this is my first trip.' A small lie.

'You'll love it,' Olly said, as if it was a law. 'I suppose your manager and your musical director have been here a few days already.'

'Good Lord. I haven't got a manager or a musical director. The only thing I've got is an agent, to whom I pay ten per cent.'

'He's here, then.'

'No.'

'But why not?' Olly sounded amazed.

'He's petrified I'll fail out here, and if I do he doesn't want to share it with me, but if I'm anything of a success he'll be out on the next plane saying, "Didn't I tell you you would be great?" But he's fairly confident in me. Before I left he sent his dress suit to be cleaned.'

In the slight embarrassed pause that followed Sid looked out of the darkened side window and watched Vegas silently glide by.

'Where are you from, Olly?' Sid asked.

'Here.'

'No, I mean, where in England?'

'Can you still tell, then? I thought I'd lost my English accent completely.'

'No, you've still got a touch left. I'm pretty good on dialects. I'm no Professor Higgins, but I can usually tell, and listening to you I would say, north. Where were you born?'

'Gateshead.'

Sid laughed out loud. 'Don't be ashamed, Olly, I won't tell anybody here.' Olly forced a grin. 'Any family at home?' Sid went on.

It was the kind of conversation Olly did not want. 'A brother,' he quietly murmured. 'I've been here in the States since I was a young man. I'm an American citizen now,' he said proudly.

'Why aye, yer bugga,' Sid said in almost perfect Tyneside.

Olly gave him a stiff smile. 'You won't be able to use anything like that in your act here,' he said. 'They won't understand a Newcastle dialect here.'

'I was stationed in Newcastle during the war,' the driver said over his shoulder. 'Well, a few miles outside of Newcastle to be exact.' He looked at them through his rear-view mirror. 'They were very nice to us Yanks.'

'That's as maybe, but this is Vegas,' Olly said sharply.

'You can say that again. It sure as hell is.' The driver said it more to himself than to anyone in particular.

'You think they won't understand the way I talk here?' Sid asked.

'If you slow down a little they might. They've got to get used to you and the sound of your voice,' Olly told him.

Sid said, 'Can you understand me?'

'Sure I can, but that's –'

'Driver,' Sid called, 'can you understand me?'

'Jesus, sure I can. I can understand you better than some guys from Texas.'

'I'd still advise you to slow down and have a good look round and listen to people,' Olly urged. 'This town's a one off. I know lots of New York comedians who mean nothing here. They're big mommas and poppas in New York and the Catskills, but here ...' He made a derisive laugh. 'Here, they can't draw their breath. Comics from Chicago sometimes mean nothing. Acts from LA, which is forty minutes flying time away – I've seen them bomb out. Then suddenly one guy hits it big in Vegas. It could be anyone. It works out about the same odds as winning a jackpot. It could be anyone from anywhere – even a Mex. If he makes it here, he's a star all over the country, but not always the other way around.'

'Who was the last British comic to make it big over here?' Sid asked.

Olly closed his eyes as if thinking. After a few seconds he said, 'Charlie Chaplin and Stan Laurel.'

'Oh, come on,' Sid cried.

'Okay. You tell me who. Go on, who? Sure, you'll get one or two who earn a fair living in Vegas, or even the whole of the States, but big, who?'

It was Sid's turn to close his eyes and think. 'Engelbert Humper-dinck.'

'He's not funny.'

'He makes me laugh.'

'You can't think of anyone, Sid. Singers you got, pop groups you got, comics you ain't got. The only time a British comic does well here is when he plays an upper-crust Englishman, who talks with a lisp and takes the piss out of himself. Then maybe – and only maybe – he might get by. But stand-up comics, they started here. This country's had smart-arsed comics while England was still laughing at Dan Leno playing dame in pantomime. You can't compete. What can an Englishman do? First of all they think, why is he talking like that? Then they think, what's he talking about? You go out there and mention one English politician and they won't

163

know who you're talking about, including the Prime Minister. There's only one politician you can name, and that's Winston Churchill, and half the audience don't realize he's dead.' Olly nervously lit a cigarette, thinking he had probably gone too far. Sid remained quiet. After a couple of lung fulls of smoke, Olly asked Sid if he was nervous.

'No,' Sid said confidently. 'Of what? What's the worst thing that can happen? I get paid off, that's the worst thing that can happen. They pay me for not working, so I'm walking about in eighty degrees of sunshine. I'm not talking too fast for you, am I? I'll still be staying at the best hotel, so for two weeks I'll be able to live it up on their money. Now that's the worst that can happen to me. At home, there may be six other comics rubbing their hands together and cadging drinks from each other saying, "He failed. Isn't that great. He failed. He flopped in Vegas." And they will be thrilled and the papers will be the same. "Last night in Las Vegas at the MGM Grand Hotel, Sid Lewis flew over (first class) to fly the British flag and failed. Yes, readers, he failed, and the once great British flag is now only fluttering at half mast." They won't mention that I tried. The other comics won't say, "Well, at least, he got the offer. We didn't." Oh, no, they'll just say he failed and be pleased because half of those comics would not have the nerve to have a go out here and the other half could not get booked in a concert party on the Isle of Wight.'

'I was on the Isle of Wight on D-Day,' the driver said.

'They're still talking about you,' Sid retorted and the driver laughed. 'If I fail here, I'll still be a star at home. The comics won't make any difference, nor will the newspapers. Don't forget, the hardest thing to find is yesterday's newspaper. When I get home after the failure, my agent will be there to meet me and help me carry the money to the bank.'

'You don't like your agent, do you?'

'It's not that. My agent doesn't like me.'

'Oh?'

'Yes, he's upset because I get ninety per cent of his salary.'

Silence took over again. The only thing you could hear in the car was a digital watch on the driver's wrist.

Olly broke the silence saying, 'Three more miles and we'll be there.'

'Five,' the driver said.

'Five, is it . . .? Are you married, Sid?' Olly asked quietly.

'Yes. She couldn't come with me. She couldn't leave our daughter, Elspeth, on her own.'

'How old is Elizabeth?'

'Elspeth. She's fifteen.'

'If you want any company just let me know.'

'I'm happy with you,' Sid grinned.

'No, I mean, female company. You know, black, brown, Jap, anything. Just let me know. Here's my card,' Olly whispered as he slipped Sid a piece of pasteboard with his name and phone number on it. 'Any time. Just let me know.' Olly winked.

Sid smiled to himself as he thought of Bobbers and Robin. They had been there three days already. 'I'm not like that,' he lied, while at the same time putting Olly's card into his top pocket.

'Of course not . . .' Olly said. 'But you know . . .' he trailed off. Then, quickly, 'Well we're almost there.'

'Oh, good. Are there any fairy croupiers at the tables, Olly?'

Olly ignored Sid's question. 'You can see the MGM up ahead.' Olly pointed, and had to admit to himself, 'Each time I see it it's magnificent.'

The size of the hotel alone was breathtaking. The car gently stopped and as it did a young man in beige pants and a dark red jacket opened the door for them to alight. Sid left the air-conditioned car and went into the hot sunshine again. Fingers were snapped and two more attendants were taking luggage out of the boot. Olly beckoned that Sid should follow him. Sid carried his British Airways bag and a raincoat over his arm. The coat was Carrie's idea. It was getting more stares than Olly's pants and shirt. Looking up at the clear, hard, blue skies, he knew he would never wear it while he was there.

An attendant held the door of the hotel open for him as Sid followed the kid from Gateshead. Sid stood there looking at the size of the place. Olly stood with him, obviously used to the surprise of visitors and first-timers. Sid was looking at an area as big as the playing-area of Wembley Stadium. This was told to all English visitors and was perfectly true. It was packed with nothing but row upon row of slot machines, rows of roulette wheels and blackjack tables, rows of crap tables, faro wheels, change counters and a constant reminder what while you were in one of the restaurants, you could play Keno. Maybe two thousand people were walking about from machine to machine, from table to table, and wheel to wheel, in surroundings that would make Elton John feel at home, and in perfect air conditioning at four-thirty in the afternoon, and not many less at four-thirty in the morning. It is a phenomenon that only the Americans could think of. No other nation would have the know-how or the nerve to do it. It was the perfect place to bring a Socialist MP and watch him turn the same colour as the money being spent there, or a Conservative MP and listen to him spout about the beauty of free enterprise. There was no pushing, you always had an empty machine, and if any trouble occurred it was dealt with so swiftly you never saw it. Sid looked around this enormous room and noticed there were no windows. This was because 'they' did not want you to see the great weather outside. On this ground floor there were six restaurants, a cinema, two theatres as big as the Palladium, a lounge – where acts were also performed – tennis and swimming outside, a shopping arcade as big as any Arndale Shopping Centre, and health clubs. It cost one hundred and twenty million dollars to build and boasted two thousand one hundred rooms. It was also built within a year.

On the left as you walked in was a long reception desk manned and womanned by twenty people, all flashing teeth and begging you to have a nice day with about as much sincerity as an undertaker's get well card. Every two seconds a soft melodious bell would sound, followed by a voice asking for Mr So-and-So to pick up a house phone. Sid signed in, while Olly organized yet another attendant to see that the luggage would end up in the right room. They then walked to a row of six elevators, which took them almost three minutes. The lift door opened. It was empty and large. Sid remembered thinking he'd played smaller theatres than the lift. A line of flashing buttons at the side of the sliding doors made you feel that if you pressed the wrong one you could start the third world war. Sid left all those things to Olly.

Olly pressed a button with 'Penthouse' written above it. They arrived at the floor seconds later. At the same time the luggage arrived, being pushed along the corridor by yet another attendant who was wishing everything that moved to have a nice day. The three of them went into Sid's suite of rooms, the attendant wheeling the luggage into the bedroom – the bedroom with the sunken Roman bath. Sid gazed round the room. It was beautiful and tastefully decorated, and, of course, large. It had, in one corner of the room, its own fully-stocked bar, with enough stools to seat ten people in comfort. Phones were everywhere; bathroom, toilet, three in the living-room, two in each of the three bedrooms. Help was everywhere hidden in a dozen buttons, phones and walled intercoms. The room, door and corridor were on permanent video in case of the slightest trouble. On that floor there were only three suites.

For the first time since he had signed the contract in England, Sid felt nervous. It was only a passing fear of, 'Jesus and money too, I hope they like me.' It was also a passing fear of self-preservation. If he did well and they liked him it would be 'Many happy returns' for a long time to come.

Sid heard the crackle of a new five dollar bill changing hands as Olly tipped the All-American full back. He now waited for, 'Have a nice day.' The man said it, but only once. Sid thought that for a five dollar tip they should have been given a 'Have a nice day' each. As Olly sat down and lit a cigarette, Sid looked out of his window to the distant blue mountains, thinking, If those early pioneers could see what happened to their dream ...

Olly shattered his thoughts. 'Well, Sid, satisfied? Room okay?' His smile was almost a leer. He knew we could not compete at this level. He was the epitome of 'Gotcha,' or even, 'Now you know why I left Gateshead, Henny.' Sid turned to him with a little jealousy in his heart. They looked at each other and both decided to keep it on a friendly basis with an invisible handshake. 'Okay, Sid, I'll leave you to unpack, unless you want me to do it for you?' He looked at Sid briefly, then carried on: 'You know, you're not used to people like me, are you? But my job is to look after your every need. I recommend you make the most of it. It may never come your way again. But if you make it here – who knows? You may have this life style for the rest of your life.'

'What's your home like in Vegas?' Sid asked him.

'Big. Almost as big as Gateshead.' Olly smiled. 'I'm also well off. Back home I'd be known as a rich Yank, and I've still got a few more years left to earn even more money. If I had stayed in Gateshead what would I have been doing? I'll tell you. Saved like hell for a holiday in Whitby. Four weeks from now I'm taking my family to Acapulco for a whole month. First class flight and hotel. The hotel is owned by this group so I get it almost free. So don't remember me to Gateshead, Sid. I've got a home that the Lord Mayor of Newcastle would be proud to drink his Newcastle Brown in. Then, if he's not thirsty, he can go and lie by the pool, or go into the games room and shoot a game of pool. It's a bit different than playing snooker over Burton's Fifty Bob Tailors, so I ask you, what could Gateshead offer my particular talents, eh? They couldn't

167

offer me a damn thing. I've no love for Gateshead or England. When I left school at fourteen years of age I wasn't willing to go down the mines or work on the docks, so I was known in my family and by all the neighbours, as a lazy little bugger. I joined the Merchant Navy when I was fifteen, just to get away. The farthest I'd been in those days was an overnight stay in Wembley to see "Wor Jackie" win the cup for us again.'

'Well, I'm glad you've got that off your chest.'

'Sid, don't underrate us. This is a big concern.'

'I'm not.' Sid laughed loudly, which spurred Olly on to more rhetoric.

'We know everything about you. This organization knows everything about you.'

'What do you mean?' asked Sid.

'Well, you've been checked out. Your politics. Where you live. We even know your taste in girls ...'

'So why did you ask me in the car?'

'I'm letting you into secrets now, Sid. We even know where your in-laws live. In Hampshire, and you let them stay in your cottage for almost nothing. That your mother-in-law hates you and your father-in-law is a lush.' Sid just looked and listened in amazement. 'We also know that you already have a girl here and the room she's in.'

'I don't know what you're talking about,' Sid lied.

'Room 1190.' He handed Sid the phone.

Sid dialled 1190. He listened a few seconds, then put the phone slowly down. 'Okay, so I do know what you're talking about, but tell me one thing – why?'

'Well, you're an investment and you're getting a lot of money and my job – and it is a job – is to see that you get all the treatment this organization can offer. If you don't accept it, that's okay, but I guarantee you that before you leave you will have pressed every goddamn button in this hotel to get the treatment.' He lit another cigarette quickly and tried to cover himself with smoke.

'Well that was some speech, Olly.'

'As I said, just protecting our investment. You have to be checked.'

'What about 1190? How did you find out?'

'That's not my department. I don't know. I haven't even seen the girl anyway. It's nothing to do with me. I'm only briefed. The only thing I know is that she's downstairs with her husband and she's waiting for you to arrive. Two at once? She must be a hot number. Anyway, I'll go and I'll see you downstairs at what time?'

'Do I have to be there?'

'No. I just thought you'd like to see backstage and meet a few people. Eat, that's all.'

'Eh, let's say five-thirty then.'

'Could you make it six? I've got to drive home and back.'

'Six it is.' Sid and Olly shook hands. 'It's been very interesting meeting you, Mein Herr.'

'My pleasure. I'll see you at the reception desk at six.' Olly put the room keys on the writing desk and left. Suddenly Sid was alone. He walked into the main bedroom to unpack and saw his raincoat on the bed. He thought of Carrie and smiled gently. He soon unpacked and dived into his Roman bath.

Sid had bathed and, while in the bath, slept for half an hour. He then took a cold shower and felt completely refreshed. How long it would last remained to be seen. Jet lag hadn't set in. He picked out his best dark suit, along with his new white shirt and his most expensive Pierre Cardin tie. I'll show those bums how to dress, he thought. He felt good and felt he looked good. He looked at his gold, extra thin watch. He hated those great big watches that made your left arm stronger than your right one, and took you a minute and a half to find out the time. The moon and the tides you could work out instantly, but the time was sometimes difficult. But then, if you couldn't get the time, you could, on some of them, get a breezy little melody, so while you were trying to find out the time you were also being entertained. He worked it out – it was five-forty. He picked up a phone and dialled 1190. It buzzed its single buzz a few times before he realized his heart was thumping faster than the one Boris Karloff had in the jar at home. After a couple more buzzes and thirty-six heartbeats Bobbers said, 'Yes?'

'Sid here. Can I talk?'

'No,' she answered in a very cool English voice.

'I'm in the penthouse called Regent,' he said very quickly.

'I see.'

'When will you phone?'

'But operator this is the second wrong number in the last, let me see, I would say . . .' (pause) '. . . two hours.' Then the phone went dead.

Sid put the phone back in its cradle and burst out laughing. 'God, that was cool,' he said out loud, followed by, 'After that I need a drink.' He looked again at his watch. Five-forty-two. As he poured a large Scotch he thought, If I'm back here in two hours. That's seven-forty odd. He swigged down the drink and it hit his empty stomach like a mallet. It burned and tasted strange. He looked at the label on the bottle – Bourbon. That's the one to avoid, he thought. He picked up his door key off the desk and left the suite.

He was downstairs at ten to six. He looked around and walked along an aisle of slot machines. At the end of the aisle was a change desk. He took out of his pocket a five dollar bill and asked the lady for five dollars worth of quarters. He said, 'Thank you,' and was answered with, 'You're welcome, sir.' He looked for what he thought might be a lucky machine, one that would give him a jackpot right away. He saw a woman leave a machine. Sid put in a quarter and pulled down a still warm handle. He lost his five dollars in three minutes flat, thinking, Good God, if Carrie had seen me do that she'd have fainted on the spot. He slowly made his way back to the reception desk, passing and watching other addicts feeding the steel boxes with money. Some were playing two machines at once, others hypnotically putting money in with a definite rhythm. Away to his left he heard a woman scream and a light on top of a machine lit up and flickered like a police lamp on Kojak's car. He walked slowly by a crap table surrounded by men putting money all over the table, while another man with a long, thin walking-stick shouted, 'Nine's your point.'

He arrived at the reception area as Olly was walking through the main doors. Sid almost laughed out loud. Olly was wearing a yellow suit, yellow shoes and socks to match, and an open-necked yellow shirt. He looked like a well dressed banana. Olly was almost next to Sid before he saw him. They both smiled. Olly spoke first.

'I'm not late, am I?'

'No, you're bang on time.'

'Good. Have you had a gamble yet?'

'Yes.' Sid smiled. 'I lost five dollars.'

'Oh, so you're the high roller they're all talking about.'

'What's a high roller?' They both started to walk towards a dark area that was a bar. It was so dark Sid would not have seen it if Olly had not known where it was.

'A high roller,' Olly explained, 'is a guy whose living is gambling and who has to come to win or lose heavy money, sometimes maybe as much as fifty grand. Well, once he's been checked out and he's

170

known, he gets everything on the house: accommodation, food, drink – although very few do drink. Anything his little old gambling heart desires.'

'How long does he stay for?'

'It's up to him.'

They entered the dark bar. All Americans seem to like darkness when they drink. They probably think they're doing something wrong so they have to do it in the dark. Sid thought that Olly was wearing a bright yellow suit so that it could be seen by the waitresses. No sooner had they sat down than a black waitress appeared, dressed in black tights and a small apron that made a mini-skirt look old-fashioned. Sid was trying to adjust to the darkness when Olly said, 'What'll it be, Sid?' While Sid was trying to read the drinks card, Olly talked to the waitress. 'Hi, Marie.'

'Hi, Mr Hunter. How you bin?'

'Fine thanks. And you? I'll have a Bacardi and Coke.'

Sid was still trying to read in the dark. 'Oh, I'll just have a Scotch and water on the rocks, please.'

'One Bacardi and Coke and one Scotch on the rocks.'

'With ice,' Sid said.

'Oh, sure.'

'Thank you.'

'You're welcome,' said Marie and stepped back into the black-ness.

Sid asked Olly, 'How did you know she was there?'

'Pardon?'

'Nothing,' Sid replied.

They sat waiting for their drinks in silence. Olly lit a cigarette. The light from his lighter showed the contours of his face. Sid re-alized that up till then he'd been looking at another fella thinking it was Olly.

The drinks arrived in a couple of minutes. Marie came out of the blackness into the darkness of their table. Sid was tempted to ask her where she kept her white stick and seeing-eye dog, but thought better of it.

'Alrighty,' Marie said, putting down two coasters, two tissue napkins, and the bill. She walked away without saying another word.

Sid asked, 'What time do they stop saying, "Have a nice day"?'

'What do you mean?' Olly asked.

'It's okay,' Sid answered, grinning to himself in the darkness. His.

eyes were now getting a little more used to the dark. He could actually see the outline of his drink. 'Cheers,' he said.

'Cheers,' said Olly, holding up his glass to be chinked, but Sid never saw it.

They watched people playing the machines and walking around the bar. One bright spark was wearing sun-glasses.

'You want to go backstage a little later, Sid?'

'Well,' Sid said, 'it's up to you . . .'

'No, it's up to you. If you do, we will; if you don't, we won't. There's lots of time. Maybe you should get settled in first. Maybe a couple of days from now.'

'Yes, that would be better.'

'Fine.' Olly thought for a minute, then said, 'Do you want to eat later, or do you want to have a drive round the town?'

'No thanks. I think I'll just hang around here and have a look at the hotel.'

'Would you like to see the first show in the room tonight?'

'Er, no, honestly. I might get to bed early tonight. You know, it's been a long flight.'

'Sure.' Olly looked away.

'Look, Olly, I know it might sound rude but you've no need to stay if you have other things to do.'

'No, nothing, but don't worry, I'll split after this drink. If you have any more drinks here, or in any other bar, or any meals you have here in any of the restaurants, just sign the tab with your name and room number. Don't pay for anything. That's all been taken care of.'

'I feel like a high roller.'

'Well, you're gambling something too, you know.'

'Tips? What about tips?'

'Ten per cent, that's fine. No one will say anything or throw it back in your face. If you want a "Have a nice day", then it's twelve per cent. If you want great service while you're here – fifteen per cent. If you want service that will knock your eye out, grumble at everything but don't leave a tip.' Olly got up to leave.

'You haven't finished your drink yet, and I've only just found mine,' Sid said.

Olly sat down. Sid tried to look at his watch but in the darkness had difficulty finding his arm. They talked about show business in general. The two people at the next table got up to go. Marie came up and cleared the table as two more people sat down.

172

'I can't see a dashed thing, dwarling,' one said.

'Never mind, dear ...'

Sid stopped halfway through his sentence. It was Bobbers. Thank God it's dark, he thought. He looked over to their table, his eyes now fully accustomed to the gloom. He could have led a group of miners out to safety. It was them all right. She looked stunning and he looked British.

'You were saying, Sid?' Olly pressed.

'What?' Sid whispered.

'Pardon?' Olly said.

'What?' Sid whispered again.

Olly leaned towards Sid. 'You were saying something about Benny and Hope, something or other ... Are you all right?'

'Fine,' Sid said very quietly. 'What's the time?'

'Pardon me?'

'What?'

'I'm sorry.'

'What's the time?'

Olly switched on the light of the clock on his arm. 'Hold on. I'll have to put my glasses on.'

Sid looked over again towards Bobbers. Marie was standing between them and him. He heard a female English voice ask for Campari and soda.

'Alrighty, and how about you, sir?'

'I can't see the list, dwarling. It's so dwark.'

'Six-fifty,' Olly said.

'Thanks,' Sid murmured.

'Have a Scotch, Robin,' Bobbers said.

'But I don't like Scotch, do I, dwarling?'

Marie moved her weight from one leg to another. Sid tried to time his movements so that his face was hidden by her bottom as it swayed from side to side.

'Maybe I should come back, sir,' Marie said. Olly was looking at his watch again.

'Er, no, I'll have a er ... What do I like, dwarling?'

'You can't have that here,' Bobbers laughed.

Olly was still looking at his watch.

'Oh, naughty Bobbers,' Robin whawhad.

'Have a Campari and soda, dear.'

'No. It tastes like that nasty medicine Nanny used to give me.'

'I think my watch has stopped,' Olly said.

173

'How can you tell?' Sid inquired.

Marie switched her weight again. Sid leaned forward as she moved. Olly picked up the tab and signed it.

'Have you got a Draught Bass?'

'A what, sir?'

'A Draught Bass.'

'I don't think so.' Marie was getting tense and Sid was looking at Bobbers through Marie's legs. 'I do have other tables, sir.'

'No, this one's fine, thank you.'

Sid heard in the darkness a black voice whisper, 'Jesus.' He thought it was time to leave and tapped Olly on the arm and nodded his head towards the lights and freedom. Olly rose and left the tip, then followed Sid, who was leaving the bar walking like Groucho Marx.

Sid arrived back in his suite at seven-thirty, after losing another five dollars on the same machine. He was starting to feel a little tired now, but the excitement was keeping the adrenalin flowing. He switched on the television and started to watch a panel game give-away show. As he watched, a man won two thousand dollars and a car for answering questions like, 'Who played the lead in *The King and I*? and 'Who was buried in Grant's Tomb?' It made shows like 'Blankety-Blank' seem intellectual.

As Sid sat there, all of his eleven phones rang. He picked one up. 'Hello,' he said.

'Bobbers here,' said a laughing voice. 'Can I talk?'

'A lot better than your husband.' Sid laughed and continued, 'I was down in the black hole of Calcutta while you were there with him.'

'No!' she exclaimed.

'Oh, yes. What drink did he eventually order?'

'You're not going to believe this.'

'Try me.'

'A port and lemon!'

'I don't believe it.'

'And the waitress brought a glass of port and a slice of lemon.' They both laughed into the phone. 'Poor man, he's lovely really.'

'When can I see you?' Sid asked.

'Probably tomorrow, if I can arrange it.'

'Where are you now?'

'In the Ladies, or as they say here, the Powder Room.'

'I don't suppose there's any chance of seeing you tonight.'

'Well, it is a little early in our marriage to start saying I've got a headache.' Sid smiled. 'I'll try and get to you somehow tomorrow. Where are you going to be in the morning?'

'I could be here about lunch time. I think I could arrange that.'

'All right, Sid, I'll ring you about one. And keep off the drink. Remember what happened last time.'

Sid looked at the glass in his hand and drank it straight down. I'm on the wagon as of now, he thought.

'I must go, darling,' Bobbers said. 'I'll see you tomorrow.' The phone snapped down quickly.

Sid went back to the television, watched for a while, then went downstairs for a snack, put another five dollars in his own machine and watched the person next to him win a jackpot. That night he slept like a baby and dreamt he was covered in quarters.

The sound of the phone ringing in the bedroom finally penetrated Sid's sleepy head. As he woke up to daylight coming through the curtains, his jumbled senses at last marshalled themselves into some order. He automatically put out his hand to pick up the phone near his bed. As he touched it, it stopped ringing. He looked at his watch. It was two-fifteen. He tried to work it out. He remembered he went to bed fairly early – about nine-thirty. He hadn't left a call. Had he slept through seventeen hours? The phone call was probably Bobbers. She said she'd ring around lunch time. He sat up quickly and rang 1190. He waited but there was no reply. He gave it a couple of minutes but nothing happened. He slowly put the phone down but kept his ear to the receiving end to the last second.

He looked out of his window. The weather was just the same as yesterday and probably the last hundred yesterdays. He thought of his raincoat hanging alone in the wardrobe. He bathed, dressed, and rang down at two-forty-five in the afternoon and ordered breakfast. It would be in his room within fifteen minutes. The hot food would be hot, the cold food would be cold. No one complained that he wanted flapjacks, bacon and eggs, fruit juice, coffee and toast at two-forty-five in the afternoon. Very similar to a British hotel, but he couldn't remember which one it was. After breakfast he rang 1190 again but with the same negative result. He then rang Olly, who was out, but a young voice took a message saying she would get him to ring at about sixish.

Sid was at a small loose end. He felt great. He'd slept the clock round and he'd had a cracking breakfast. He looked at his watch.

Now what time is that in England? he wondered. He knew England was so many hours back, but not how many. Anyway, I'll ring Carrie, he decided. He dialled direct.

His call was answered by a sleepy voice saying, 'Hello?'

'Hello, darling.'

'Who is this?'

'It's me, Sid.'

'Sid who?'

'Me, Sid. Is that you, Carrie?'

'Carrie's asleep. This is Carrie's mum. What's the idea ringing at this time of the morning? Who are you? You're not the police, are you?'

'It's me, Sid,' he shouted from Las Vegas to North Finchley.

'He's in America, thank God,' and with that she slapped the phone down.

Sid was left over four thousand miles away looking dumbly at a silent phone. He threw the receiver down with such force it rang out once as if in pain. Out loud he said, 'The old cow! The stupid old cow! She's staying in my home and rings off. The bitch! I swear one of these days I'll kill her and laugh and applaud all the way to the funeral.' He walked round his suite slowly cooling off.

Over four thousand miles away, Carrie's mum took a cup of tea up to her daughter. Carrie was awake and her mum knocked and walked in with the tea. 'Oh, you're awake then?' she said.

'Yes, I heard the phone ring downstairs. Who was it?'

'A crank. I told him where to get off.'

'Did he say who it was?'

'No,' Carrie's mum lied. 'He just breathed heavily and said some dirty things.'

'Oh dear.'

'I think you should change your number. You don't want that going on while your husband, what's-his-name's away.'

'I'll tell Sid when he comes back.'

'No, you should do it now. Once these vile people have your number they ring and ring and they tell their friends to ring. No, I think you should change your number. I'll do it for you later on today.' Carrie's mum spoke with a certain authority. 'And if I were you, you'd better let me answer the phone for a while. I don't want you hearing the kind of filthy things they say, and I'll tell Elspeth not to answer it either.' Her mum left the bedroom with a smile.

Sid thought, I'll ring back later. He rang three more times and kept getting his mother-in-law, who always told him the same thing, to stop being filthy, which he couldn't understand. After about three days of trying, he couldn't get the number at all. He eventually wired Carrie to ring him. When the wire arrived at his home in Finchley, his mother-in-law thanked the postman, put the wire under the doormat and never mentioned it to anyone. Sid had been in Vegas almost a week now. He'd had one letter from Carrie, saying that everything was fine but up till writing the said letter she hadn't received any mail from him, but then America was a long way away and if he remembered the last time they went to Spain his mother didn't get their card till they'd been back home a week and they posted it the day after they'd got there. That afternoon he rang Leslie, his agent, and told him to get in touch with Carrie. Leslie rang and rang but the number was unobtainable.

Meanwhile, back at the ranch, Sid was getting bored. He'd been backstage, he'd met all the people he should have met. He was keen to work. He had worked hard on his act and thought sensibly he would cut down on the dialogue and keep in as much mime and business as possible. He'd only seen Bobbers once more and that was by the pool. She looked fabulous in a swimming costume so small she would have had to use a magnifying glass to get it on. She left a note for him at the desk saying that she and Robin were off to LA for the last week of their honeymoon and she would try and see him in England some time.

Sid's opening night came. He didn't cause any waves, but at least he wasn't paid off. He played his ten days and left Vegas making neither enemies nor friends. It was a part of his working life that Sid hardly ever spoke of. He was disappointed to say the least, but although he was never asked back, he always felt inside that he had not failed. He said the difference between American and British show business was that in Britain you could have failure and be remembered for your success, while in the States you could have success and then be remembered for your failures. And, as he once said with a rueful smile, 'The money's different, too.' But Sid felt when the Americans said goodbye it was permanent. Sid had Olly sent a half a dozen cans of Newcastle Brown with a note that said, 'If the Lord Mayor of Newcastle ever stays with you, these should make him feel at home.' He never received a reply.

15

Carrie's father dropped dead suddenly in a pub an hour after closing time, and just after getting the barmaid to say she'd see him upstairs later. Everyone said, 'That's the way he would like to have gone.' Yet the look on Carrie's father's face just before he hit the floor seemed to say, 'No, it isn't.' The last thing he heard in this world was someone saying, 'No, this is my round.' The last thing he saw was the barmaid looking at him and laughing as if to say, 'Haven't I got big tits?' And the last thing he thought was, 'Hasn't she got big tits?' Embassy, St Bruno, and Castella smoke enveloped him. The drunks, the locals and the local drunks had laughed at and with him all evening. He hit the floor hard, with surprised, unblinking yet fearlessly open eyes. Well, the left one was open. The right one was closed, because when his maker called him, he was winking at the barmaid. Laughter, noise and the general hubbub of pub life faded within three seconds of Carrie's father actually hitting the floor. Some wag shouted, 'Give him another drink, then throw him out.' The ambulance arrived and took him to the hospital.

When the phone rang, Carrie's mum answered it. The police explained what had happened. Very gently they told her he'd dropped dead.

'Pardon?' she whispered.

'He dropped dead. The doctor thinks it was a heart attack.'

Very slowly she put the phone down, sat on the chair next to the phone, and quietly sang, 'Nuts, whole hazel nuts, Cadbury's take them and they cover them with chocolate.' She sang it three times, made a cup of tea, and went back to bed.

Sid made all the arrangements for the funeral, secretly wishing it was for his mother-in-law. Carrie took it extremely well, as did

Elspeth. Carrie's mum reacted as if it was the death of King George VI. She went into mourning and seemed to expect the rest of the country to do the same. She wore black from the day after he died until the night she remarried, two months later. She spoke of her dear departed as He and in the best royal tradition said, 'When one loses one, one should keep one's memory of one.' According to Carrie's mum, 'Carrie's Dad didn't die, he became deceased.'

Sid, who quite liked the old boy, sent flowers from many different stars. The stars never knew and Sid paid for them. The wreath from Lord Olivier was very nice. It simply said, 'Alas, poor Yorick,' signed Sir Lord Olivier. Carrie's mum wanted to know who Yorick was. Sid spent over two hundred pounds on flowers from the stars. As the coffin left the cottage it looked like the scene from the gangster film where the Mafia had bumped off Mugsy and then given him a great send off with thousands of flowers. It took the four carrying men almost five minutes to find the coffin under the flowers at the cemetery. As the four men, dressed in black, carried the coffin towards the church they were followed by the family. Carrie's mum leaned heavily on an embarrassed distant male relative. She sobbed and moaned, all in all enjoying every second. Carrie, Elspeth, and Sid followed close behind. Sid was stopped twice for his autograph, once by one of the gravediggers, who told him it wasn't for him as he didn't think he was any good anyway. It was for his sister's boy, who was in hospital. The other time by a boy of about sixteen, who asked him if he could do it four times for his mates, then asked him if who they were burying was anybody famous and could he get Charlie's Angels' autographs for him?

The family slowly moved on towards the church. Bringing up the rear was an old man in a wheelchair, being pushed by a middle-aged lady. Sid had never seen them before. He nudged Carrie and with his eyes got her to look back. She smiled at the old man in the wheelchair. She turned back to Sid and said quietly, keeping her eyes forward, 'Dad's older brother, my Uncle Luke.'

'Luke?' Sid asked out of the corner of his mouth, rather like a ventriloquist.

'Yes,' whispered Carrie, without moving her lips.

'And the old girl pushing him?'

'His daughter, my cousin Daisy,' she said through her handkerchief.

'How come I've never heard of them?'

'I'll tell you later.' She spoke into the hankie as if to wipe a tear away. Sid looked forward towards Carrie's mum as she staggered behind the coffin, moaning and crying. The unfortunate distant relative was almost dragging her along, trying to look quite normal, which he was finding very difficult. Elspeth's mouth had not closed for the last fifty minutes with surprise at the antics of her family. Her gran was almost at screaming point. Why? Elspeth thought. Good Lord, she didn't even like grandad, let alone love him. Elspeth was fascinated. Mummy's so calm, she thought, Daddy's trying to look serious and gran's playing the part of the bewildered widow. Look at her thumping the distant relative on his back.

The church door came nearer. It was a very old church. The vicar came from the darkness of the porch through the solid, wide, two-door entrance. One half of the door was shut and had been for the last 130 years, leaving only half an entrance. The Reverend Dennis Hoddinutt put his head round the door and looking towards Carrie's mum, ranting, raving and thumping her distant relative, then looked towards heaven and quickly ducked back into his church. Probably running up the aisle shouting, 'Sanctuary, Sanctuary', thought Sid.

The last twenty-five yards towards the church entrance was downhill, about one in four. The coffin carriers had automatically quickened their pace and were now almost running towards the half door, carrying the coffin on their shoulders rather like a battering ram. Carrie's mum and her distant relative ran close behind, Carrie's mum on rubbery legs and her distant relative trying valiantly to keep her from falling. The four men in black were now getting away and rapidly lengthening the distance between the family and the body. The men were all professionals and knew this church well. Two seconds before they entered the church the leader on the right shouted, 'Hup,' and with amazing grace all four went into single file, lifted the coffin on to their heads and without a moment's pause went through the single door and disappeared into the dark church. The rest of the mourners rushed into the church slightly out of breath, all except the wheelchair, which was jammed between the church wall and the edge of the door. The impetus threw Uncle Luke forward out of his wheelchair as a car crash throws its front seat passengers through the windscreen. Carrie, Sid and Elspeth heard the cry of, 'Look out!' from Cousin Daisy. They stepped quickly to one side to let Uncle Luke fly by them without his chair. Carrie's mum was inside the church shouting, 'Why have they taken him?' to the distant relative, when Uncle Luke landed in the small of his back and the distant relative was suddenly taken from her too. She then collapsed on top of Uncle Luke and the distant relative with a scream that made the church brasses ring and twenty-four church pigeons leave the tower for a new home in the nearby woods.

The four carrying men put the coffin down on the spot indicated by a look from the vicar, who had now realized his biorhythms for that day were not good. He now spoke fondly of a man he'd never met. He spoke of his strength, his love of his family, his work for charity, his love of animals and children. Carrie's mum sat there rubbing a bruised knee wondering who the vicar was talking about. The vicar finished his sermon with, 'This God is our God for ever and ever. He will be our guide even unto death.' The organ started to play the intro to the chosen hymn, verses one, four, five and eight: 'Thou judge of quick and dead, before whose bar severe, with holy joy or guilty tread, we all shall soon appear.'

The coffin was once again picked up and followed out of the church to the freshly-dug hole. Daisy had fortunately retrieved the wheelchair and was consoling her shaken father, who was now back in the chair having missed the service. The distant relative limped along with Carrie's mum. They were near the open grave when Carrie's mum fell to her knees and shouted, 'Why? Why?' to the vicar. She then grabbed both legs of the distant relative, who was standing at the head of the grave and not expecting her to grab quite so high. He jumped out of the way like a startled rabbit, immediately lost his footing on the mound of newly-dug soil and fell feet first into the grave. He stood there six foot below ground level with the vicar and mourners looking down on his balding head. It took quite a while to get the poor man out, and only then with the help of the coffin ropes and two gravediggers. His black suit and black shoes were ruined with light brown clinging mud. Carrie's mum kept shouting, 'Come out of there. It belongs to my husband,' and then tried to hit him with a heavy wreath that had been sent by Paul Newman. The vicar's face was almost as white as his surplice.

Eventually the coffin was lowered into its final resting place. Unfortunately the hole was too small to accept it. It stuck, with one end a foot higher than the other. Carrie's mum screamed, 'He doesn't want to leave me,' as the vicar stamped on one end with his foot. Carrie's dad ended up in his final resting place with his head six feet down and his feet four feet up. The gravediggers, on a nod from the vicar, started to fill in the grave as everyone walked back to the cars. They were then taken from the cemetery back to the cottage for a boiled ham tea.

16

2 DECEMBER 1979

Sid, with Carrie, walked up the magnificent winding stairs of the Grosvenor Hotel, Park Lane, London. It was a stairway wide enough to take four couples abreast and long enough to make you out of breath walking down it. From the balcony it swept down straight into the large ballroom that was below ground level. The evening was now almost over. Sid had said his goodbyes to his guests and most of his friends. He was drunk. He knew he was drunk. He felt sophisticated, but could not say it. It was two-thirty am and apart from a few people in the ballroom talking and settling bills, the staff now outnumbered the guests. It had been a great night, especially for Sid.

As Sid and Carrie slowly made their way up the stairs, Sid spoke to Carrie: 'Hasn't it been a great night, eh? Hasn't it been a great night? Truthfully now, hasn't great a beenight . . . a great night? Bloody great night, eh?'

'Don't swear, Sid.'

'Bloody isn't swearing. In kids' books they say bloody. "He had been shot and his chest was bloody." '

Carrie and Sid had almost reached the top of the stairs leading to the balcony. 'You'd better let me have the car keys,' she said. 'I'll drive.'

'Okay, that's a good idea, Olly.' Sid gave her the car keys from his pants pocket mixed up with loose change and a crumpled fiver. Carrie kept all of it just to be on the safe side. She was happy for Sid. He'd just won the biggest award, the Star Award. He was very drunk but in a way entitled to be. He'd worked hard and had become what she had thought he could never become – a star – although she still wondered why.

Sid was ecstatic. 'You know this was the big one, eh? This is the one to have. This is the one, eh?' Sid was now at least four stairs behind Carrie. He'd had to stop to talk. He knew he was in a state and wouldn't be able to do two things at once, like walk and talk. He could walk or he could talk, but he knew he couldn't walk *and* talk.

Carrie was at the top of the great staircase, looking down towards her husband. His evening jacket open, his tie off, his shirt out, he was now walking slowly backwards down the stairs. 'Stop there, Sid. Just stop there,' Carrie said, and walked back down towards him.

To give him his due, he stopped. He stood there waiting for Carrie, grinning and holding on to the wall side of the stairs in the way Tensing and Hillary must have scaled Everest. Carrie reached him at the same time as a waiter coming up the stairs did. Between them they brought him to the top.

'Thank you, gennelmen,' he slurred. He looked over the rail down to the ballroom floor. Drunken tears came into his eyes. He looked at the Star Award in his hands. It was a beautiful thing. Gold and shaped like a star with six long thin points like a large sheriff's badge. He had done all the jokes in his 'Thank you' speech. He had put it on his jacket lapel and said, 'Get offer yer horse, Kincaid. The only good Injun is a dead Injun. White man speak with forked tongue.' Then he'd had a comedy shoot out from behind the drums with the special Star Award presenter, James Stewart, one of the greatest cowboys of all time. Mr Stewart had said some wonderful things about Sid – things you should only hear at a memorial service or a Jewish wedding. Admittedly he'd read them off a script, but that was not the point; he'd said them. He said them about me, Sid thought, Sid bloody Lewis from bleeding Potters Bar. He remembered everything about the evening. He always would. It was a night no one could or would erase from his mind. Every second was there in his memory. As he looked down from the balcony he saw it all again in a flash, right from the cheer that went up when his name was announced, his friends standing, Carrie squeezing his hand, other stars saying, 'Well done,' his speech, the walk back to his table, the seemingly never-ending applause, the dancing and, of course, the drinking – all in his mind. The only thing he couldn't remember clearly was coming up that great staircase. Carrie touched his arm and he turned to look at her. She saw the tears in his eyes and for a moment they held one another gently.

'Come on, Sid,' Carrie said at last. 'Let's go home.'

'A bloody great night, eh?'

'Yes, Sid, bloody great.' She guided him out from the balcony to an exit.

'I'll have to work harder to get this again next year. Nobody has ever won it twice. Nobody.'

'You will.'

He stopped and grinned. 'I'll bloody try, sweetheart.'

'Yes, I know, dear. Stop swearing, Sid.'

They moved towards the Park Lane exit, through people saying, 'Well done,' 'You're the greatest!' 'You deserve it,' 'When are you coming back again on television?' They eventually made it outside to Park Lane. It had been raining, but it was now a lovely clear night. Sid swayed a little more out in the fresh air. By now his grin was like a permanent fixture. Carrie told him to fasten his jacket, which he did still holding his award, and talking to anyone who came out of the hotel. Carrie's idea was to go into the subway and cross the dual carriageway, get their car, and pick Sid up in about five or six minutes.

'Sid, are you all right outside,' she asked,' or would you rather wait inside while I get the car?'

He smiled at her. 'I'll go inside in a few minutes. The fresh hair his doing me good, I think.'

'All right, dear.'

'Bloody great night, eh?'

'Yes, dear.'

She left Sid gulping fresh air into his lungs and made her way towards the Green Street subway to take her across the road. Sid was swaying and saying good night to everyone who came out of the Great Hall entrance. He waved to some people as they passed him. A taxi driver, thinking he was waving for a cab, swerved suddenly towards Sid. The road was still slippery from the rain and the taxi skidded over the kerb. The cab was doing no more than ten miles per hour, when the mudguard hit Sid. He saw it coming and instead of jumping out of the way turned his back to it. Carrie looked round in time to see Sid hit and the impact send him against the wall of the hotel. He was still holding on to his award as he hit the wall. Two of the points pierced his heart. It took Carrie six seconds to get to him but he'd already been dead five.

A group of noisy people came out of the Great Hall exit, happy, merry and laughing. They looked down at Carrie holding Sid's head in her lap and one of them said, 'Never mind, love. He'll be sober tomorrow,' and walked away.

Index

Miss Elspeth Lewis (daughter) now lives in a small village in central Brazil, where she is the common-law wife of Mr Ferdo 'Rats' Matuka, a black preacher who is wanted for questioning by Interpol, regarding a shipment of hymn books from Hong Kong. When opened they were found to contain packets of high grade cannabis, worth on the streets one and a quarter million dollars. Brazil has no extradition rights.

Mrs Carrie Lewis now lives in Miami, Florida, USA, and is married to Mr Daniel Crawford. Mr Crawford is a tax consultant. It is confidently said that if Dan had been in the Nixon administration there would have been no Watergate. Mrs Crawford runs an English-style wet fish shop called The Holy Mackerel in down-town Miami. She also heads the committee of TITS (The Independent Tribune Society).

Miss Serina French (Rene Ellenberg) married Mr A. Keppleman. They live in Golders Green. Miss French is resident singer at the Starlight Rooms, East Finchley.

Mr Loose Benton has his own dress shop in New York, USA, called the Loose Change. He still sings occasionally.

Mr Jimmy Parker (James O'Toole) died suddenly of a liver complaint while filming a TV medical series.

Miss Estelle Fuller married a middle-Eastern emirate and is now Princess ༖ༀ༖ (translation: First one in the harem).

Mr Leslie Garland left the MGM agency to form another theatrical agency, the Thompson, Garland, Weinstein and Ulanova Agency (TGWU).

Mr Lennie Price left show business and now lives in Blackburn, where he is an importer of genuine Moslem prayer mats with built-in compasses, which are specially made to point only to the East.

Mr Ed Low died halfway through a 'pull-your-pants-down sketch', while appearing in pantomime at the Essoldo Theatre, Market Rasen. He was eighty-two years of age. He was cremated in Louth and his ashes were strewn all over the crematorium floor by his elder brother dropping the urn.

Mr Ivor Nolan married Ann Clyde (Bonnie). They moved to Australia and worked in television. Miss Clyde became very popular with her afternoon programme, 'Goodday, Mrs Aussie'. It is said in both Sydney and Melbourne that her afternoon programme was so popular it caused Kerry Packer to invent night cricket. In Australia she is an authority on fashion. She runs her own chain of hairdressing salons; two in Mundiwindi, two in Brunette Downs, one in Noonkanbah, one in Meekatarra, and one in Bopeechee. Mr Nolan is the chief cutter in Mundiwindi.

Mr Oliver Hunter died while on holiday in Gateshead. He fell down in the Mayor's Parlour, split his head open and was dead on arrival when he reached the hospital.

Miss Shelley Grange (Minnie Schoenberg) married Mr Giorgio Richetti. They went to live and work in Italy, where she is now serving a twenty year jail sentence for the murder of her husband and his mother, Mrs Angelica Maria Sophia Juanita Louisa Richetti. She drugged both of her victims, put their bodies – while still alive – into a large, air-tight, sea-faring wardrobe trunk. She sent the trunk by sea, c/o Miss Serina French, the Starlight Rooms, East Finchley, London, NW11. Fortunately for Miss French, the dockers at the port had a blacking on all Italian ships that week, on account of an Italian restaurant owner in Galashiels who had sacked a drunken Scottish waiter for throwing hot spaghetti over three Irish customers. The boat went back to Italy without unloading its cargo. The police found the bodies in the trunk and arrested Mrs Giorgio Richetti and charged her with murder. The last words uttered in court by Mrs Richetti were, 'Stuff Italy and all its wops,' which, in the opinion of her lawyers, Vittorio, Vittorio, Vittorio and Vittorio, did not help her appeal.

Miss Roberta Moor-Roberton (Bobbers) is now Roberta Loose-Leggit. Her first husband, Mr Robin Archibald Glazebrook, committed suicide. He took an overdose of sleeping pills while on a business trip to Berlin. Her second husband, Mr Ryan Rutt-Rutter BARNRT, accidentally drowned in his bath while on a business trip to Berlin. Her third husband was Lord Hawkins Saville Picavance Phealphree ALBrMACUBCFRSOOmVC and Bar, MP (Labour). He died after falling in front of an underground train while on a business trip to Berlin. Her fourth husband is Sir Clifford Evershed Kalvin Loose-Leggit MCMM, attached to the British Embassy in Berlin, Germany.

Mr Manny Keppleman sold his half share of the Starlight Rooms to his brother Al and opened a Jewish take-away restaurant in Brixton.

'The author and the lovely Sid Lewis were more than good friends. The book? Well, it's divine, divine, divine, and a little naughty. I'll give it three divines and one naughty.'

Hilary Flowers,
Gay World

'His flies are self-tied to a two pound breaking strain nylon leader. With his first effort he's made the ginger quill his own. If his next book is half as good, he's into the big marlin.'

'Cocky'
Fly Fishing Annual

'The author, like Sid Lewis, is a genius. He understands Sid so well. He writes about him with such care and affection. He is undoubtedly a great, new talent and should write for *The Times*.'

'Mr Lonely': Music and lyrics by Peter & Daniel Davies.

Also available in Methuen Paperbacks

These and other Methuen Paperbacks are available at your bookshop or newsagent. In case of difficulties orders may be sent to:

Methuen Paperbacks
Cash Sales Department
PO Box 11
FALMOUTH
CORNWALL TR10 109EN

Please send cheque or postal order, no currency, for purchase price quoted and allow the following for postage and packing:

UK CUSTOMERS

45p for the first book plus 20p for the second book and 14p for each additional book ordered to a maximum charge of £1.63.

BFPO and EIRE

45p for the first book plus 20p for the second book and 14p for the next 7 books thereafter 8p per book.

OVERSEAS CUSTOMERS

75p for the first book and 21p per copy for each additional book.

While every effort is made to keep prices low, it is sometimes necessary to increase prices at short notice. Methuen Paperbacks reserves the right to show new retail prices on covers which may differ from those previously advertised in the text or elsewhere.